SUDDEN DEATH AT A LONELY CAMPFIRE

Martin Iturri cast a glance at the sheep huddled in close to the wagon and bedded down for the night, a mass of pale white against the darker-hued terrain. As he did so, his dog suddenly sprang up growling, his neck hairs rising to sound an alarm.

"Easy," he murmured, as he set his empty coffee cup on the big steps of the sheep wagon. When the dog rushed forward, the Basque knew it was more than a coyote—perhaps a grizzly bear.

Martin swung about with the intention of getting his rifle out of the wagon when the chilling sound of a rifle splintered the uneasy silence. The heavy-jacketed slug broke his spinal cord and punctured into his lungs. He was dead even before he pitched forward, with his head slamming into the wagon's rear step, the blood spilling from his broken nose mingling with the blood gushing out of his mouth.

The sheepdog attacked the shadowy form of the horseman breaking out of the night. A snap shot from a revolver seemed to catch the animal in midstride and it tumbled over and over in dying agony.

ZEBRA'S HEADING WEST!

with GILES, LEGG, PARKINSON, LAKE, KAMMEN, and MANNING

KANSAS TRAIL   (3517, $3.50/$4.50)
by Hascal Giles
After the Civil War ruined his life, Bennett Kell threw in his lot with a gang of thievin' guntoughs who rode the Texas-Kansas border. But there was one thing he couldn't steal—fact was, Ada McKittridge had stolen his heart.

GUNFIGHT IN MESCALITO   (3601, $3.50/$4.50)
by John Legg
Jubal Crockett was a young man with a bright future—until that Mescalito jury found him guilty of murder and sentenced him to hang. Jubal'd been railroaded good and the only writ of habeus corpus was a stolen key to the jailhouse door and a fast horse!

DRIFTER'S LUCK   (3396, $3.95/$4.95)
by Dan Parkinson
Byron Stillwell was a drifter who never went lookin' for trouble, but trouble always had a way of findin' him. Like the time he set that little fire up near Kansas to head off a rogue herd owned by a cattle baron named Dawes. Now Dawes figures Stillwell owes him something . . . at the least, his life.

MOUNTAIN MAN'S VENGEANCE   (3619, $3.50/$4.50)
by Robert Lake
The high, rugged mountain made John Henry Trapp happy. But then a pack of gunsels thundered across his land, burned his hut, and murdered his squaw woman. Trapp hit the vengeance trail and ended up in jail. Now he's back and how that mountain has changed!

BIG HORN HELLRIDERS   (3449, $3.50/$4.50)
by Robert Kammen
Wyoming was a tough land and toughness was required to tame it. Reporter Jim Haskins knew the Wyoming tinderbox was about to explode but he didn't know he was about to be thrown smack-dab in the middle of one of the bloodiest range wars ever.

TEXAS BLOOD KILL   (3577, $3.50/$4.50)
by Jason Manning
Ol' Ma Foley and her band of outlaw sons were cold killers and most folks in Shelby County, Texas knew it. But Federal Marshal Jim Gantry was no local lawman and he had his guns cocked and ready when he rode into town with one of the Foley boys as his prisoner.

ROBERT KAMMEN

THE ELKHORN MARAUDERS

ZEBRA BOOKS
KENSINGTON PUBLISHING CORP.

ZEBRA BOOKS are published by

Kensington Publishing Corp.
475 Park Avenue South
New York, NY 10016

First Printing: April, 1994

Printed in the United States of America

One

Where the cattlemen sprinkled along the eastern reaches of the Bighorn Basin damned the intrusion of sheep onto lush grazing land, the golden eagle found them easy prey. The eagle was ghosting up near a feathery batch of cirrus clouds being burned away by the rising heat of day. The eagle seemed motionless—the lord of these high western skies—with an occasional slight movement of a wing, it changed direction but held to a circling pattern at around eight thousand feet.

As more sheep were brought into the basin, so came more golden eagles. This particular eagle had a tattered patch of broken feathers near the center of its breast—caused by an encounter with a wolverine. And it was lord of this patch of sky stretching south from the cowtown of Elkhorn and down to a series of ribbony creeks. The eyes of the eagle, glittering hotly brown in their large sockets, were settled on a few sheep that had wandered away from a band of around three hundred. Still, the eagle held high over the basin, the rays of the morning sun shielding it from the one thing it feared—a Basque sheepherder named Iturri.

The Basque was still hunkered by his campfire, savoring his last cup of coffee. This was the summer of his second year away from Vitoria, a small Basque village in the province of Alava in northern Spain. What made this lonely life bearable for Mar-

5

tin Iturri were the serrated mountains touching around the basin in an almost circular pattern. And of course there was the Basque hotel in Elkhorn, which he would not see again until winter swept in.

"Angelita," he murmured, as he brought a straining eye to the eastern fringes of sky to have sunlight pierce into his squint. Half of his mind still held an image of the hotel owner's comely Basque daughter. Other sheepherders like Iturri held a dream clutched firmly in their thoughts . . . asking for Angelita's hand in marriage—a woman still promised to no man. But Iturri knew that she would never marry a sheepherder. Still, it was nice to have such a dream . . .

His eyes held skyward, Iturri knew that the eagles would return to have a go at some of his sheep, as would coyotes and other predators. He couldn't understand why such a craven bird as the eagle was held in such high esteem in this country, for where the coyote killed cleanly, the eagle wounded far more animals than it killed outright. Though grizzly bears were the worst of the lot in that they were like a man who'd waste a whole goose just to taste *pate de fois gras*, A grizzly could slaughter seven or eight ewes in one night just to sup on their udders.

Iturri used his boots to send loose sand splaying over the dying embers of the fire and was reminded of a story he'd heard in Elkhorn: A golden eagle had come to an untended bank of sheep, perched on the back of an older ewe and dined on her rear end while she walked around—and after that one died, it flew over and perched on another. Iturri had already packed the rest of his gear, and now he stowed the empty cup in a saddlebag and climbed aboard his seedy gelding.

For the last two days he'd been sleeping in his bedroll, ranging farther and farther from his sheep wagon as dictated by the feeding whims of the sheep. They always went away from the morning sun and would water down around midday. Then they'd drift back away from the afternoon sun. And sheep—be it here

6

or back in his homeland—liked this high and dry country. Moisture was their worst enemy, causing their hooves to grow long and curl at the ends and infesting their bellies with worms. Despite this, they could survive a winter with little more to eat than sagebrush. He'd watched a band of them during the windier days of last summer turn away from a lush pasture of timothy and clover to lunch on the bitter leaves of chokecherry bushes.

"Sometimes," he murmured as he gazed ahead at the dog wagging toward him, "they are harder to understand than the lovely Angelita."

He let the gelding pick its own walking gait, as it lowered its head to pluck out a clump of prairie grass. The camptender, according to Iturri's calculations, would arrive today to move his sheep wagon. Other than that there'd be no break in the solitude of this day or of his thoughts. Now the sheep began funneling into a lowering draw, which Iturri knew would bring them to more open country.

As the Basque lowered out of the range of its vision, the golden eagle thrust earthward in a long gliding swoop. Much like the hunting tactics of a cheetah, the eagle kept its eyes boring in on its intended prey, plummeting in an angling dive in which it seemed to skim the tree-stippled slopes of the Bighorns. Its flight pattern brought the eagle passing through another draw and coming in on a few stray sheep, mostly ewes and newborn lambs and yearlings.

Rapaciously the eagle honed in on a lamb, fluttering its wings as it descended onto the lamb's back, and driving its talons deep into the chest cavity. Bleating its fear, the lamb managed to break away, the other sheep scattering out. Now the eagle beat into the sky again and wheeled over to attack a yearling. The eagle realized its talons couldn't penetrate into the lungs of this bigger animal, and when it attacked, it was at the head, striking at the eyes in an attempt to puncture the brain. As the yearling staggered away blindly, the eagle rose to soar away. It would return—for the eagle knew both animals would eventually die from their wounds—coming back the following day or week to feast on gourmet bits of brain and head skin.

When some of the missing sheep began trickling over an elevation into the draw, the Basque went for his sheathed Winchester and spurred the gelding up the shaley draw wall. Ducking away from the wide limbs of a juniper, he worked the lever as he caught a fleeting glimpse of the eagle framed in the upper reaches of the draw, pushing up into the Bighorns.

"Damn," he muttered savagely. He refrained from firing, mostly because of the hot sun glaring into his eyes and his concern for the killing handiwork of the eagle.

With the rifle laid across the front of his saddle, Martin spurred the gelding into the adjoining draw and down toward its narrow grassy floor, where some of the sheep had gone back to grazing as if nothing had happened. He rode in on the yearling standing with its head down in confused blindness, licking at its own blood and bleating now at the creaking sound as the Basque swung down from the saddle. A short distance away the lamb stumbled after the ewe. Iturri could hear the air whistling out of holes punched into both sides of the lamb's chest. There was little he could do other than wait until they died, and it sickened him. Unsheathing his knife, he eased closer to the yearling and quickly slit its throat. Then he caught the lamb, and after killing it, carried the body and that of the yearling through some brush, where he piled rocks over the bodies. At least, he mused angrily, the eagle wouldn't have its way.

Going back to his horse, he climbed into the saddle to begin hazing the strays back through a low cut in the draw and toward the main band, with the dog coming to help. Soon the strays were grazing along as if nothing had happened. The Basque picked out a distant plume of dust, checked out the sky again, and settled stoically into another day of solitude.

"Angelita . . . she might be married by now . . ."

TWO

At first Samuel Alderson couldn't be sure—it might be just a turkey vulture lifting out of the high reaches of the Absarokas westerly. Alderson and three other basin ranchers had pulled off the stagecoach road to give their horses a breather. Everyone had swung down to check saddle cinches, and while the others congregated under a shading juniper, Alderson stayed out in the open with his eyes honed skyward.

He judged it to be around midmorning and about as still as it got in the basin. It was a late June day, and except for a brief cold snap last week, summer had really taken a grip, as had sheepmen on a lot of acreage east of the Bighorn River. Now disturbing rumors had come to ranchers like Alderson that the Varney brothers, the biggest sheep outfit in Idaho, were going to bring sheep across the Bighorn River. At first the Varneys had run sheep in the Great Divide and Sweetwater basins, and then three years ago they'd expanded their Wyoming operation by coming up here. There had been a few incidents, but so far nobody had gotten killed—but if they brought sheep across the river, Samuel Alderson knew a range war would break out.

You could read it plain in Alderson's long weathered face that he'd been through some tough times as a rancher. Even so, he wasn't an unkindly man—sometimes he would keep a good 'poke on the payroll rather than let him go to ride the grub line over a long winter. He had a big frame that was gaunted out some from hazing broncs so much. His hair was smoked-out with age, like grayish smoke lazying away from a campfire stoked with juniper wood. Though the others were packing sidearms, he'd stowed his old Colts in a saddlebag. As part of their worries was word coming out that Treech Rincon had been released from territorial prison.

Alderson could make out now it was a golden eagle, but still an eye-squinting distance away and high-flying easterly. "Sheep," he grunted, "is the reason so many are back in the basin."

"Hey, Aldy," called out rancher Milt Tyman, using Alderson's old nickname. "This sippin' whiskey ain't bad."

Turning, he stepped along the length of his bronc, who twisted its head back to sniff at Alderson's coat pocket. "Nope, mite early for me with that stuff."

Another rancher, Carsey Kemmerer, had caught sight of the eagle, too, and he drawled, "Maybe if enough come in they'll take care of this woolie problem."

"Too many of them cleft-footed locusts," spoke up Tyman, with his eyes going to Lazy C owner Jim Graham. There'd been rancor in his words; Alderson figured that some of it had been brought on by the whiskey Tyman had been drinking.

By noon they should be pulling into Worland, one of several cowtowns strung along the Bighorn River. Worland fringed on the beginnings of land taken over by sheep-growers, but that was as far as it went, as anyone connected with woolies—the Basque sheepherders and others working for the Varney brothers—stuck to Elkhorn and sometimes Ten Sleep. It was Alderson's quiet comment that brought them back into the saddle. He was the last to mount up, and when he did, he reined his bronc in alongside Jim Graham's deep-bellied gray, allowing Kemmerer and Tyman to canter along the rutted road ahead of them.

The sun was sending out golden sparks through clouds that

were forming just above the Bighorns. One look from Jim Graham told him the clouds were dust-dry and they'd disperse before long. He was of an equal age with Samuel Alderson, but somewhat smaller and younger looking and a widower. His place down along the Greybull was called the 2-by-2, referring to the pair of daughters and sons raised by the Grahams. Sadness had dampened his spread with the passing of his wife, Callie, going on seven years now. He was like Alderson in many respects—cordially quiet, clannish, with a firm grip on his personal dislikes. After Callie had passed away, he'd built a grotto out near the home buildings, much like the stone cairns erected by Basque sheepherders, and had installed an old church bell in the grotto. Jim Graham had said it was to hold guard over Callie's grave site.

But only Samuel Alderson had glimpsed the reason why neighboring rancher Graham had put up that grotto. The man could not get over the death of his wife, the grief over her passing simply holding in. Once he'd ridden in unexpected-like to find Jim Graham with dark shadows lining his eyes, and he knew without asking that Graham had been shedding a few tears. Before—to Samuel Alderson's remembrance—whenever Jim Graham walked into a crowded room and his wife wasn't there, it was as if the man entered a room empty of people. And now as he rode, envy cropped into Alderson's mind—for what had been between Jim and Callie was still the purest of all loves.

"Can't believe Treech Rincon got an early release from prison—"

"Maybe he'll head for other parts," Jim Graham ventured.

"No, Treech'll be back," Alderson said flatly. "Others testified against Treech, too." The unspoken part (and this is what Samuel Alderson was worried about) was Treech Rincon's unveiled threat to gun down Jim Graham and Jim's oldest son, Marty. It wasn't just Treech but those cousins of his, the Yardleys, and in Samuel Alderson's opinion just some ignorant honyockers out of Montana. This bunch and Treech Rincon had ranged freely in the basin, claimin' to be after wild mustangs, and though they caught some, they rustled a heap more cattle, hazin' this stolen beef up into Montana. Then Rincon's luck had run out when they'd hit the Graham ranch, for in a running gunfight Treech Rincon had held back to let the Yardleys make their getaway. A slug in his leg and his horse down, Rincon had no choice but to give up.

The trial for Treech Rincon had been short and sweet, everyone expecting him to be doing some sky dancing. Rincon's five-year sentence was still chawed about a lot as being a miscarriage of justice. Nary a word was pried out of Rincon about his cousins, the Yardleys, being his rustling partners, and now after nearly four years that bastard, in Alderson's opinion, was a free man.

"At least," Alderson said, "since Treech has been gone them Yardleys have laid off'a rustling. That hardscrabble place they call a ranch lays just south of Moses Quinta's 77 spread."

"They stole some cattle from Quinta. He has that rep as being a gunfighter—probably why them cowardly Yardleys held off from stealing too many 77 cows. I tell you, Aldy, I figure Rincon is just another blowhard."

Chuckling, Alderson said, "Probably sweet-talked the warden into that early release. As I recollect, he never did have much use for Worland as a place to chase the elephant. He outta know if he shows up, other ranchers such as me and Milt and Carsey will back you up."

"I know that, Aldy."

"What I figure on doin' is passin' on an ultimatum to Rincon through the sheriff's office that he's no longer welcome in the basin."

"Rincon's damned prideful."

"Man's pride goes away in a hurry when his rear end is weighed down with 30-06 rifle slugs." Talking with Jim Graham about Treech Rincon's possible return had taken Alderson's thoughts away from his reason for going to Worland.

Then where the road curled around a shaley hill, he got his first glimpse of the Bighorn River, to fix in on an eagle winging out of a cottonwood. The bird flew over the river and went due east—into sheep country, Alderson mused. Much as he wanted to swing around and head for home, a certain loyalty held him headed for Worland showing yonderly. "Well," he muttered softly, "the good Lord willin' all of this will blow over." But deep inside he knew different, and he let a sigh of regret go drifting to his backtrail . . . for what happened from here on was out of their hands.

Three

Seven years was a long time not to pack a gun, but Moses Quinta had no regrets about this or about yoking up in marriage with ranchwoman Celia Farnsworth. Though he'd taken over running her 77 spread, Celia still hung in there sharing the yoke of work and whatever problems cropped up.

Up here in the basin, folks tended to forget Quinta had been a notorious gunfighter, though once in a while his name would come up in a cowtown saloon—talk that connected him with demised cattle king Charlton Talbot. That early trouble had seen Talbot trying to shove out a lot of small ranchers including the 77 Ranch. Then Quinta had come up in response to a letter sent to him by Celia Farnsworth, to hire out his gun to Celia, but mostly to even the score with Talbot.

At the moment Moses Quinta and his wife were loping their horses down into the Bighorn River floodplain, with Quinta thinking about how he'd gunned down Charlton Talbot up near Sheridan. Folks tended to forget that Talbot had once been Quinta's partner in crime down in Oklahoma and the Nations, remembering him only as a cattleman gone bad. Maybe, Quinta mused, Talbot's the lucky one. For there were times when a room got awful quiet when Quinta walked in. It got so that he held out at the ranch more'n he should—that it would be Celia barking at him to hit for Worland or the basin and get in to a poker game, as she couldn't stand having him underfoot anymore. He drew closer to her loping bronc and reached out to touch her shoulder.

"I still can't figure it out . . ."

Smiling back at Moses, she said, "When to use that extra fork?"

"I'm not talking about that wedding supper . . . but about us . . ."

"You mean after Sara gets married?" In her late thirties, Celia Farnsworth had a few threads of gray in the chestnut hair pinned up under her brown hat. She was still a comely woman, with high cheekbones and a few weather lines around her eyes. She brought a gloved hand over and touched Moses' forearm—a comforting gesture. Wistfully she thought about how, after they'd managed to get her herd over the Bighorns to Sheridan, Quinta had left without saying goodbye. And how she'd tracked him down to Buffalo. The deal Celia Farnsworth struck was that if she won all of Quinta's money in a high-stakes poker game, they'd be married. "You know, you really folded some good hands back there."

He grinned, his teeth a white line against the bronzed planes of his ruggedly handsome face. He was tall, and though packing on a little more weight, it didn't show all that much. Deliberately he'd left his six-gun at home, the sheathed rifle just a standard part of his saddle rigging. Or, he mused, there was an off-chance of them encountering the Yardleys on their way in to Worland.

He hadn't seen hide nor hair of that unkempt bunch of rustlers ever since Treech Rincon had been hauled off to territorial prison, even though that strip of land claimed by the Yardleys enjoined the 77. But about a month ago one of Quinta's 'pokes had come across Harge Yardley over at Manderson—just a fleeting glimpse of the high rider pushing out of town after his three brothers. There was Dyson and Eli and Jake, all on equal terms when it came to breaking the law.

What Moses hadn't divulged to Celia was that a county com-

15

missioner came out last week with the news Sheriff Cy Eldridge had suffered another heart attack. It seemed the commissioners had gotten together and decided that if Eldridge wasn't able to continue on as sheriff, their choice for the job was Moses Quinta. Just until fall elections, he'd been told.

They rode past an old roping corral gone seedy with weeds growing around the few posts still standing, and a rusted-out mower, the road bending now to have them come in past Spilway's blacksmith shop hogging the east side of the wider road turning into a street. Now that he was here, Moses got to mulling over just why the commissioners had so magnanimously picked him out for the lofty office of sheriff of Washakie County. And it wasn't, as he'd been duly informed, that none of the deputies were qualified. What they wanted was a man with a reputation to pack that tin star if hostilities broke out between cowmen and sheepgrowers. The more he thought on it, the more rankled he got. Here it had taken him seven years to make a lot of folks forget about his checkered past.

"Something bothering you, Quinta?"

He snaked a glance at Celia regarding him through somber eyes and drawled, "You know, don't you . . . ?"

"Buck spilled the beans about them wanting you to be sheriff. I dragged it out of him. It isn't just Cy Eldridge coming down sick, is it?"

"Nope, I reckon not. I'm no gunhand anymore, Celia. Probably couldn't bust a knot in a fence post with my Colts." A deep sigh fluttered away as he added, "Seems my past just won't go away."

"Moses, I just want you to know that this is your decision to make."

Nodding, he said, "Anyway, it'll only be until election time. Got to say, hon, I just don't cotton to the notion of being sheriff. Medran, Josh Medran—now doggonit, Josh would make do in that job. I reckon that's what I'll tell those county commission-

16

ers—make Medran sheriff and just let me go back to the ranch-in' business."

"Whatever," she said vaguely. "I'm going over to Beth's. You know how she is, Moses, you're either there at noon sharp or you go hungry."

"Yup," he grunted, as he watched Celia spur her bronc off onto a side street. "Noon sharp—sounds like a warden I knew once."

"Well, Mr. Quinta, that meeting was like sending a steer year-lin' out to breed some cows."

They stood near the shading wall of the grange hall waiting for some other ranchers to come out, and Moses Quinta smiled back at Alderson adjusting his big-crowned Stetson. The sun was lowering, but it was still hot enough to cause them to seek wall shade or move under cottonwoods growing in a line along-side a lane. Moses and Samuel Alderson weren't wearing their gunbelts.

As Alderson had just said, the meeting had turned out to be a shouting match over what to do about the growing number of sheep being brought into the basin. About fifteen ranchers had shown up, and right away Carsey Kemmerer had tried to take charge. Moses knew about Kemmerer owning land east of the Bighorn River, though most of the rancher's land holdings lay in the central part of the basin. There'd been a wait-and-see attitude until one of the county commissioners had arrived, bear-ing a telegram sent over from Ten Sleep telling of how that sheep company had hired the Yardleys to help guard its scattered flocks of sheep.

"You know Kemmerer better'n anyone."

"Nope," snorted Alderson. "I don't think anyone really knows what makes Kemmerer tick. He's a man doesn't do much talking, an' kind of ambitious, too."

"They've more or less made him their leader."

17

"Some of the ranchers have, Moses. Like the office of church secretary—nobody runs for that job. I do know this, there's some dark days in the offing."

Out of the meeting hall came Jim Graham and Milt Tyman. The four of them cut under the cottonwoods and up the lawn, heading for the beckoning batwings of a saloon. The cowtown was spread out for quite a ways alongside the river. It was here a lot of ranchers came for their supplies, bypassing some smaller places to do so. Quinta's intentions were to have a couple of beers, then head over to his stepdaughter's place for a late supper. Now as he filed into the saloon, he looked about with a long practiced glance, a habit he hadn't been able to shake. They came in four abreast to stand at the bar, where Quinta's double eagle bought the first round.

Jim Graham said quietly to start the conversation, "Each of us has to make up his own mind about getting involved in this thing."

Tyman said, "That choice was taken out of our hands when those sheepmen put the Yardleys on their payroll. Still and all, we've got families to think about . . . an' runnin' our spreads . . ."

Moses Quinta absorbed this as he stared at his reflection in the back bar mirror. There was, he realized, just too much animosity between the two factions. Violence of some sort would occur. He didn't have to get involved, but the cold fact remained—and he knew it—that all of them had to take sides. Not to do so would be like a man standing in a dry creek bed after a cloudburst. In a way it was a price he had to pay for the respectability he'd earned, and he wondered how it would feel to strap on his guns again. Once one of the Yardleys—he reckoned it had been Harge Yardley—snickered out that he would sure like to square off with that old son'bitchin' gunhand named Quinta. If that ever happened, Moses knew the other three Yardleys, and maybe Treech Rincon, too, would be at his backside.

As another glass of beer was slopped before him, and his shot glass refilled, Moses tried to ponder the logic of why anyone would hire on the Yardleys—men hated by ranchers and lawmen alike. They were agents from hell when it came to taking out a lonesome 'poke checking on a herd of cows. But except for Rincon, they had no big reps as gunhands.

He glanced at Jim Graham chuckling at a sordid tale being spun out by Aldy Alderson. Moses cocked his ear to what was being said, remembering the threats spouted by Rincon that he would gun down Graham and his sons.

Milt Tyman said, "Moses, I've heard that yarn before. But you, you're more used to stayin' at the home place than coming into town."

"I was just thinkin' that at least Treech Rincon's confined to the territorial prison," Moses said softly.

"You haven't heard? Suppose not, Moses, but Rincon's out of prison."

His slate-gray eyes narrowing, Moses blinked away his surprise at the news. Finally he murmured, "Just doesn't add up."

"You don't suppose," Tyman speculated, "these sheepmen had anything to do with it?"

Through the mirror Moses saw the batwings being pushed inward, and he turned away from the bar when Deputy Sheriff Josh Medran ambled in and upon spotting Quinta came over. "Howdy, Mr. Alderson, gents. Been looking for you, Mr. Quinta, to tell you . . . to tell all of you . . . that Cy Eldridge just passed away."

"I knew about that bad heart of his," Alderson said quietly. "Sorry to hear that, Josh. Reckon I'll mosey back to my hotel, as it seems the sun's set."

They followed Alderson out onto the boardwalk, where the deputy drew Quinta aside, and Medran said, "Hogan, one of the county commissioners, sent me over. I know about that offer they made you, Mr. Quinta, and I don't resent it being made. Though they could have at least waited until Cy had died . . ."

"Josh, I want you to tell Hogan that I'm—".

The ear-puncturing sound of a rifle cut away Quinta's voice. Instinct slapped his right hand down toward his hip as he went into a crouch, and Medran exclaimed in disbelief, "Jim Graham's been shot!"

Once he'd cleared the shards of light coming from outlying buildings, the horseman reined off the road and riverward, where he drew up and held for a moment. He couldn't chance being spotted, now that he had unleashed the violence.

He was still displeased over how some of these wimpy-assed ranchers had conducted themselves at the meeting. Though the ones that counted had come to see things his way. Now, with a final probing gaze uproad toward Worland, he felt it was safe enough to keep his meeting with the man who'd killed Jim Graham. And of course he'd attend Jim's funeral, for he expected to be asked to be one of the pallbearers.

When he came down close to the river, he rode along the narrow strip of sand to where the river widened to form sandbars, out to a small island thick with scrub trees. Here the wet sand clutched at his horse's hooves, and it splashed through small pools of water and into a shallow arm of the main river, where prints made by another horse told him the killer had arrived, though he could already feel the eyes of the man taking in his approach.

On the island he urged the bronc into the midst of the concealing trees but didn't bother to dismount. The man who'd been taking his ease on a fallen tree rose, the tailormade he was sucking on brightening as he inhaled to reveal his gaunt face.

"Like I said, Mr. Kemmerer, that went—"

"Don't you ever use my name again!" Kemmerer lashed out. "Here or any other place or so help me—"

"Easy," the other man said, as his eyes glinted back just as hotly.

20

"So, you did your killing job here. I might have more work for you." Carsey Kemmerer dipped a hand into his coat pocket, lifted out a small leather pouch, and tossed it to the killer. "I know you're acquainted with Moses Quinta."

"I'd take him out for nothing."

"It seems they've talked him into taking over as sheriff. This could be a problem. But don't do anything until I give the word, or—"

The rancher wheeled his horse around and came out from under the trees. Once he was clear of the river, he headed into Worland. The day had gone well for him. The fact that a neighboring rancher had been murdered by his order was brushed away. Anyway, Graham was too unreliable, he thought. Control . . . that's what it all came down to, control of his life and those around him . . .

Four

The worst part of the trip for Treech Rincon was heading north through windswept Shirley Basin. There'd been places where the wind had thrown up pebbly sand, but he'd blundered on, sucking on a whiskey bottle and lunging in free air.

His release from that stone-walled hellhole at Laramie had come as a complete surprise. And good behavior had nothing to do with it. He'd given as good as he'd gotten back there, in bare-knuckle brawls that had seen some get crippled up awful bad. Rincon had gotten a few missing teeth and more scars, and the worst he'd suffered was his left earlobe getting bitten away. But he'd survived, which was all that mattered.

"Never trust a gent bearing gifts," Treech Rincon muttered, and the passengers seated facing him in the stagecoach studiously avoided his red-rimmed eyes. He'd gotten on at Casper, with his thoughts on when the iron gates of the territorial prison had slammed shut behind him and there'd been this suited gent waiting in a carriage to give him a ride into Laramie.

"Mr. Rincon—"

Slinging his possibles bag over a scrawny shoulder, he gazed at the man in the carriage. Finally he spat out, "You a lawman?"

"I represent the people responsible for securing your release from prison, Mr. Rincon."

"The hell you say?"

"Yes, but this is no place to discuss business."

By rights, Treech Rincon mused, he should have been taken out and hung. But like the judge had said, hanging a no-account bastard like him wasn't punishment enough. "That judge will sure be pissed off once he finds out I've been sprung. Business you say . . . I don't like doin' business with some two-bit lawyer . . ."

"Harge Yardley said you'd be owly as hell about this."

"Harge in on this?"

"Get in the carriage and find out, Mr. Rincon."

Treech Rincon discovered that the people who had secured his release from prison wanted him back in the Bighorn Basin. When he'd left Laramie it had been aboard a horse, which he'd sold in Casper. For a week he'd boozed it up around town, putting a big crimp in the two hundred dollars he'd received from that lawyer. Still mean drunk, Rincon had taken the stage out, and now the southern end of the Bighorns and the Bridgers framed into his line of vision. It was around one o'clock on a clear blustery afternoon, and a day and some four hours later Treech Rincon was gazing moodily out a side window at a creek beyond which rose the lower elevations of Cloud Peak in the Bighorns.

He was still in a drunken haze, having slopped it up at every stage station along the way and in Bigtrails and Ten Sleep, too. He didn't know what he was getting into, and it didn't matter a tinker's damn to Rincon as long as his cousins, the Yardleys, were involved in it. In Casper he'd paid considerable for a matched set of .44 rimfire Colts fit into holsters and a gunbelt checked with fancy scrollwork—though before he'd gotten by with only one gun.

"'Pears we're almost at Elkhorn."

Rincon didn't respond to the carpetbagger leaning to peer out of a window, as all he wanted to do was vacate the stagecoach and head to the closest place serving beer. If Harge and the rest were here, all the better. When some buildings flashed by the rolling coach, he reached up and pulled the brown Stetson down over his forehead. In the dark blue cotton shirt and Levi's he appeared to be just another cowpuncher in reach of a ridin' job. That is, until you honed in on Treech Rincon's moody gray eyes, narrow pitted face, and missing earlobe. Then you knew trouble had come to Elkhorn.

Main Street was about as Rincon had anticipated—a wide patch of ground lined by false-fronted buildings and shadows elongating easterly as the sun was settling in behind the Absarokas. Like a halfblood Sioux he'd pulled some jobs with, Rincon didn't know if it was Monday or going on Friday. His whiskey-reddened eyes picked out a barmaid framed in the open door of an upstreet saloon, and he swung open the stagecoach door. The pointed toes of his high-heeled boots thudded onto the hard dusty street. He swung about and called up to the shotgun clambering onto the coach roof, "That new saddle is mine an' them saddlebags wrapped around that Yellow Belly . . ."

"Ain't I seen you a'fore . . . ?"

"Probably have," Rincon admitted as the saddle was handed down to him. Then hefting his saddlebags, he peeled onto the boardwalk to come out of the shadow of the Gallagan Hotel. Sullenly he took in what was happening along the street before it dawned on him that he didn't have to be dodging twilight shadows at least for a while, as he'd been given a conditional release from prison. Breaking into an off-key whistling rendition of *Buffalo Gal,* he went into the Ornery Bull Saloon.

Had not Treech Rincon's senses been dulled by corn whiskey, he would have noticed there was more to Elkhorn than the one long forlorn street. He'd have seen other businesses on side streets: the new log building going up where town and ranch children would attend school, the houses of worship—Faith Baptist and St. Thomas Catholic Church—and the town hall farther to the east. And the other hotel, the Navarre, which was run by a Basque named Arnaud. But most important to hardcase

24

Treech Rincon was the stone building splashed with white stucco a block west of the saloon where he'd sought refuge, and in which the Varney Brothers ran their growing sheep operation in the Bighorn Basin.

While in the saloon all Rincon had eyes for was one of the barmaids—along with slopping down three quick steins of cold foamy beer and matching glasses of rotgut whiskey. While she—she'd told him her name was Shirley—quickly gauged that here was her windfall for the month. She wore a clever pink gusseted dress which concealed a lot of lumpy places, cut low a'purpose to expose her ample breasts but with a low-ankled hemline as though to show she had some traces of modesty left. As Rincon's hungry eyes had raked over her fleshy attributes, she'd quickly been matching him drink for drink. Shirley's female instincts told her this uncouth 'poke hadn't sampled a woman's favors for a heap of Sundays.

Now Rincon's braggin' words filled in what she'd suspected. Pulling the barmaid close, he blurted, "As Billy the Kid is my witness, you smell damn good."

"Why, mister, you an owlhooter, too . . ."

"That Kid can't hold a candle to Treech Rincon."

"That so?" she giggled.

With one arm around Shirley's rounded shoulder, Treech Rincon, a boot planted possessively on the bar rail, allowed a grin to circulate amongst the tables. Farther back an oldtime cowhand was nursing his drink at a table, and he sat merged with the back shadows, doubtful that the braggart at the bar could even see him. By name he was Chesty Moore, in his seventies, and still clear of mind but stoved up a lot from too many years spent saddlebound.

He wasn't a man to draw attention to himself. Though pridefully he could claim, if he had a mind to, that he'd help settle the basin. Troubling Moore at the moment wasn't so much that he'd recognized Treech Rincon, but what Rincon's presence back in the basin meant. "This sheep outfit . . . hiring on those Yardley brothers. They were just as guilty as Rincon," he muttered.

Up at the bar Rincon had established what he wanted with the barmaid and now pushed her toward the staircase, leaving behind all of his worldly possessions. Those at the tables took a short break to watch the barmaid bulldogging her present customer upstairs, a sight they'd witnessed many times before.

Rincon dropped the whiskey bottle on the stairs, and solemnly someone intoned," A damned waste."

As everyone tucked in to what they were doing before, a man detached himself from the bar and ambled over to where Rincon had piled his belongings on a bench nestled in under one of the front windows. The only one it seemed observing this was former cowhand Chesty Moore. Moore was about to leave anyway and head halfheartedly back to his rooming house, but he refrained from sipping down the last of his whiskey. He took in the man—just some drifter judging from what he wore—reaching a covert hand in to wrap it around the long stock of the Winchester rifle.

Pushing up from the table, Moore's long-booted stride carried him up along the front wall, and he was there as the drifter latched on to the saddlebags. A long bony hand still containing a steely grip held the drifter's collarbone, and now Chesty Moore said in a voice raised so those at the tables could hear, "Was I you, mister, I'd put that rifle and saddlebags back where you found them."

Quizzical eyes came from the tables and up along the bar to take in what was happening. As for Moore, he let the moment build, for he realized that he was the only one who'd recognized Treech Rincon. There was a moment of sad reflection, too, for the aging cowhand, in that he knew the Yardley brothers had been hired on by the sheepgrowers, out of which would only come trouble. Trouble which would erupt now that Rincon was back in the basin.

26

"That's it," he said to the drifter. "Now, hombre, best you vamoose."

Once the drifter had hurried outside, Chesty looked about and said through the impatience of those wanting to get back to their card games, "Just didn't want to take the chance of that drifter gettin' gunned down by Treech Rincon." He took a step toward the door with the intention of leaving.

"Chesty, what'ta hell you talkin' about?"

Without breaking stride he said laconically, "That was Treech Rincon headin' up yonder staircase with Shirley."

The batwings swung back after Moore's leisurely departure to take in the uneasy glances being exchanged by those still in the saloon.

"Rincon, here?"

"Once he links up with the Yardleys . . . shit, deal me out, I'm goin' home . . ."

For over a week the Yardley brothers had been out checking on the bands of sheep owned by the Varney Sheep Company. The sheep were scattered out clear down to Kirby Creek, they'd found, and then westerly almost to the Bighorn River and to the north, away past Manderson. Harge, older brother to the rest of them, had put up with their griping over having to ride every day. Then quit, he'd told Dyson, along with reminding his brother this was the best deal they'd ever come across.

They were spurring on through a late evening rainfall. The clouds were low and moving fast, and patchy to reveal a few stars. Out front Harge Yardley rode with Eli. Harge was a square-bodied man, the yellow slicker making him look even more bulky. When things got a little hairy up in Montana, he'd made the decision to relocate down here. Before they'd just been roaming cowpokes, and Harge counted it lucky they had latched on to some land in the basin.

Eli Yardley groused, "How much farther to Elkhorn?"

"How the hell do I know—five miles, maybe," Harge snapped back.

"We should have nighted in that old trapper's cabin."

"We would have, Eli, and got just as soaked as it had no roof to speak of."

"Yeah, checking on these stupid sheepherders gives a man a certain stink. But . . ."

"But we're gettin' a regular wage."

"It ain't the money, Harge. They're some kind of foreigners—"

"Basque, out of Spain, I've heard."

Eli Yardley grinned toothily. "I hear that some of them go plumb loco after a couple of years of tending them woolies. You never did say, Harge, how that deal went over at Worland . . ."

Sidling his horse in closer, Harge said, "Don't you ever let it out I was over there. That's your trouble, Eli, you can't let things go. Anyone finds out I was there that night, the law'll be hot on our asses again."

"At least Eldridge won't be bothering us no more," he said sullenly, holding on to the sudden flash of resentment at his brother.

"Eldridge—he weren't much of a starpacker. But Moses Quinta, he's a different breed . . . an' it don't make no sense him being appointed sheriff. I see some lights ahead."

Lapsing into silence, Harge Yardley still could see the look of shocked surprise on Jim Graham's face. Killing the rancher was something Treech Rincon planned to do anyway, and for Harge there were no remorseful afterthoughts. He saw, at least for the moment, no reason to tell his brothers that they were getting paid by both the sheep company and by cattleman Carsey Kemmerer.

Now there was a sly one, that Kemmerer, and cold-blooded as they came. Unlike a lot of the other basin ranchers, Carsey Kemmerer wanted hostilities to break out. Harge knew that Kemmerer had broken bread at Jim Graham's table many a time, and they'd held roundups together and spring brandings. It was after the Yardleys had been hired on by the Varney sheep outfit that Kemmerer had secretly contacted him, Harge mused. He ducked away from a low-hanging branch of a cottonwood tree hovering over an outlying building and briefly noted the clouds dispersing over Elkhorn.

Harge was impatient and short-tempered, but he could keep his brothers in line up to a point. He wasn't one to plan ahead, or to plumb too deeply the reasons behind other men's actions. Still, he'd been puzzling over what Carsey Kemmerer hoped to gain from starting a ranch war. He'd made a deal with the rancher to gun down Graham and there was more—the details of which he'd tell his brothers when they hooked up with Treech Rincon. That Harge Yardley was working both sides of the fence by being paid by both a cattleman and this sheep outfit was, in his opinion, just opportunity knocking.

Coming in on a dark and deserted street, he lifted his eyes to the moon just floating into view, and he said acidly to himself, a'fore long it'll be stained with blood.

When hanging about Elkhorn the Yardleys stayed at the Gallagan Hotel, their rooms and other expenses being picked up by the sheep company. Coming in on the hotel after leaving their horses at a downstreet livery stable, Dyson Yardley, a thin, moon-faced man in his thirties (as were his brothers) said, "Hotel's closed down. Anyway, I'm cravin' a drink after that mangy wet ride."

Stepping past the hotel in the middle of the empty street, they looked about at the darkened business places, the town appearing even more gloomy since there were no street lamps. Up ahead some three blocks, a saloon was still open, one of four in operation in Elkhorn, with one more due to open in a couple of weeks. Closer beamed the beckoning lights of the Ornery Bull Saloon, with Harge Yardley letting his brothers hold out in front of him. He'd have a few drinks, then it was his intention to head for the hotel and roust out someone to prepare some hot water, as Harge needed a bath to rid himself of this sheep stink he imagined he was riddled with. All of his life he'd been a confirmed sheep hater, and if they hadn't been down on their luck and Treech Rincon in jail to boot, he wouldn't have hired on to do gunwork for the Varneys.

"But cowpie stinks, too," he muttered, trailing behind into the saloon.

They didn't pull up to the bar but commandeered a table, as all of them were worn out from days in the saddle and not taking too kindly to their wet clothing. "Eli," Harge said gruffly, "go up there and fetch back a bottle."

A reluctant grimace brought Eli Yardley up from the chair as Harge peeled his eyes about the interior of the saloon. By his tally there were about fifteen men hanging on until the place closed, and just two cowhands huddled in close at a table, as this was sheep country. Sinking lower in the chair, Harge removed his wet Stetson and tossed it onto an empty chair, and then he ran a tired hand through thinning strands of brown hair. His eyes lidding down some, he said by way of conversation, "Tomorrow we go see Babcock, and just maybe get paid."

"Yup," Jake Yardley said reedily around the tailormade occupying one corner of his wide mouth. "Good idea, as I intend to go on a bender." His clothing was trailworn and his boots run down at the heels. He suppressed the urge to cough, as he had consumption, and he figured if his lungs didn't play out first—what the hell, some waddy with a gun would get lucky. Jake Yardley's dark brown eyes lazed over to take in the action at a poker game.

As Eli came back bearing two bottles of whiskey, Dyson Yardley said, "Wonder what's keeping Treech? You know we owe him a heap for what he done." He had a long sober face but was prone to getting ugly when drunk. Dyson had ambitions—he wanted to strike out on his own, which meant leaving horses and sagebrush behind as he craved seeing San Francisco. The bartender came in behind Eli easing back into his chair, and from the tray the bartender carried, Dyson latched on to a sliced hunk of deer sausage.

The bartender said nervously, "Welcome back boys"—his fawning eyes slid to Harge—"Mr. Yardley. I can cut up some more sausage and cheese; that's fresh bread."

"Was Gart Babcock in here tonight?" inquired Harge.

"Was, but he left around nine. I'll put what you drink on the sheep company tab."

"Just keep them bottles coming, bardog."

"There was someone else asking about you."

Every eye at the table honed in on the bartender.

"Someone . . . man by the name of Rincon."

"I'll be damned, Treech came back."

"You think he wouldn't?" snapped Harge.

"Took Shirley upstairs," the bartender went on.

Eli Yardley let out a loud whooping snort to expose what teeth he had left, and he exclaimed, "This'll be the grandpappy of all benders."

"I thought *you* was sweet on Shirley?"

"She ain't the only filly in town," rejoined Eli, as he swung up from his chair to head with the others over to the wall staircase and tromp upstairs. One hand clamped on to a whiskey bottle, the other stuffing sausage into his mouth, he swung left with Dyson and went searching down the west wing of the hallway for their cousin, Treech.

In the lead, Dyson found a likely looking door, swung it open without bothering to knock, then veered across the hallway and whistled to announce he'd found Treech Rincon. The hardcase and the plump-bodied barmaid lay naked and snoring on the feather bed, and Dyson remarked dryly, "'Pears Shirley's got a bigger roll around her midriff than Harge; a wonder what them corsets can do."

31

"Yeah," grinned Eli, "reminds me of a sow we had up in Montana. Let's wake up Treech."

Dyson responded to this by yanking out his Smith & Wesson and triggering a bullet out the open window, the flat crackling sound jarring into their ears and causing Rincon to jackknife to a sitting position, his eyes flaying open wide in fear before it dawned on him his kin were here.

He cursed out through a drunk, sleepy smile, "Dyson, you ornery son'bitch, me and her is jaybird naked."

Now the barmaid was awake, too. Dyson said, "From the looks of her she's about ready for the butcher's block. Here, have some of this poison."

Almost of its own volition the hand of Treech Rincon swung the bottle toward his mouth, and he began guzzling it down, the spillage slopping onto his chest. Coming in now were Jake and Harge Yardley, with Harge scooting aside to let the barmaid, who'd covered herself with a bedsheet, pass out of the room. Harge whacked his hat at her rotating backside, then he shouldered in past his brothers and grasped Rincon's outstretched hand.

"Just want to tell you, Treech, you're in the sheep business now." The smile in his eyes held as the expected explosion came from Rincon.

Rincon's face was blank, as if what Harge had said hadn't registered. Then a scowl appeared, and with his eyes sort of rolling around in their sockets, he said, "Woolies? Did you say, *woolies?* Dammit, Harge, I know we've done some lowdown skunky things before—but woolies!"

"Yup, woolies."

"You mean—"

"Yup, old pard, sheep money got you out of prison."

"You want to hear more, Treech?"

He swung his eyes to the grinning Dyson. "Don't hold back nothin'—"

Harge cut in with, "For now that'll have to do, as we're all bent out of shape after bein' on the trail for a week or so." What he meant was that with the return of Treech Rincon, they'd be doin' some heavy celebrating and spill out most anything when they were boozin' it up. Afterwards—when they were drying out and still headachy and hung over—they'd be plenty mean enough then to get to their killing job. He knew the money would make the difference, as once they started, the basin would be one vast killing field.

"Okay, okay, Harge, I can wait until you spell it out for me," said Rincon. "But I'm flat busted."

"Don't matter as this sheep company is pickin' up all of our expenses."

"Maybe woolies ain't so bad after all."

Five

When Moses Quinta returned to Worland, it was as a lawman. As he'd told the county commissioners, he wasn't versed in how to handle the duties of a sheriff. One thing that helped was his having Celia's support, but he could see in her eyes that she was fearful of what could happen. Especially now that he'd heard Carsey Kemmerer had hired on some gunhands.

Before leaving the ranch, Moses had oiled up his six-guns and tried them out, only to discover that his hands were kind of stiff and his swift draw a thing of the past. But once he'd settled into it, he could punch slugs into some tin cans he tossed into the air with a degree of accuracy. On the way in to town, he'd puzzled over just who it was that had bushwhacked Jim Graham. Most said it was Treech Rincon. Or maybe one of the Yardleys. At Moses's insistence, telegrams had been sent out, one coming back from Laramie telling of Rincon's release from territorial prison, another from the law over at Casper saying that on the day Jim Graham had been shot Treech Rincon had been sighted in Casper.

The wooden pew cutting into his back, Moses Quinta pondered over the shooting and the rancor it had stirred up amongst the ranchers as the preacher went on with his sad droning eulogy. Every pew was filled, and some chairs had been set up along the wall aisles and back of the pews. The dead air was

34

still as if listening, and Moses was beginning to perspire some. He'd left his guns back at his hotel room, refusing the offer to stay over at Celia's daughter's place. He knew as sheriff he'd have to get used to some irregular hours.

Gazing about, he picked out a few people he didn't know and glanced at the pallbearers occupying one of the front pews. The pine box bearing the body of Jim Graham had been nailed shut, and Moses took in Marty, one of Graham's sons, turning his head to gaze over at where Carsey Kemmerer was seated. Though Marty Graham's face was stamped with grief, his eyes, Moses couldn't help noticing, held a silent accusation.

Now the sound of the piano brought everyone to their feet singing *Rock of Ages,* and the pallbearers moved to lift the coffin and wend their solemn way toward the front door. Once he was out of the church, Moses Quinta broke away from the procession heading out to the cemetery and claimed his horse taking its ease under an oak tree. There would be lunch afterward in the church basement, but Moses had other things on his mind. One incident which Deputy Sheriff Josh Medran had filled him in on was the matter of some sheep being killed near the northern forks of No Water Creek. Mounting up, he reined out from under the tree and onto a graveled lane but checked back on the reins at a hold-up wave from rancher Samuel Alderson.

"Seems longer than four days," remarked Alderson as he reined in alongside Moses, and they headed back toward the heart of town at a walk.

"Cy Eldridge was laid to rest yesterday," said Moses. "Now we bury another good man."

"I expect you know they're startin' to kill sheep."

"What Medran told me."

"Among other things, I expect."

"Meanin' that Kemmerer is doing some hiring—"

"That . . . and Moses, that Treech Rincon is back. Over at Elkhorn, I was told."

"At least we know Rincon didn't gun down Jim Graham."

35

Moses glanced to the southwest at the funeral procession reaching to the cemetery, which was guarded by a low bluff. Though Graham would soon be buried proper, it was expected that he find Jim Graham's killer. Somehow he knew the Yardleys were involved, perhaps figuring that by killing Graham they'd be doing their cousin Treech a favor. The fact remained that he was grasping at straws, as he was there when it happened—Graham getting gunned down—and Tyman and Carsey Kemmerer. And so'd been the man he was riding with, but he ruled out Alderson as being anyone's target.

To himself Moses said, wasn't so long ago I was a gun for hire. Could be one of the enemies I thought I left behind when I turned respectable. Or Kemmerer—now there's a man who's made a few enemies with his heavy-handed ways.

Like Alderson, Moses didn't believe the gunman's target that night was Milt Tyman, as Tyman had a small cow spread that made just enough to eke out a living.

"Tell me about your neighbor, Carsey Kemmerer."

Alderson whistled softly through his handlebar mustache while sort of grunting out, "Gets kind of uppity at times. You know he once shined up to Graham's wife . . ."

"No, Aldy, that's news to me."

"Callie—Mrs. Graham—she was some looker. Sometimes she'd single me out"—he stroked his mustache—"at one of them moon-kickin' barn dances an' we'd hoof up a storm. Yup, Moses, in my day I was some sparker. But me and Callie, it was like she was my daughter. Proud to say I'm godfather to two of their younkers. Now, Carsey Kemmerer—seems to me Carsey found himself a woman about a year after Callie got hitched to Jim—at least that's my recollection."

"They were neighbors."

"Weren't at first until Carsey bought land adjoining Graham's ranch. After that he helped out the Grahams more'n most."

"He was with us when Jim got killed," Moses said pointedly, as they swung past Guymon's Barber Shop on Maple Street.

36

"I get your drift," countered Alderson. "Did Kemmerer have anything to do with the killing? Another good question would be—did he ever get over losing Callie to Jim Graham?" Aldy Alderson turned his head away and spat out tobacco juice. He turned back, wiping his mouth with the back of his hand to add, "Only Carsey could answer them puzzlers, Sheriff Quinta."

"Yup, now I'm sheriff, which is another puzzler. As you and everyone else hereabouts knows, I've no qualifications for the job other than my old rep as a gunhand. I don't even know how to serve papers on someone. For when they came for me a'fore, Aldy—lawmen that is—it weren't with paper but with cold steel. An' see these gray sideburns; there's more gray piled up under this beat-up Stetson."

"You sound, son, like you need some firewater under your belt buckle."

"I do indeed, and I'm springin'."

"You ought to, Sheriff, as you're employed regular now."

It pleased Carsey Kemmerer all of the talk spreading through the basin that sheepmen were behind the murder of Jim Graham. To fan the flames of hatred and distrust, Kemmerer had gone up to the basin and Greybull, as he'd told his foreman to take in some cattle sales, but in reality to give a firsthand account of that killing. From here others carried the story to outflung cowtowns and ranches.

Once he was clear of the cemetery, Carsey Kemmerer didn't reroute back to the church, heading instead with a couple of other ranchers for the Calumet Saloon, a quiet, out-of-the-way bar favored by cattlemen. On the way there, he couldn't help noticing how subdued the town felt, draped in mourning but with a deeper undertone of expectancy.

From what Harge Yardley had told him, he knew that the Varney Sheep Company was sending in some hired guns from such places as Utah and Idaho. This suited Kemmerer's purposes and his next course of action—part of which involved forking out hard cash to a couple of top guns. And from what he'd just been told, Wayford Clark, owner of the Double C, was doing the same.

Unlike the Great Divide Basin and that Casper town, there wasn't any late afternoon wind shrilling into Worland. And if any wind did come into the basin, it didn't last long. Through the open saloon windows came the sound of an anvil as a blacksmith hammered some iron into shape. The voices of the ranchers were low-checked where they sat up near the bar. Kemmerer swiveled his eyes to the four hunkered over a game of cutthroat pinochle, and to a drunken swamper barely able to keep himself planted on a bar stool. The other rancher at his table, Bailey Smith, a ruddy-cheeked man with big lumpy hands and his hat tilted carelessly to one side of his large head, was all full of talk they should hit more'n one band of sheep at a time.

"Confuse the hell out of them," said Smith.

"Won't take much," threw in Wayford Clark, "as some of them sheepherders ain't all that swift."

"Perhaps," said Kemmerer. "But we've got ranches to run. At the most we can spare two, three 'pokes. Reason this meetin' is set for tonight. Not only to build up our war chest, but to get more ranchers to come in with us. We start too hot and heavy, a lot'll shy away, but once they're committed—"

"Yup, Carsey," said Wayford Clark. "Then there's no backing away. What about Graham's son, Marty. Anybody has a right to gun down some sheepmen it's him."

"With Jim just being buried today," said Kemmerer, "and the rest of his family here, too, we'd best give the Grahams a little time for mourning."

"I expect so." Wayford Clark flicked a welcoming hand as a couple more ranchers—Art Littlejohn and Corvin Baugh—sidled in and grabbed chairs on their way over to the table. They had ranches in the Grass Creek area. Littlejohn slid another round table in closer.

"A long ride for you boys."

"Especially when there's no watering holes betwixt where we pulled out of and here."

The bartender came over with some more shot glasses and a bottle of whiskey. Corvin Baugh said, "But we did manage to fatten up on trailkill." A grin lifted his flat cheekbones.

Scratching at his neck, Art Littlejohn murmured his thanks as Kemmerer reached across to fill the shot glass, and then Littlejohn drawled out, "Can't believe both Callie and Jim are gone." Solemnly he picked up his shot glass and added, *"Salud."*

The glasses clinked down; nobody spoke for a while, their wind-scoured faces set in pensive lines. In the silence the bottle was passed about, and then the talk began again as Corvin Baugh reached a quiet hand into an inner coat pocket and lifted out his leather wallet, out of which he extracted some greenbacks. "Me and Art sold some livestock. Being a far piece away, we're sort of isolated from all of this sheep trouble. That don't mean you haven't got our support." He reached across the table and placed the money before Carsey Kemmerer. "If you boys need more, why, just give me and Art a holler."

Staring at the money, Kemmerer brought his eyes sweeping about, with a smile for Corvin Baugh and Littlejohn. "I've been doing a lot of soul searching of late. We don't know who killed Jim Graham. Treech Rincon? Nope, but then who? We don't know either if this sheep company was behind it, either. Now if we took out after one bunch of sheep, they could retaliate by taking out after our cattle."

"Could," pondered Wayford Clark.

"What we don't want to be is a lynch mob or a vigilante committee . . . as we have to respect the law. At least to a certain degree."

"What are you drivin' at Carsey . . . ?"

"There is a way to avoid bloodshed." This was the last thing that Carsey Kemmerer wanted to happen—that or a truce between these men and the sheep company. But he'd spoken with a deliberate callousness simply to show these men that he was no hotheaded cattleman intent on exterminating their enemies. The truth of it was that this was a ploy to cast suspicion away from himself and away from what would happen tonight. "What I'm getting at is that we could send a delegation over to Elkhorn to talk to this sheep company. At least try to stave off a ranch war."

"You could," muttered cattleman Bailey Smith, "bring this up at tonight's meeting. But what happened to Jim Graham tells me it won't hold much water."

"Maybe," said Carsey Kemmerer as he took out his turnip-shaped watch. "But at least it'll show this sheep company we're honorable men. Supper time—I'm heading for the Westerner Club with the intentions of paying for your food and drinks, gentlemen."

For Moses Quinta—passing along a night-shrouded street— there was a sense of unreality, caused chiefly by the badge glittering where it was pinned to his leather vest. He was making the rounds of the saloons and gaming joints in the company of Deputy Josh Medran. What they were picking up on was the tenor of emotions still gripping the cowhands and ranchers who'd come in for this afternoon's funeral. Though Moses still considered himself a rancher, the sight of his badge got some to clamming up when he entered a barroom.

And he said wryly, "You know, Josh, I used to have a powerful dislike for badgepackers."

Medran laughed softly, as he matched Quinta's stride along the boardwalk fronting parts of Cedar Street. He was tall and lantern-jawed, sandy haired, and a southpaw as attested to by the gun thonged at his left hip. As for Moses Quinta, he'd found out that Medran had gotten divorced a couple of years ago but was trying to patch things up with his former missus, and not having all that much luck with it. This gnawed at Moses, as he didn't want a deputy that was distracted by other things; and then there was Josh Medran's habit of wanting to use his fists rather than that hogiron when he went to make an arrest. Otherwise, in Moses's opinion, the man was solid.

"Kemmerer is looking for trouble."

"Hiring those hardcases—'pears that way."

"An' now Wayford Clark has done the same thing. Sort of out of character for Wayford."

Medran said, "Just some unprideful gunhands goin' after sheepherders. When d'ya think they'll hit another band of sheep?"

"I was hopin' Mr. Kemmerer could tell me. Despite all that talk about just bein' one of the ranchers, they sort of look to him for leadership. Interestin' what Alderson told me, or maybe you knew that, about Kemmerer having an interest in Jim Graham's wife."

Coming in on another saloon, they paused in the light pouring out of a window, with Josh Medran kind of shrugging as he said, "Way I heard it, that was a long time ago. Why?"

"Don't rightly know," said Moses, as he held in his mind the way Marty Graham had acted over at the church this afternoon. Just an angry shading of the eyes, and it could be, thought Moses, he was reading too much into it. Maybe he should concentrate his efforts on what was happening tonight in Worland. The only training he had for this job as sheriff was the old, long-buried instinct of a man swift with a six-gun. In an ironic way the county commissioners weren't too prideful when it came to picking him. Running scared—that's what they were—fearing the dire and damn real possibility of a ranch war, and their lawman a middle-aged gunfighter with a rusty rep to back it up. There was his place, too, and there was Celia to protect and honor and love. Though she'd sure as sin put slugs center-bore into anyone loco enough to come against the 77 spread. Which reminded Moses that he hadn't availed himself of any free meals over at Beth's.

"Nope, that noon-sharp stuff doesn't cut the mustard."

"Come again?"

"Aw, Josh, you mosey in to this saloon. Think I'll go upstreet for some coffee and some grub."

He went on alone, under a wide sweeping veranda hooked to a mercantile store, mindful of the fact that he hadn't walked this far in cowboy boots for a spell, and that the heels were rundown some. And mindful of the chat he'd had with the mayor and one of the county commissioners, in which a notion had been thrown about that Moses Quinta should head over to Elkhorn and lay down some ground rules with this sheep company.

More fat had been thrown in the fire because of those damning front-page articles in the *Worland Star Journal,* accusing both the Yardley brothers and Treech Rincon of murdering Jim Graham. Just as inflammatory were other articles telling of the incoming invasion by sheep interests. Moses was beginning to believe that taking this badge was like shaking hands with a rattlesnake. Wouldn't be long 'fore he'd need some antidote. 'Cause he knew that sidewinder'd try to do him harm. An' his tinny star made a fine target, too.

The worry of his thoughts in the slant of his stare fixing on the Worland Hotel, Moses began cutting across the street, but checked his stride to let a buggy roll by. Main Street still had a lot of traffic. He'd been lucky to get a room at the hotel due to folks coming in for the funeral. Then he was stepping onto the boardwalk, with Marty Graham pushing out of the lobby, and he threw Moses a curt nod.

"Evenin', Quinta."

"Could you spare a few moments, Marty?"

In his middle twenties, Marty Graham wore a black suit and hat and a hesitant smile, which faded away as Moses Quinta moved up closer. He was slope-shouldered like his father had been and wasn't wearing a gunbelt. There was about him a look of bitter sadness and resignation. "Okay, fire away."

"I've known you, well, since I came to the basin. Your pa,

42

they don't make them like that anymore. I'll sure miss Jim." He thought about what Aldy Alderson had told him this afternoon, that Carsey Kemmerer had been an admirer of his mother, but Moses knew this was not the time to rake that story over the coals. "You know about tonight's meeting?"

"Expect I do, Sheriff," he said pleasantly.

"You going?"

"Debating it."

"You know these people, Marty. If the son of Jim Graham joins forces with Kemmerer and his supporters, it's the same as an open declaration of war."

"That's a pretty strong opinion, Sheriff. Like the other ranchers, I've got a spread to run . . . now that dad's . . . gone . . ."

"Yup, he left you more than the ranch."

"The decision of what to do is up to me. 'Spect I don't like sheep same as any other cattleman. But so far they haven't shown up in my part of the basin."

"What I hear is they're drifting them closer. You know, son, your pa always respected your judgment—reckon that's good enough for me."

Marty Graham gave Moses a searching look, through which came a pensive smile. "Have to tell you, Moses, he took a shine to you even though you'd had a checkered career packing a gun. But pa was like that—always willing to give a man a chance. Even—"

A steel-jacketed slug sent Marty Graham's hat fluttering from his head, then shattered a lobby window. The ugly rifle snarl that followed came out of an alleyway across the street. For a moment Marty remained framed in the square of light pouring out of the lobby, then Moses grabbed his arm and pulled him toward the meager shelter of the porch support pole. Crouching now, Moses unlimbered one of his Colts as he snarled at Graham, "Get back into the hotel."

"But—"

"Do as I tell you, dammit." Moses swung up to dart out

43

toward the three horses tethered at a tie bar, and then he pushed out to break toward the opposite boardwalk, dread thick in him of catching a slug from that Henry rifle.

As he crossed the boardwalk to hug in close to the buildings, it suddenly dawned on him that only one shot had been fired. And when he eased into the alley, he found out that the rifleman was gone, though he had left behind the steel-jacketed casing. Moses picked it up and stuffed it into a vest pocket.

Holstering his Colts, he stood there, half turned so that he could survey the front of the hotel, where he could make out curious eyes peering cautiously out of doorways and windows. Back there, he sorted out, he knew he'd been shielding most of Marty Graham's upper body from the view of anyone hidden in this alley. Maybe that was it—why the only damage was to young Graham's Stetson. Still, it just didn't feel right—

The city of Worland had graciously loaned those attending the meeting called by Carsey Kemmerer the use of the board-framed schoolhouse, situated up at the eastern end of Cedar Street. Behind this rose a bluff stained with layers of red rock and topped by scoria. Horses and buggys ringed the two-story building, and one latecomer came afoot to sneak in as Carsey Kemmerer was finishing up his middle of the meeting speech.

For Kemmerer there'd been some displeasure over a handful of holdout ranchers, men more inclined to view a gunbattle from as far away as they could get. Again there wasn't even the slightest hint of breeze to chase away the heat of day, and men were perspiring even though the windows and doors were ajar. Some of them still had on the suits they'd worn when attending the funeral service. They'd duffed coats and ties, as had Carsey Kemmerer, who was dragging a checked handkerchief across his brow.

"It all comes down to the hard fact that we have no other choice in the matter. These sheepmen are the invaders. I just

44

took a swing over along Nowood Creek. And, gentlemen, if only you could see how these sheep have literally destroyed the grass. Bailey Smith, do you have something to add?"

"Won't take long," grumbled out the rancher as he pushed up from the side table he'd been using as a chair. He was hatless, had rolled his shirtsleeves up to the elbows, and was brushing away at a mosquito. "The thing is, gents, we've dealt with this kind of situation before. Indians, them homesteaders, what all. Back then when I was a heap younger it was the law of the land to use whatever means necessary to hold on to your rightful property. Now this, woolies."

He hitched at his trousers tucked into buffed dark brown boots and said, "Hey, Eddie, d'you remember, back a couple of months, as I recollect—we was up at Tater Drew's place in Manderson guzzling down some prime stuff when all of a sudden this awful stench come in through the batwings. It was some crazy Basque pushin' a band of sheep right down Main Street. Smellin' sheep dung that close damned near—"

Boots thudding onto the front porch steps cut away Bailey Smith's words, and he turned toward the front door, which was framing one of Wayford Clark's cowhands, who exclaimed loudly, "Someone just tried to kill Marty Graham!"

Six

The evil-eyed men who had come to Elkhorn were a source of worry for Javier Dominquez, the sole proprietor of the Navarre Hotel. That they were hired by the Varney sheep outfit to protect Basque sheepherders meant little to Dominquez, himself a Basque from the province of Basse Navarre. He brought his worry from his downstairs room in the hotel into the spacious kitchen. He lit one of the lamps hanging from a ceiling beam. Then he turned toward the large cast iron stove, not bothering to look at the wall clock ticking away. For he knew it was around four o'clock in the morning, his usual rising time.

Despite the solid shock of gray hair, his thick mustache still retained traces of coal-black hair. His eyes were a clear steely blue, those of a man more accustomed to the mountainous plateaus in the basin. In fact, fifteen years ago Javier Dominquez had quit tending sheep out in Utah and Nevada to drift about for a time with his wife and only daughter. Now here he was in Elkhorn, having been here for about seven years, and at that time this building had been an abandoned hotel. Today, at least in Dominquez's opinion, it was the finest hostelry within miles.

A fire began sending out heat from the kitchen stove, and he set about making a pot of coffee. Afterward he would prepare food for the meals they would sell during the coming day. He cooked the old traditional Basque way, took pride both in his cooking and in their beautiful daughter, Angelita. And of course, the Navarre, a home for the many Basque sheepherders working out of the basin.

From his own experiences Dominquez knew that a hotel such as this was an ethnic haven for Basques braving the High Plains and the mountains. It provided the herders with an address, a place to leave their town clothes while working on the range, and a home between jobs. Staying at the hotel were a half dozen Basques who had recently left Spain and were unversed in English—and so he was expected to serve as their interpreter. Traditionally, too, he extended liberal credit and cash loans to temporarily strapped herders. Never had one of his fellow Basques failed to pay him back.

By six o'clock he had several pots heating on the stove and rolls and bread baking in the oven. Around him he could hear the hotel coming to life, and soon after, Elena—his wife of twenty-two years—appeared. Like her husband, Elena Dominquez had been born in Spain, coming to America as a sprightly girl of seventeen. Some ten years younger than Javier, her hair was shiny black, which sat well with her deep brown eyes. Coming to him, she placed a hand at the base of his neck and leaned in to receive a kiss.

"You smell good," he murmured.

"And you smell like a loaf of bread." They laughed together, sharing this quiet moment, as within the next half-hour the dining room would occupy their time.

He reached to a shelf to lift off a porcelain cup, which he filled with coffee, and stood holding it patiently as she tied an apron around her ample waist. Framing a scowl, he said, "That man who runs this sheep outfit, what is his name?"

"Isn't it . . . Taggart?"

He handed her the cup. Now he lapsed into Basque, an incomprehensible tongue to those not having heard it before, and which they call *eskuara,* or clear. Some claim it was the only language to escape the Tower of Babel. But all Basques agreed

47

that the devil himself once tried to learn *eskuara* by hiding in the attic of a Basque home. Some seven years later—so the story went—he had mastered only the phrase *Bai, anderrea!*—Yes, ma'am.

"Wait, my husband, for why should you be concerned about this sheep outfit bringing in men to protect the herders? Did not Martin Iturri say this is all for the good?"

"Iturri, he is just soft on our daughter. Besides, he is out there, isolated from all of this. I tell you, Elena my wife, these men have the eyes of the devil."

"Papa, are you starting on that again."

He swung away from the chopping block to frown at their daughter coming through the door leading into the dining room. Every time Javier Dominquez had to pause in what he was doing to take in Angelita's radiant beauty. He never expected at the age of forty-one to get married, much less have such a daughter come from his loins. She was to both him and Elena a blessing from the highest heavens.

Angelita wore a flowing skirt and sandals and a summery white blouse, her black satiny hair dancing well below her shoulders. Her eyes had a purplish cast, and they rarely lost their teasing smile. She was twenty, full-bodied, with captivating mannerisms. Most of the Basques staying here had never married, as befitting their lonely way of life—and Angelita flirted with them as much as they played up to her. Though she was in no hurry to get married, one of the Basques who'd just arrived from Spain had gotten her attention—Zalba Goyeneche, from Alava, so shy he blushed every time they encountered one another.

"Well—" snapped Elena Dominquez, from where she was lifting a pot off the stove, "we've got men to feed. You, Angelita, see that the silverware is in place. The *chorizo,* Javiar, is it cut—"

"And the *salchichon,*" he told her, adding silently, Better I had stayed on as a herder. Up until now this had been his domain, but with daybreak he would take over the chores of running the bar and lobby, and now he was bringing platters of hot food into the dining room.

Fifteen Basques, the only residents of the hotel—though at times a salesman or traveler would come in to seek a room— were clustered around the long table dominating the dining room, although smaller tables stood before a series of windows. Fresh white paint covered the walls, the high ceiling was underslung with oaken beams, and the hotel faced southeast away from the prevailing winds. Everybody waited for the hotel owner and his wife to join them and Angelita, while chatting quietly in their native tongue.

"Come, come," Dominquez said impatiently to his wife, and when she entered the dining room, it was to sit alongside her daughter at the back end of the table.

At the head of the table, Javier Dominquez picked up the bottle of good Spanish whiskey and filled his glass, then he passed the bottle on, to have the other Basques fill their glasses. The women poured a little sweet wine into their glasses. It was always this way at breakfast. Dominquez held up his glass and said by way of a toast, *"Osagarria*—a good life."

He smiled at the responses from his boarders, and he eyed one man and said, "Pascuala, so you go out sometime this week?"

"Out to herd, yes. It is good here in the basin, plenty of shelter and grass."

"You worked for this sheep outfit over in Utah, as I understand. These Varneys, are they honest men?"

"There is only one of them, Adolph Varney, I believe. The other brother went away to start another business. To answer that would be difficult, as I do not want to alarm those who've just arrived from home. But those we work for are heavy-handed at times, I suppose. But when one is out there alone with the sheep"—Pascuala shrugged—"what else matters. A good life—*Osagarria.*" He drained his glass and bent to the task of eating breakfast.

As did everyone else, partaking of the hot fresh rolls and thick slabs of bread upon which they piled the dry salami, *salchicon,* and the Basque sausage, *chorizo.* And deep cups of *cafe con leche* or hot chocolate, rich and thick as a pudding. And to top this off was a slab of *membrillo,* a quince jelly so stiff it was eaten out of the hand like candy. And this morning there was a special treat made by Elena: plates of hot crisp strips of fried dough sprinkled with coarse granulated sugar known as *churros.* Finally, a little more whiskey was consumed, during which time Angelita shaped a teasing smile for young Zalba, who in his blushing confusion slopped whiskey onto his woolen shirt.

A Basque with the pretentious name of Beltram Yparraquirre retorted through his smile, "My good Zalba, how can you claim to be a herder when you can't handle a little whiskey. Eh, tell me?"

Young Zalba Goyeneche rose and fled the dining room to a crescendo of friendly laughter. Shaking his head, Dominquez looked the length of the table at his daughter and said, "You shouldn't tease Zalba like that."

"You know Angelita," his wife said. "Now scat everyone, get to work, and if you don't have a job yet, go outside and do your smoking there." She rose to call out to her husband, "Don't forget we're almost out of olives and pine nuts . . ."

He waved back at her while continuing on into the barroom, where he went around the bar and opened a closet door. Reaching for a broom, he turned to see that Pascuala had come in and was settling a red beret over his shaggy black hair. The Basque was thick through the shoulders with muscular arms and a square-jawed face. Dominquez knew that Pascuala, along with the others, would go over to the holding pens to began separating sheep into bands of at least five hundred. When a band was ready, one of the Basques would take it out to an assigned parcel of land and would not return until wintry weather set in. As for Pascuala, it was evident something was troubling him, for the man followed after Dominquez as he headed for the front door.

"You know, Mr. Taggart will not heed our advice."

"I know," said Dominquez. "He has his orders, I suppose, which is to keep pushing the sheep into places where they aren't wanted. These men he has hired, they are to protect the herders? Bah, better they try to stop a chinook from sweeping into the basin. I tell you, Pascuala, I can smell it, the winds of violence."

"Without us and the herders like Martin Iturri, they would have to pull out."

"Running solves nothing. Tell me, what is their name these men with guns?"

"I hear they are of one family—brothers. Except for the one that just arrived."

"Yes, the one that just got out of prison, Rincon." He began sweeping out the interior of the enclosed porch and paused now to gaze with hooded eyes at the herder. "They walked by here yesterday, when my daughter was out back doing some washing. I saw him, this Rincon, as he strutted in to where she was working. I saw those lustful eyes of his. Though Angelita told him to leave, I know he will be back."

"I have a gun."

"And I have one under the bar," countered Dominquez. "To use on rats and burglars. Men such as these are killers. This Rincon"—he forced a smile—"men like him shouldn't live in mountainous country as their brains do not get enough . . . what do you call it . . . oxygen. Go now, my friend, to your job. And leave all of this to me."

During the warm summery day the Navarre Hotel saw a few locals drop in to eat and others to while away a little time in the barroom. By four o'clock, out of the twenty rooms only two were vacant—some salesmen renting rooms and the new schoolmistress rented one also; she was around thirty and from Ohio. Javier Dominquez went out to buy some supplies and to stop off at the Citizens Bank, where he made a deposit.

On his way back to the hotel, Dominquez passed the red brick building owned by the Varney sheep outfit. Out back some horses were tethered, and though he didn't know them, Eli and Jake Yardley were squatting in the shade of a cottonwood. Lazy bums, he mused, and he took a firmer grip on the reins as his buggy came abreast of the building. Some time ago he'd stopped wearing a beret, knowing that if he were to be accepted out here, he would have to adopt local customs. One barrier was Javier Dominquez's Spanish accent and the fact that he just couldn't pronounce some of the new strange-sounding words. Another was that as a Basque he hadn't been asked to join any civic groups.

"Time heals everything," Dominquez murmured, as he caught a distant glimpse of the holding pens, and beyond those, a herder taking out a band spread out over a hillock. Which meant to him that tonight there'd be one more empty room, and in the days to come, more of the same as other herders went out.

As a rule the herders were lightly armed with a pistol or rifle to use on scavengers like coyotes or bear. All of them were aware of the growing hostility displayed by basin cattlemen. The newcomers—Zalba Goyeneche and Ciriaco and a few others—were no more than twenty, though ages old when it came to handling sheep. They had a propensity for arduous work and by reputation were honest and loyal. But how, Dominquez wondered, would they react if and when some cowhands attacked their band? One herder against ten or twelve horsemen, with common sense fleeing before a burst of anger, and if a Basque fired back, he would surely go down. Dominquez had a bad feeling for these hired guns brought in by the sheep outfit. If asked, he would say that he was filled with many superstitious beliefs. All Basques had an extreme aversion to snakes, believing that all snakes were venomous and could poison their victims with both their tongues and tails. The Basques were a tribe shrouded in mystery as to their origin and often said, "We are like honest women; we have no history." Dominquez considered himself fortunate that he hadn't gotten sagebrushed as so many Basques had out here—gone loco from the isolation, the long and lonely weeks. *That crazy Basco* was an expression he'd heard flung around many times.

"I'm afraid these things will come to an end before very long. These gunmen hired by Mr. Taggart . . . they could start the violence . . ."

"What was that, Papa?"

Lost in the worry of his thoughts, as Javiar Dominquez reined in behind the hotel, he suddenly realized that Angelita had called out to him from where she stood hanging clothing and linen on the long clothesline put up alongside the barren patch of ground where his Basque boarders played *pelota,* their favorite game.

Under the wide brim of the straw hat he regarded her curious eyes and grumbled, "It is just that prices have gone up. Come, you—"

At that moment his wife opened the screen door and came outside. "Finish hanging up the clothes. I'll help your father." She came in closer to sniff at his mouth, then smiled and kissed him lightly on the cheek.

"No, I did not stop and have a drink."

"That is your business."

"Oh, is that so?" he said with mock severity. He clambered down and began unharnessing the horse. "I saw a band of sheep going out—it could be we won't be seeing Zalba Goyeneche for some months."

Elena Dominquez said, "Quit teasing your daughter and put the horse away. Supper waits for no man in my kitchen."

When he had the horse stabled in the large shed out back of the hotel, he let his worries of the day ebb away. He knew those

53

gunmen would be leaving again. In another week, too, all of the sheep would be out of the holding pens and taken to grazing land by Basque herders. Then Elkhorn would settle back into a summery routine of hot days and cool evenings. He went out the back door to grasp a pitchfork thrust into the large pile of musky-scented hay.

Dominquez paused to gaze westerly and far across the basin to where clouds held the upper reaches of the Absarokas in hock. While the alpenglow of the lowering sun was cutting away quickly, and it occurred to him that in a sense the Basques rooming in his hotel were also in hock—to him—until they settled their bill—and to this sheep outfit. He thought about the mortgage, though he hoped to pay it off within the year, that the bank held on the Navarre.

"To be totally free, is it just a wistful dream? Or must we be in hock until we die . . . ?"

A whistled command from Pascuala brought his dog up from its haunches and sprinting in a circling pattern to head off some sheep that had wandered away from the band. With the dog nipping at their heels, the sheep swung about and went bleating back, and now Pascuala threw a pleased smile at the other Basques standing by the open gate of the sheep corral.

"The trick, Zalba, is to use your dog only when necessary, since sheep are high-strung and will not put on weight."

"But a dog like that, it costs a lot?"

Pascuala replied, "I have her offspring. They are about a year old now and I've been training them. How much, you asked?"

One of the older Basques, Arnaud, said, "Oh, Zalba, to deal with such a one as this Pascuala; he will hold you up. Now, my young friend, I have some dogs, too. The best, I've been told."

As Pascuala stood there still retaining a smile, he saw the horseman passing through the corrals, and this time he was glad that the man they worked for was alone. This time Burt Taggart was riding his roan gelding instead of the more skittish bay. It was around supper time, and the presence of Taggart at this hour meant that another band would be heading out tomorrow. "The sheep—get them back into the corral. And Zalba, I cannot sell one of my dogs to a friend. Tonight you can pick the one you want."

As the sheep started flowing into the corral, Taggart drew up to the south of the pole structure but held to his saddle as Pascuala hurried over. Burt Taggart was big and chunky, and not overly friendly to the Basques. Smoke curled away from the cigarillo he was chomping on. The low brim of his hat shielded dark brown eyes. He wore a western-cut suit, and today he didn't have a gunbelt strapped around his waist.

"Sheep look good," he began.

"They'll put on more weight once we get them out to summer pasture."

"I figure"—he took in through assessing eyes the encircling ring of sheep corrals—"we can form at least five more bands."

"Now that Ciriaco left with a band, there are six of us left," said Pascuala.

Folding his hands over the saddle horn, Taggart lapsed into silence as he gauged his next move. He already had fifteen bands of sheep scattered out over the basin, another having just left Elkhorn. The sheep company employing him was well-heeled when it came to hard cash, even though he had orders to keep expenses down. But Burt Taggart considered himself his own man—he had to be to ramrod a bunch of sheep and Basque herders in cattle country.

He fixed his pondering eyes back on Pascuala, a man he considered to be the spokesman for the herders. "Our plans for next summer are to railroad in more sheep." Again he considered what he said in that deliberate way of his, and inhaled deeply of the cigarillo. If anything, there was in him a well of stubbornness—he considered sheep or Basque herders to be expendable items. He knew that once he gave the order to bring sheep across the Bighorn River there'd be gunplay.

At first he'd been reasonably certain Harge Yardley and his brothers could handle anything that came up. But even after Treech Rincon came back to hook up with the Yardleys, doubts had been tripping through Burt Taggart's mind. He needed more guns to face what he knew was coming. To get run out of the basin by the cattlemen would mean the end of sheep coming in here. What he'd done was to send a telegram to the home office in Utah telling of his concern, and just today a response had come back, curt and to the point—he was to use his own judgment in the matter. So tomorrow Taggart planned to get word out to men he knew to strike for Wyoming.

"Six, you said?"

Around a nod Pascuala said, "I promised that all of them would have jobs."

"How about camptending . . . ?"

"You are the boss."

"No," Taggart muttered. "Split what's left into six bands. I want all of the sheep out of here within the next three days. You come up to my office and I'll show you my maps." He swung his horse away, leaving behind the bitter scent of strong tobacco.

Pascuala, happy that things had gone his way, hurried over to the other herders waiting for him by a corral, his dog sniffing at his heels. "We leave this week," he told them.

"Are there enough sheep for six bands?" questioned Zalba Goyeneche.

"There aren't, which is the reason you are buying me drinks tonight at the hotel. Because of my eloquent argument with Mr. Taggart you will become a western herder, my good Zalba. So, it is supper time."

As it was back in Spain, the same custom ruled at the Navarre Hotel of having supper start around nine o'clock. In the barroom

Dominquez came around the bar to pour more wine into large water glasses, received appreciative smiles from his Basque customers sitting at small round tables. He went on to the front table occupied by the schoolmistress from Ohio.

"Miss Calhoun," he said pleasantly, "will you have some more wine?"

"Really, it is delightful, Mr. Dominquez, but I—"

"Just a little more," he urged, "as supper is about ready. As you know, these men are Basques, as I am. The *entremeses* taste so much better quenched with wine and good conversation. That man over there, he is Arnaud. What he just said is that you are very beautiful." He called out in Basque to the others. "So, a toast to the beautiful Margaret Calhoun."

Her eyes sparkling, she said, "Do they have wine every night?"

"Before supper, yes. But tonight is special, as this week all of them depart with their sheep, for months sometimes. But for now—*Osagarria!*" He went behind the bar and along it where bowls of appetizers were spaced: olives, almonds and pine nuts, and toasted filberts. Up front at a table sat a trio of carpetbaggers nursing their beers. Now Dominquez bent to lower the empty wineglass into a bucket, and as he straightened, Elena came to stand framed in the door leading into the dining room.

"Come, we are ready," she announced, moving in to stand by the back end of the bar, where Dominquez handed her a small glass of wine. She waited until the barroom was empty, then she threw her husband a smile.

"I hate to see them leave."

"Yes," she agreed, "but not as much as Angelita."

"Bah," he said. "This Zalba, he is just a puppy that needs weaning."

"Javier!"

The way she'd spoken, and the fact she'd used his first name, held him behind the bar.

"This Zalba is all Angelita's spoken about these last few days.

57

Flirtation, you keep saying." She waggled a finger in front of his face as wine spilled out of her glass. "Hardly, since he is so shy he hasn't even spoken to our daughter. But it isn't words that worry me; these eyes see that they're in love."

"Zalba leaves, fortunately, tomorrow. She will get over him."

"But tonight, it is their time."

His graying brows widened over his questioning eyes. "I do not like the sound of that, my devious wife."

"It is not we who'll decide for Angelita who she'll marry."

"But . . . Zalba Goyeneche?"

"Come, the food is getting cold."

During the supper of a fine Basque soup called *porrosaldo,* and the *codido,* of meats, vegetables, and beans, it finally began to come to Javier Dominquez that his daughter was now a woman, that he had no claim on her life any longer. Gazing at her seated next to Zalba, a sigh erupted from his belly as he released the sadness he felt. Around him there was plenty of conversation, and wine bottles being passed around. Along with the Basque sheepherders, there were the carpetbaggers, one of them talking to the new schoolmistress, and sprinkled about were some camptenders. They had the singular task of wagoning out supplies to the scattered bands of sheep. Two of them were Basques, older men who no longer wanted to brave the solitary world of the herder.

Now Dominquez turned his eyes the length of the table to his wife laughing at a story being told by Pascuala. He glanced at Angelita talking quietly to Goyeneche, who had finally, it seemed, found his own voice. Once in a while a basin cowhand would drift in and have a meal, just on the off-chance of gazing upon Angelita, and there were some locals, too, including the banker's obese son.

"No, a lazy oaf," Dominquez muttered, as Arnaud rose and said, "Our last week here . . . and so why should we be sad? It is what we were born to do. So tonight I have my accordion, it my good friend Javier will let us dance out on his patio."

* * *

Lantern glow was diffused by moonlight ambering palely over Elkhorn. Those out back of the Navarre were wrapped in the closeness of the night, reining away what daylight would bring. As for a lot of townfolks, they were thronging southerly on Main Street where a circus had set up its tents. It was here the local law, Marshal Ray Zent, had gone to try and cadge some free vittles. His rotund presence had been duly observed by Eli Yardley, trying his hand at firing a .22 caliber rifle at a spinning wheel displayed with the bonneted heads of several renowned High Plains Indians. All that registered to Eli was the glint of a badge as his woman of the night yanked the gun away and suggested loudly they head back uptown for more pleasurable entertainment. Embarrassed to a sorryall by his errant shots, he meekly submitted.

While out behind his hotel, Javier Dominquez was enjoying the music and the dancers swirling about on the patio. In spring he had put up some poles with hooks that now held lanterns casting out a cheery yellow glow on his wife, Elena, dancing with one of the carpetbaggers. There was the schoolmistress and a Basque, but his immediate thoughts were for Angelita dancing with herder Zalba Goyeneche. Through the haze of all the wine he'd consumed, it was slowly dawning on him that she wasn't Angelita but the woman he'd married some twenty years ago.

An elbow nudged rudely into his. "The *anguilas,* the tiny baby eels, how well they were sauteed in olive oil and butter."

"Si, Arnaud, then came the lamb chops," said the Basque, Bertrand, "so small you must savor each bite. And . . . then the wine . . ."

With a sweeping gesture that brought him back to his table, Dominquez speared out a smile and said with a connoisseur's gift of lore, "The sea, and the women in bright oilcloth aprons and rubber boots. How they brought us, on crushed ice, the fish and shellfish—"

"The squid and eel," remembered Pascuala. "And how exquisite the gooseneck barnacles and limpets, and the periwinkles and sea snails." Laughter exploded with a drunken loudness out of the Basques; now an apologetic smile. "Ah, fish from every size from slim anchovies to tuna so big it took three women to lift it. And row upon row of lobster and shrimp. But most of all"—his eyes darted around the table—"there were the crabs scuttling around in wicker baskets." He wiggled his fingers and laughed again. "But we are here, casting our lot in this new land."

Bertrand, of the stolid frame and older by five years at thirty, replenished their wineglasses. None of the Basques wore berets and somehow seemed younger, gripped as they were in the sanctity of this hotel. Any weapons they owned were packed in their gear, simply because they saw no need to bear arms when not out with their bands of sheep. Pascuala grimaced at the music being played by a Basque who considered himself capable with a guitar. Pascuala shoving up from his chair to say, "Music like that is why so many get divorced."

Javier Dominquez spoke up. "He wasn't so bad. What do you say, Arnaud, Beltram?"

"That we check out the whiskey in the bar. Though I would like to dance with the schoolmistress."

"Arnaud," said Dominquez, "you are too old for her. Come I cannot stand the sight of Zalba Goyeneche's cowsick face anymore."

"He could become your son-in-law," said Beltram as he opened the screen door for the others.

"How I know," mumbled the hotel owner as he strode on by.

Now that Pascuala had added the musical notes of his accordion to the plunking of the guitar, Angelita suggested to Zalba that they dance, and they rose from the table together. For this dance he swept an arm around her slim waist to bring her a

60

little closer than before when they'd danced, though he cocked a wary eye in Elena's direction. "I am not so good at this."

She said, "See, bring your left foot out this way more . . . that's it . . . and now we swirl around again."

"Angelita, I wonder, when I come back—"

"I'll probably be married to somebody else by then." A smile revealed her even rows of teeth as a frown creased his forehead. "Yes, you will come back, Zalba. Then go out again as a herder. It is a lonely life not only for you but for the woman you'll marry someday."

Engrossed in one another—as was everyone out on the patio in the music being played by Pascuala—nobody seemed aware that several men had filtered out of the deeper shadows of a side street and were angling toward the back of the hotel. Closer, lights from the patio tore the shadowy masks away to reveal Treech Rincon and the Yardley brothers.

Spreading out, the others held back a little as Rincon swaggered toward Angelita, a lustful glitter in his eyes. He was smoking a tailormade and had his left hand hooked in his gunbelt. Angelita whirled to face the gunhand.

"Told you I'd be back, honey. You"—he jabbed a finger at Pascuala—"just keep on a'playin', as this filly and me is gonna do some high steppin'."

"No," spoke up Zalba Goyeneche, stepping in front of Angelita. "Go . . . you are not welcome here . . ." In close like this, he couldn't slip away from the sucker punch thrown by Rincon, a blow that struck the Basque squarely in the mouth.

Pulling out his six-gun, Treech Rincon slammed the barrel at Zalba's forehead, and he fell heavily at Rincon's feet.

He broke out in a snickering laugh, holstering his gun and reached out quickly to snare Angelita's left arm. "As I said, honey, me an' you is gonna—"

Just like that, Rincon's black sombrero was whipped away from his head by a shell piercing out of the barrel of the Remington rifle fired by Javier Dominquez. Disbelief etched in

61

his eyes, Rincon staggered backward while stabbing for his holstered gun.

Again Dominquez's rifle belched flame, the slug nicking away at Treech Rincon's remaining earlobe. The hotel owner shouted angrily, "Do it and the next bullet will find your heart! You other black brigands, unbuckle your gunbelts."

"The hell you say!" snarled Harge Yardley.

Countered Javier Dominquez, "There are three of us with rifles! I will count to three . . . then we will open fire. So do it!"

"Dammit," Harge spat at his brothers, "do as the bastard says . . . unbuckle 'em." Carefully he obliged the hotel owner by unbuckling his gunbelt and easing it slowly to the ground. Then the Yardleys began slinking away, joined by Rincon raining back curses and wanting their guns turned over to Taggart at the land company come sunup or else.

Dominquez shouldered through the screen door and stood gripping his rifle as Pascuala went about gathering the discarded gunbelts, which he brought into the barroom. There Beltram and Arnaud were seated calmly on stools at the bar.

"Where are your rifles?"

"There were only five of them. Besides, the way Dominquez can handle a rifle there was no danger. Whiskey?"

"Damn right I want whiskey. Can you believe it, these are the men who'll watch over us out there. I don't like this. I fear . . . for all of us . . ."

"We can quit and find work elsewhere—"

"Perhaps," murmured Pascuala after he'd downed a half a glass of straight whiskey. Gasping, he added, "A little more won't hurt."

Outside, Dominquez placed his rifle on a table and went over to embrace his daughter. He gazed at Elena, who had helped Zalba onto a chair and was treating the gash knifing across his forehead. "They are evil men. I swear . . . I swear this will not happen again. They . . . they respect nothing, not even our women."

Beltram nudged Dominquez's shoulder, and they moved to one side, where Beltram said, "I think it would be better if we took their guns over to that sheep company office tonight. Inside that recessed porch. And then Pascuala and I will go over to the Gallagan Hotel and tell Mr. Taggart what happened here tonight. For only he can control these men."

"Yes, a wise thing to do, Beltram. The sooner Taggart knows, the better. Tomorrow I will speak to him myself. These men are killers, but at least they'll be working for this sheep outfit if trouble breaks out with the ranchers."

Seven

The trail left by the carcasses of dead sheep headed upslope, with the pair of horsemen scaring up turkey vultures and a few golden eagles. After three days the stench of the dead sheep picked at their nostrils. Scrub pine trees and shaley rock covered the slope, tapering off at rimrock. Sheriff Moses Quinta reined up first, and gazed in dismay at the sheep that had been driven over the bluff to fall to their deaths. As Deputy Josh Medran pulled alongside, Moses let out a few low-muttered swear words around a cigar gritted between his teeth.

"We can blame Carsey Kemmerer for this."

"Damned fool," agreed Moses. "Now that Marty Graham has thrown his lot in with Kemmerer, well, Josh, we've got our work cut out."

"They didn't kill all of the sheep."

"Nor, from what we heard, that sheepherder. These Basques are tough hombres. I expect we'll find him around here some-place."

"Could be he's scoping in on us right now." Medran nodded off to the southeast, and then Moses picked up on the reflecting light of a field glass.

"For damn sure we won't be welcome."

"An' Moses, some of these Basques don't speak English."

"I just hope he knows what this badge is all about asides

makin' a tempting target. Sheriff—it still don't fit right." He reined after Medran, retracing back through the junipers.

Once they were away from the slope, Moses twisted in the saddle to look back at the dead sheep. A lot of mutton gone to waste, he felt. Down here the ground was covered with prairie grass chewed short by grazing sheep. Around him the terrain was made up of low tawny hills separated by draws in which an occasional creek cut through. Except for a few places, it was barren of trees. Off a ways Medran was loping his horse along as he sought out hoofmarks left by the sheep marauders. Both of them were heading due east, and it wasn't long before they viewed Nowood River glinting under the afternoon sun. Waving his deputy over, Moses drawled out, "That higher ground across the river is where that Basque has driven his sheep. If he's got a rifle, he can pick us off when we cross over."

"I'd probably do the same if someone killed my livestock." He watched as Moses untied the bandanna from around his neck and then reached down to unsheath his Winchester.

Tying the bandanna around the barrel, Sheriff Quinta held the rifle aloft and waved it back and forth while spurring at a walk down toward the riverbank. Crossing, he got to thinking back to a situation about the same as this, when he'd been hired by a cattle baron to track down some cattle rustlers. The water depth had been about the same, coming up just below his stirrups, but the river wider and four guns opening up at once. Then he'd taken that crossing at a scared gallop and somehow survived to capture those rustlers. His title then had been that of high-priced bounty hunter.

Halfway across, a bullet scoured the river surface a short distance away, the rippling afterburst of sound tearing into Moses' ears. His bronc skittered sideways; he yanked on the reins and yelled at Josh Medran, "A warning shot."

"What do we do?"

"We sure as hell don't fire back." Clearing the water, he waved his rifle again, catching a glimpse of the sheepherder settled in amongst high rocks of a higher thumb of land spilling away from a long spiny ridge hooked onto the lower elevations of the Bighorns. Reining up, Moses swung down, and as Medran pulled alongside, he untied the bandanna from the rifle barrel and thrust it back into the scabbard. "He might not open fire if I go the rest of the way up there on foot."

"And if he does?"

"Well, then you're the new sheriff."

Medran grinned, then let it fade away. "I could ease over there and come in around that other rise. You know, Moses, that sheepherder might be just a plumb bad shot, the way he missed back there."

The sheepherder was up there, a good quarter of a mile, but it was as if he'd been eavesdropping, for his rifle cracked again. Josh Medran's hat tore away from his head, and in his fear of the moment Medran jammed his spurs hard into the flanks of his horse. The horse fishtailed into the air and spun around in choppy galloping strides, with Medran grabbing for the saddle horn just to stay mounted.

"Guess that answers Medran's question," Moses muttered anxiously. "Helluva shot from that range. Now, no sense stallin' about this." He began walking ahead of his horse with a deliberate uphill stride. Moses knew the Basque was watching him through a field glass, and was probably scoping in on the badge pinned to his vest. Some moments passed before the sheepherder pushed to his feet to stand with his legs apart in a poise of arrogant defiance.

Some fifty rods out now, Moses yelled up, "I'm Sheriff Quinta, out of Worland." Removing his hat, he swiped the bandanna across his sweat-beaded forehead. "Are you gonna use that rifle, or what . . . ?"

Martin Iturri smiled coldly as he pulled the beret from his head, the gesture of a man filled with contemptuous anger, but he held back from using his rifle by a cautious inner reserve.

66

"If you walked more, Sheriff, and rode less, you'd lose that paunch."

"That ain't no lie," Moses grunted. "I'm finding the good life can creep up to ruin a man." He labored up farther, and it was here that the Basque pointed out what remained of his band clustered below the long tree-stippled ridge. "They sure didn't have to kill all of them sheep."

"They know no other way. They came at night, shooting, riding fast and hard. My dog started barking a few minutes before. But you know how it is out here: coyotes, bear . . ."

"You have a campfire going?"

"Yes, Sheriff, I did."

"Like you, these men were weaned on guns. If they'd'a wanted to they could'a punched your lights out. Still, they did enough damage. And they'll have to answer for it."

"I am Martin Iturri, a Basque, and very doubtful that these fools will ever be brought to justice." He turned and began moving over to angle down the southern flank of the ridge.

Moses called after him, "Where are y'going?"

"To start a campfire; make coffee and eat. Join me if you like." Iturri slipped downslope.

Turning, Moses took a stride and he grimaced when his boot came down on a sharp protruding rock. "The hell with this walking," he grumbled, climbing onto the saddle, and he lifted his hat to give it a come-on-up wave to Josh Medran who was holding uncertainly down west of the tapering ridge. As Medran began riding upslope, Sheriff Moses Quinta took a cigar out of a shirt pocket, then he found a sulphur match. He was puffing on the cigar when Medran arrived.

"Where's the sheepherder?"

"Probably puttin' some poison in that coffee he's brewin'." Quinta allowed a brief smile to show as he surveyed the bullet hole in Deputy Medran's wide-brimmed brown hat. "That Basque told me he was aimin' at me."

"Hoss shit, Moses, that hombre could have punched us both out."

"Well, let's go and pick this herder's brains as to what this sheep outfit is up to."

What they found out around the noonday campfire was that Iturri had pulled out of Elkhorn with a band of sheep long before the Yardleys had been hired by the Varney Sheep Company. Sipping coffee from a tin cup he'd taken out of his saddlebag, Moses felt a pang of guilt, for he suddenly realized that Iturri was about out of grub. Slowly he pieced out from Martin Iturri that out of fear for the rest of his sheep he was trying to herd them back up closer to Elkhorn, and in doing so, had lost contact with the camptender out there someplace with supplies.

"My wagon," Iturri explained, "is east of the river you just crossed. I expect the camptender has found it and is probably wondering where I am."

"We've got some grub," said Josh Medran, "and you're welcome to it. Like you said, Mr. Iturri, they came at night. So you didn't see them all that close."

"Only that they were cowhands."

"Your boss, Taggart—what we've heard is that he plans to bring sheep across the Bighorn River. Which is pure cattle country. Tell me, Iturri, how do'ya cope with being by your lonesome for months at a time . . . ?"

"Cowhands, I know, hole up in line shacks during the winter."

"Yup, but generally they pard up with someone. Even then when spring comes some of them do strange things until they get the kinks out of their brains. Yup, being alone for months at a stretch is no kind of life."

"As you said, Sheriff, you don't believe these men will be back to kill the rest of my sheep."

"Maybe not your bunch, but I figure this is just the beginnin' of this thing—and me being sheriff, an' with a helluva lot of territory to watch over ain't easy. Josh, I reckon I'm gonna mosey on over to Elkhorn for a talk with this Mr. Taggart. Once we line out Mr. Iturri with what supplies we've got left, strike back to Worland."

"You could run into Treech Rincon."

"Without them Yardleys to back his play, he's a yellowbelly, which, Mr. Iturri, is—"

"We have them, too, Sheriff Quinta."

Josh Medran said, "I'll tag along, Moses, to make sure Mr. Iturri hooks up with that camptender. Then cut back."

"One final question, Iturri—just where in tarnation did you learn to handle a rifle, as you sure parted Josh's hair."

"It was from my father. He was a smuggler, running things in from France. Then he died; a rockslide. So I came here. Sheriff, I can tell that you want to find the men who killed my sheep."

"Yup," Moses answered laconically. And by doing so, he would be going against fellow cattlemen. But he saw no need to reveal this, for it would downgrade his credibility with Martin Iturri.

He cast away the remaining coffee from his cup and rose to step over and rummage through his saddlebags. He came up with some beef jerky and a small pouch containing coffee and a can of peaches. "It ain't much, but it'll keep you goin' until you run into that camptender."

"Or I can butcher a sheep," said Iturri, as he stood with Josh Medran, watching Sheriff Quinta climb into the saddle and rein westerly.

Light from a quarter-moon guided Moses Quinta the final few miles to Elkhorn. He'd last been here going on seven years ago, when sheepmen were starting to take hold and the town was about half the size it was now, as he found out when he came in past the schoolhouse to one side and clapboard houses opposite on a tree-lined street.

Wearily he brought his bronc upstreet past the Gallagan Hotel in search of a livery stable. He figured it was the day side of nine o'clock, as some stores were still open. His eyes went to baskets of vegetables and fruit displayed along the facade of a grocery store, and his stomach rumbled hungrily.

At a wide intersection, he cocked an eye at light pouring from the gaping doors of a livery stable, and just beyond that, a big two-story building called the Navarre Hotel. "That's sure enough a Spanish name." And he got to wondering how his deputy and that Basque were faring. He knew Medran could handle most anything that came up. But if those sheep killers came back—worry eeled away at Moses as he rode into the stable to find the hostler was gone.

After tending to his horse, along with giving it a quick rub-down with a curry brush, he left the stable and eyed the hotel again. Before he and Celia had stayed at the Gallagan, which catered to ranchmen, or at least had before Elkhorn became known as a sheep town. Along with a room and a hot meal, he needed to get the lay of things here. And if that hotel, as he suspected, was owned by a Basque, it was a good starting point.

Ambling on, Moses knew his first duty tomorrow would be to find the sheep company office and relay the bad news about Iturri's sheep being killed. Another matter was how to handle Carsey Kemmerer. Those aligned with Kemmerer would back any story he came up with, which meant to Moses that he needed a lot of hard evidence to throw not only at Kemmerer but at the others. They'd be sure to toss Jim Graham's murder in his face along with the recent attempt to kill Marty Graham.

When Moses entered, the lobby was empty, the open door to the barroom drawing him in, where he nodded civilly to Javier Dominquez tending the bar. The bar stools were empty, a handful seated at the tables nursing their drinks.

"Evening," Moses said, as he eased onto a stool. He speared his eyes at whiskey bottles lining the bar. "I see some of that stuff is imported. Whatever . . ."

As Dominquez filled a shot glass, he shrewdly judged

Quinta's overall appearance and the badge, which had imprinted on it, *Sheriff, Washakie County.* "The other one—Eldridge—I heard he died."

"He was sheriff, alright—until a heart attack done him in. I'm Moses Quinta. More or less filling in until fall elections." He extended his hand.

"Javier Dominquez. I own the hotel."

"You are Basque, I take it?"

"Yes, Sheriff, by birth. And now an American."

Moses grinned. "Guess that makes us about even." He downed the whiskey, to have Dominquez refill it. "I expect the herders stay here when they're in town."

"They're all gone now, but yes. It is for many the only home they have over here." He reached down the bar and picked up two baskets, which he placed at Moses' elbow. "We also have some sausage and cheese."

"I had more like a hot meal in mind."

"We can handle that."

"Well, reckon I just might bunk down here, if you've got a spare room."

Dominquez nodded, judging by the way Sheriff Quinta had spoken that the man had something on his mind other than acquiring a room or a meal. "Come, I'll show you to the dining room." He picked up the bottle and another shot glass as Moses eased off the stool and stepped back along the bar.

In the dining room the hotel owner called back through an open door, "Elena, we have a customer." He sat down at a table across from Moses and added, "Have you had Basque cooking before?"

"Yup, long time ago down in Nevada. Enjoyed it then, Mr. Dominquez, an' I'll take whatever you've got on the griddle." Removing his hat as the hotel owner spoke in Basque to his wife, Moses noted just how scrub-looked everything was, from the flowery curtains to the fresh white paint covering walls to the lacy tablecloths. And there was a look of dependability about

71

Dominquez. Rubbing at his stubbled jawline, he added, "A number of things brought me over here, though my chief concern is this sheep outfit hiring on the Yardley brothers."

"They are evil men," Dominquez said. "Gunhands. There was a little incident the other night . . ."

"Want to tell me about it . . . ?"

It took a moment for Dominquez to compose his thoughts, then he said flatly, "One of them, this Rincon, came lusting after my daughter, Angelita. Only I drove them off at gunpoint, Sheriff Quinta. Much to my relief they left town this morning."

"Too bad, as I surely would like to have a few words with Harge Yardley, and Rincon, too. As far as I'm concerned they're murder suspects. I ran into a herder out there—Martin Iturri. Seems a couple of days before, a lot of his sheep were killed by marauders."

"Iturri, was he hurt?"

"I reckon not, as this first raid was just a warning, Mr. Dominquez. What do you know about the intentions of this sheep outfit to send woolies west of the Bighorn River?"

"Mr. Taggart could answer your question, Sheriff. He isn't an overly friendly person, at least to us Basques." He fell silent as Angelita appeared bearing a tray.

"Why, obliged, ma'am," smiled Moses. "Those vittles sure have a tangy smell to them."

"This is my daughter, Angelita."

Moses shoved up from the chair and said, "Me, I'm Sheriff Quinta, from out Worland way. Mr. Dominquez, you sure have a beautiful daughter." Easing back onto the chair, he gazed at the hotel owner refilling his shot glass. "This is pretty potent stuff."

"Good Basque food is better enjoyed with good whiskey. Sheriff, if there is more trouble, it will be the Basques and sheep that'll suffer. I know—I was a herder out in Utah, and in Nevada."

"In a way that first raid was done in response to a rancher getting murdered over at Worland. A few days later his son was

72

shot at from ambush. Now, Mr. Dominquez, if the Yardleys were over here at Elkhorn, they didn't have a hand in that killing. Folks back there don't care, as they're blaming both the Yardleys and Treech Rincon. Now this sheep outfit hiring on these scum is just about an open declaration of war. And me smack dab in the middle of it."

"I do not envy your position, Sheriff."

"Between you and me, I'm still a rancher. By rights Cy Eldridge should be sittin' here talkin' to you right now. Anyway, I'm here. Sworn to uphold the law, even though by doin' so I just might have to throw a lot of friends in the calaboose." Moses raised his shot glass and smiled. "There's this Basque word that's used to throw mud in your eye."

Dominquez smiled back and reached for his glass. "I think I like you, Moses Quinta. So to better times—*Osagarria.*"

"A rancher you said?"

"Am now, and will shuck this badge in the fall. Before that I worked on the wrong side of the law. Done some things that make these Yardleys look like grammar school kids. Took a good woman to get me to hang up my six-guns and otherwise reform. To a good life—*Osagarria!*"

It didn't take until a little after sunup for word to spread about Sheriff Moses Quinta's arrival in Elkhorn. Before leaving the Navarre Hotel, he'd had a hefty breakfast and a few final words with Javier Dominquez. Just as he came out of the hotel with the intentions of heading over to the sheep company building, a delegation of three merchants brought him up short, as one of them said, "Sheriff, about time you got over here."

"Yes, we've got a lot at stake. And we're not going to have any ranchers chase out the Varney Sheep Company."

"Simmer down now," Moses snapped back. "You're about as steamed up as those cattlemen are."

"Well, Sheriff Quinta, these cattlemen have set their hired

hands against bands of sheep. You must realize, Sheriff, that before these same cattlemen shied away from our town, didn't hardly support us."

"What you're saying is," said Moses, "that prosperity has come to Elkhorn. And it seems to me, so have Harge Yardley and his no-account brothers."

"What could you expect if your property was attacked?"

"Can't argue none with that. I'm on my way over to see Burt Taggart and tell him not to drive his sheep across the Bighorn River. G'day, gents."

When Moses shouldered into the sheep company building, it was painfully evident from the cold stare thrown him by Burt Taggart that he would receive little help from the man. Testily Moses said, "Taggart, so far you've been on the receiving end of a lot of grief out here. I reckon the message is plain as smoke rising from a chimney that woolies aren't welcome in the basin."

"You didn't ride all the way over from Worland to tell me that, Quinta," said Burt Taggart as he removed his hat and tossed it on his desk.

"Nope, another one of your bands was hit; maybe fifty sheep killed. Bunch handled by Martin Iturri. I left one of my deputies out there to help that Basque get lined up with a camptender."

"You know who did this," the sheepman said accusingly, and even as he motioned for Moses to sit down. "I've been told you're a rancher, too."

"Look," said Moses, "I didn't go around cadging votes to get this badge. But the fact is, Taggart, I'm the law out here. Which doesn't mean a helluva lot when folks take the law into their own hands."

"Meaning your cattlemen friends."

"Meaning your sheep would have been left alone if you hadn't hired on the Yardleys. They're rustlers and worse."

Taggart opened a humidor as Moses folded onto a chair. He offered a cigar to Moses, who took it with a curt nod and bit the end away. As he lighted their cigars, the sheepgrower openly surveyed the face of the man across the desk. Inhaling, Taggart finally said, "You were a gunfighter once. I expect that's one reason why they pinned that badge on you after Cy Eldridge passed away. Cy now, he knew how to handle things. He'd come in here, we'd talk—not that we agreed on everything. But Eldridge didn't shade his words any."

"Around about the time Jim Graham was killed, just where were the Yardleys?"

"I read about that in the paper, Sheriff. And I can pretty much pinpoint the day it happened. So you can rule out the Yardleys; they'd just left here to check on what I hired them to do: play watchdog over my sheepherders."

"Just left?"

"Early afternoon the day before Graham was killed." Burt Taggart saw no need to reveal the whole truth by telling Sheriff Quinta the Yardleys had pulled out at least three days before the killing. He had questioned Harge Yardley about this—had been told, and he had to believe it, that none of the Yardleys had been within twenty miles of Worland on the night of the murder. Nor would he reveal to the sheriff that commencing in a week or two at least seven gunhands would be riding in to begin working for him.

"You know what'll happen if you cross the Bighorn—"

"Would you believe it, Sheriff Quinta, that at least two ranchers west of the river are beginning to realize there's a bigger profit to be made in sheep than in running cattle? They came here some time back to learn what they could. But so far they're holding back . . . and you know why, Sheriff."

"For fear of being branded sheep lovers."

"I'll ease your mind, Sheriff, by telling you flat out that, at least for now, my sheep will stay this side of the Bighorn. I have no intentions of this being an eye for an eye."

"Suppose you could exact some revenge by stampeding some herds of cattle over a cliff. What I'm proposing, Mr. Taggart, is that you take this matter up with the federal judge."

A sour kind of laughter bubbled out of Taggart, and mirthlessly he said, "Judges hereabouts are prone to side with ranchers."

"In the past, maybe. The way to solve this is to limit sheep grazing to certain basin counties. There's plenty of land out here."

"That may be so, Quinta, but the good grazing land is held by the cattlemen, and most of the waterways. Rivers—aren't they supposed to be public domain? What about your 77 spread? It borders on the Bighorn River. You wouldn't want anyone to come in along that stretch of river, be he cattleman or sheep owner."

"You'll protect what you have, I reckon, Taggart. So the message I'll take back and relay to the cattlemen is you'll continue to operate peaceably as . . ."

"If, Sheriff, they stop raiding my bands of sheep."

"Fair enough. You know, on the way over here I scoped in a lot more sheep than I've seen in these parts before. These Varneys—the men you work for—I hope they don't bring any more sheep into the basin. They do that, all hell'll explode." Shoving to his feet, Moses tugged at his hat as he surveyed Burt Taggart still slumped behind his desk.

And Moses said, "Like me, I expect, you have to take orders from others. Me from judges. And you from the men that hired you on. Adios, Taggart, but I'll be back. I'd sure appreciate your telling Harge Yardley that, as I want to have words with the man."

Outside on the boardwalk, Moses unclamped the cigar from between his teeth and flicked it out into the dusty street. Burt Taggart's brooding insolence hadn't set well with him. It left Moses with the feeling Taggart had shaded the truth of what he'd told him about the Yardley brothers. Now he shoved this aside, letting the gist of his thoughts settle on Deputy Medran and the Basque sheepherder.

"By now," he mused, "they should have hooked up with the camptender." But just the same Moses knew he'd better fill his

76

saddlebags and a gunnysack with extra supplies. Coming along the street, he gazed about at the awakening town, taking in some new buildings—the signs of the current wave of prosperity.

Before leaving the Navarre Hotel, he'd settled up his room and lodging bill, and now Moses began angling downstreet toward the livery stable. As he came in on the stable, a couple of horsemen just pulling into town from the east caught his eye. Entering the stable, he held by the door and watched through curious eyes as the newcomers kept heading along the street, then swung onto an empty lot next to the Varney sheep Company building. He didn't recognize them as any of the Yardleys or Treech Rincon, but sure enough they had all the earmarks of gunhands.

"Now I know," Moses Quinta muttered edgily, "just how Burt Taggart intends to keep the peace in these parts. The damn-fool liar."

Once word of this got out, Moses knew the cattlemen would respond in like manner—each side building up its gun-packing forces, not trusting one another, just primed to kill, and him caught in the middle. Darkly Moses swung about and went to claim his bronc, now thinking suddenly of Celia and how just being around her had rubbed away a bunch of nasty gunfighter habits. Saddling up, the new sheriff of Washakie County knew he'd better shove notions of sympathy and kindness aside or he'd wind up like rancher Jim Graham, and damned quick to boot.

Eight

Only once had the camptender come out, and this had been to tell young Zalba Goyeneche to swing his band of sheep about and graze them more to the west. Afterward, the camptender left to wagon supplies to other Basque herders, and the silence of his own thoughts began gripping Zalba. Despite all that he did—tending to his horse and mending any worn equipment, and even adding more rocks to an obelisk of rocks erected there by other Basques, along with the daily ritual of watching the sheep—he could not get out of his system this love he had for Angelita Dominquez.

He had set up his latest camp for the night a short distance from the obelisk, and he stared at it now, a stone tower known to all the herders as *harrimutilak,* or stone boys, wishing that from those very rocks the woman he loved would emerge. That she preferred him to the other herders was to Zalba Goyeneche a most marvelous thing. But when he brought to his mind an image of her mother's stern visage, hesitancy etched itself across Zalba's stubbled face.

"Neither Mrs. Dominquez nor her husband, I'm afraid, think I'm much of a catch for their daughter."

Tonight he would be fortunate enough to sleep in his sheep wagon, brought up only this morning by the camptender. He welcomed this, as he still hadn't gotten used to sleeping out in his tarped bedroll, and the nights were colder than back in Navarre. But to have a job and be amongst his fellow Basques, Zalba knew that he could put up with any discomfort.

Distantly he heard the bells strung from the necks of a few sheep, and a whispery wind rustled through patches of bluestem and tailgrass and stirred the crowns of fir trees growing farther up on elevations. He'd hobbled his gelding, and it was nibbling at grass. Zalba was filled with a sort of lazy ambiance, though his probing eyes were always going to the sheep spread out a little below him.

He'd been told to be on the alert for bands of horsemen, and at first he had, but as the days passed and he hadn't seen even one solitary traveler, he set his mind to other things. And as the day began winding down, Zalba went to head back a few stragglers that hadn't swung easterly away from the lowering sun, with his dog nipping at their heels.

Later he was fortunate enough to camp near a spring. The sheep crowded in to drink—and when some of the lambs got separated from their mothers, their low bleating noises came to Zalba by the sheep wagon. As his supper of beef short ribs warmed over the campfire, he fingered a mouth organ out of his woolen shirt pocket as he sat on the wagon tongue. Guarding the camp site, back of the wagon, was a low shaley ridge, the base of the ridge draped in shadows.

A smile of remembrance lit Zalba's eyes. "Ah, si, the song Angelita liked so well was called *La Borachita* . . ."

The smile holding, he let the soft notes of his mouth organ spill away some of his loneliness.

Sharing another campfire were Treech Rincon and his cousins, the Yardley brothers. But they'd found amusement of a different kind—a whiskey bottle they were sharing and a greasy deck of playing cards. Harge Yardley had deliberately brought them to this low arroyo and a nearby creek, as Harge knew that less'n two miles away a band of sheep had been bedded down for the night. Other bands were scattered about a little farther away.

Since leaving Elkhorn day before yesterday, Harge had brought them in a roundabout way that carried them to the banks of the Bighorn, on acreage belonging to a basin rancher. They had camped along the river, opposite a higher bluff spliced down its middle by a draw, which was used as a regular crossing place. Tonight they were about seven miles east of the river, coming here this afternoon to wile away the time.

"I expect," began Harge, "I'd better spell it out for you . . ."

"Why—we've been ridin' around in circles!"

"Yup, Eli, but tonight you won't be ridin' around in circles, as we've got a chore to tend to."

Treech Rincon pulled the tailormade out of his mouth and spat away a small hunk of paper, scowling as he said, "This chore, Harge, is it for the same bunch that got me out of prison . . . ?"

Nodding, Harge said, "Yup. I guess you figured it out it weren't the sheep outfit we work for that done this."

"I figured that," said Rincon. "So there's a joker in the deck."

"A real mean bastard, a rancher named Kemmerer."

"Carsey Kemmerer?" said Jake Yardley. "Hell, we rustled some of his livestock."

Harge leaned up from where he'd been resting against his saddle, and he reached over and lifted a small leather pouch out of a saddlebag. All of them were hunkered down around a saddle blanket they'd been using as a card table, and Harge opened the pouch to spill out its contents onto the blanket, his brothers and Rincon eying with rising interest the thick wad of greenbacks.

"Is that," Dyson Yardley muttered, "some of that Confederate shit . . . ?"

"That's legal federal tender. Which is just the first payment on what Kemmerer has paid us to do."

"Hold up," Rincon said. "It was *you* strikin' a deal with this rancher."

"All of us, Treech, are gettin' equal shares."

"To do what?"

"Kill some Basque sheep-dung herders." Harge let it sink in as he guzzled down some more whiskey. He sat there relishing the moment, as lately Dyson had been questioning his leadership. What Dyson needed—and which he'd tend to at some more convenient time—was to be taken out behind the outhouse and worked over. Sometimes he wondered if his brother liked getting the shit kicked out of him, for Dyson always came up on the short end. "You're looking at five thousand . . . with more in the offing. *If* we handle this right."

Eli Yardley frowned as he chewed all of this over in his mind, and finally he said, "We're hired to protect these herders?"

"We'll still do that, brother. Only with less of 'em out here, we don't have to ride so damned far."

"Harge, you double-dealin' son'bitch," laughed Rincon. "I love it."

"It was your ma," Harge laughed back, "that took to whoring."

"Who knows?" came back Rincon. "I might be related to half of Montana. So, when do we start?"

"Tonight. Reason I brought you here. Took that roundabout way along the Bighorn. Listen up now." He corked the bottle of whiskey and laid it aside.

Cannily he laid it out that after hitting a band of sheep, they'd try for another, taking out both herders, and then beeline back to where they had made camp last night.

"Once we cross the Bighorn, we ride along it for three, four miles, then recross it and from there maybe make tracks for Eriksen's road ranch. He'll fit us with an alibi that we rode in there before sundown. So now let's saddle up and tend to this killin' chore. Unless, Dyson, you've still got somethin' wedged in your craw . . ."

"Nope. Now just pass me my share of them greenbacks and I'm all set."

"Might as well give the rest of you asshole brothers your share, as you tend to listen more when you're flushed." In the general laughter he tended to this, then everyone was saddling up and eager to move out. Treech Rincon cast a speculative glance Harge's way.

"I just hope I run into that Basque I punched out back there in Elkhorn. He sure didn't like it when I latched on to that Angelita. When we hit town again, oh man—"

For a long time Martin Iturri sat around his campfire, where he let the events of the last few days control his thoughts. He had been with Deputy Sheriff Josh Medran when the camptender had shown up, and now both men had taken their departure, leaving Iturri with his sheep wagon and fresh supplies.

He had taken a liking to Medran, and through the man gained more insight into the viewpoint of the cattlemen. As for the other one, the sheriff, here was a man Iturri wouldn't like to have angry at him. This Moses Quinta—about him was an aura of cold efficiency. Sketchy details of Quinta's checkered past had been related to him by Deputy Medran, who also had a healthy respect for Quinta's expertise with a six-gun, rusty gun-hand or no.

Most likely when the camptender got back to Elkhorn, and when Mr. Taggart learned that many of his sheep had been killed, there was every possibility Iturri's remaining sheep would be mixed with another band and he'd be out of a job.

After he sipped coffee from his cup, Martin Iturri said resignedly, "Such is life—*Osagarria.*"

He cast a glance at the sheep huddled in close to the sheep wagon and bedded down for the night, a mass of pale white against the darker-hued terrain. As he did so, his dog suddenly sprang up and came growling to Iturri, its neck hairs rising to sound an alarm that perhaps a coyote was on the prowl.

"Easy," he murmured, as he turned to set his empty cup on the big steps of the sheep wagon. Just inside the wagon was his Winchester, though ever since they had killed his sheep Iturri had taken to wearing his gunbelt. Now when the dog sprang forward, the Basque knew it was more than a coyote out there—perhaps a grizzly bear.

Martin swung about and planted a boot on the lower step with the intention of getting his rifle when the chilling sound of another long gun splintered the uneasy silence. The heavy steel-jacketed slug broke his spinal cord and punctured his lungs. He was dead even before he fell forward, with his head slamming into the wagon's hard rear step, the blood spilling from his broken nose mingling with other blood gushing out of his mouth.

The sheepdog headed toward the shadowy form of a horseman breaking out of the night. A snap shot from a revolver caught the dog in midstride, and it tumbled over and over in dying agony. The bullet had come from Treech Rincon's gun—the outlaw recklessly out front as was his style—and he pumped more bullets at sheep breaking away from the wagon. Reaching the wagon, he jumped down from the saddle as the Yardleys came in—all but Harge going on to kill more sheep.

"Fine shooting, Harge."

"Later you can buy me a congratulatory drink. Now help me heave this jackass the rest of the way into this shit-kickin' sheep wagon. Then we'll torch it."

"Fried Basque; the coyotes'll like that."

When the marauders pulled out, they left behind a lot of dead sheep and flames eating at the wagon containing Martin Iturri's body. As for Harge, the high flames were a signal he worried might send a message to other herders. "Maybe not," he muttered, "as maybe sheep-dumb has rubbed off on them same's the one we just killed." Now he called out loudly, "Over there, we cut through that arroyo and go southwesterly—three more bands down thataway."

"We gonna hit them all?"

"Just one more will do. As its gettin' too damned late, an' we gotta hit into that road ranch a'fore sunup. So let's hump our hosses into a gallop."

"Yup," said Eli around a grin that shined out of the near-darkness. "Whatever you say, Harge."

To which Harge muttered, "My shithole brothers'll do anything for money. And if there's enough of it, so will me and whorin' ol' Treech . . . git now, hoss."

Nine

With a southeasterly wind pushing into his back, a sleepy-eyed Moses Quinta rode slouched in the saddle. He'd pulled the brim of his hat down to shield his face from the midafternoon sun. After pulling out of Elkhorn, he'd remembered that Celia's birthday was coming up in a couple of days and he hadn't bought her a present. She would be celebrating her birthday in Worland without him, he mused resignedly.

For some time now Moses had been snaking southerly glances at the Bridger range. Deep in one of the canyons of that range lived an old pard, a once-upon-a-time genuine plainsman named Zach Lankford. Back when Moses had hired out his guns to the 77 Ranch, it had been Lankford backing up Moses' gunplay in a Silver Spring saloon. Afterward Lankford had hooked on as cook for the 77, had been part of a crew trying to push a large herd of cattle over dangerous Granite Pass in the Bighorns. Then, with age creeping up on Lankford, he'd simply up and quit one day, and later Moses had found out about the cabin Lankford had put up in the Bridgers. He'd gone there once, around three years ago, and right now Moses was debating about detouring that way.

Coming out of a long draw, he rode up the slope of a rise and took in the sweep of the basin. The band of sheep run by

85

Martin Iturri could be within five miles of his present position or been brought another five to the west.

"And with night coming on," Moses uttered to his bronc, setting out again, "I don't want to be comin' in on that Basque's campfire. For as good a marksman as Iturri is, it won't be some hat he'll be ventilating this time."

The direction he took now brought Moses Quinta due south, toward a line of trees marking Kirby Creek. Down by the creek, he let his horse drink, as he fixed on some high granite rocks up on the mountain that were shaped like a man's head, then lowered his gaze to a canyon sweeping up toward rimrock. Pushing his horse across the creek, he cleared the shrub trees and set his horse loping along a wide stretch of dusty prairie. It hadn't rained all that much this summer; the grass was stubbly and burned out in places, and the wind plucked away at the plume of dust thrown up by Moses' horse.

Out this way, though he'd seen some stray cattle, he hadn't come across any sheep, though antelope shied away when they sighted the horseman.

Down from a mountainous height just east of the canyon fell a narrow ribbon of water, which would become part of one of the basin's many unnamed creeks. He was staring at the way sunlight was glinting on the waterfall, and thinking of lighting a cigar, when without warning an owl began hooting. Moses reined up sharply.

"Too damned early for some owl to—"

Then, his eyes stabbing about, and with him ready to pull out his six-gun, he spotted Zach Lankford tucked on his gelding amongst some limber pines guarding a ridgeline.

"You old fart!" Sheriff Moses Quinta shouted through a quick grin. "That ain't no way to greet a friend." He began spurring his bronc up through the pines.

Lankford didn't say anything until Moses had come up and pulled to a halt facing him. Gumming his uppers and a wad of chaw around in his mouth, he set critical eyes upon the badge

Quinta wore. He still wore buckskins, and usually Lankford forked along an old Indian cayuse with a short-stirruped Blackfoot saddle. He didn't seem as thick through the shoulders, as age was leaning him out. Lankford's black eyes were still deep in their sockets, but the shaggy beard was something new. In a voice that sounded like sandpaper being run over wood he said, "Sheriffing must be good for you, Quinta, as it don't appear you're so lardy-assed. You steal that badge?"

"It was thrust upon me."

"One of them-or-else things?"

"Cy Eldridge gave up the ghost, Zach."

"That so? You . . . a lawman. Seems to me I recollect your words, Quinta, spoken when we was both in our cups, that a man packin' a badge is gotta be dumber than a sack of rocks."

"A lot has happened since then, Zach." He brought his horse after Lankford's, easing around a huge boulder balanced precariously on the sloping upthrust of lower mountain, and now Moses saw the carcass of a whitetail slung over the back of a packhorse. "Venison—you sure know how to live."

"Seems to me you had a hankering for porcupine," jibed Lankford as he untied the reins from a pine branch and guided the packhorse down a game track.

After a while the track brought them to the middle floor of the canyon, and from here they went up a wider trail flowing quietly past Douglas firs. It was darker in the canyon, the wind cutting away as if someone had closed a door. Moses recalled Zach Lankford's cozy hideaway was off to the left in a dense stand of pines, though from the front porch of the spacious cabin a man had a clear view of the Bighorn Basin.

They sat on the porch after having their fill of venison and greens and chicory coffee and shared a bottle of whiskey while they rehashed some old times. Moses spoke of the troubles that had sprung up lately and his regrets over taking on this lawman's job.

"Jim Graham was too trusting."

Lankford agreed. "Graham was always there when someone needed help. I remember Treech Rincon; kind of a dumb bastard when it came to figurin' out the lay of the land. The Yardleys are a shade slower."

"This sheep outfit is bringing in more guns. Which should suit what Carsey Kemmerer has in mind."

"A range war?"

"More than that," said Moses. "He's pushin' hard to get all of the ranchers involved."

"This Basque herder you ran into—seems to me the smart thing for him to do would be to pull out of here."

Moses—staring thoughtfully off into the lower reaches of the basin—grimaced as he handed the bottle to Zach, and he drawled out worriedly, "So far the law-abiding cattlemen have been content with killing a few sheep. The Basques are armed, and believe me they can shoot. But they're scattered out, one against a dozen or so. If one of them gets killed—"

"Yup," said Lankford, "and it's gonna happen." He brought the bottle to his mouth, and then his shaggy-browed eyes squinted into watchful lines, stabbing out at a distant red speck of light, which suddenly flared brighter.

"See that, Moses?"

"They're aren't any buildings out there . . . and the sky is clear. Maybe—" He keened his ears, trying to pick up on the sound of guns. That fire, flaring even larger now, was at least ten to fifteen miles away—far to the northwest of Kirby Creek. Now he added chillingly, "Maybe they hit another band of sheep."

"And set fire to a sheep wagon," muttered Lankford.

"Guess I won't be overnighting after all, Zach." He pushed up from the porch steps, and followed by Lankford, went into the cabin and reached to a wooden chair for his gunbelt.

As Moses began buckling the belt around his waist, Lankford asked, "Mind if I tag along . . . ?"

"There could be gunfire."

"Suppose so. But I know the quickest way to get from here to there, and asides, I'm cravin' a little excitement."

"Okay, Zach, but you'll go as my deputy."

He grinned. "Always wanted to be dumber than a sack of rocks. You go saddle our hosses while I throw some grub into that sack. Make it that old Injun cayuse for me, Quinta."

"I thought that old bag of bones died of consumption a long time ago."

"Nope, and at least that old bag of bones hasn't got one of them pot bellies, Sheriff. Well, get humping after them hosses."

Worries of a different kind had brought Zalba Goyeneche stealing away from his lonely campfire sheltered by a copse of shrub trees. He had been warned about the mountain lions which sometimes strayed out of the Absarokas and prowled the lower elevations of the basin, though a few could be found in the Bighorns. All he knew was a general description given to him of a big cat that could kill a ewe or ram with one swipe of its massive paws. There were also much smaller bobcats he had to look out for and had come across before.

He chided himself for making camp amongst these trees and not in a more open space. Staring back at his camp site, a good three hundred yards to the west, he could see the sheep settling down again. With Zalba was his dog, held by his command at his heels. While along this tree-stippled ridgeline, he'd gotten a moonlit glimpse of tawny hide and cold-gleaming yellow eyes before the big cat wheeled and vanished, leaving behind a deep-throated growl of defiance. Though he had stiffened in fear, young Zalba had pressed on, hoping to get in one good shot with his rifle.

Now the dog, a spotted black and white mongrel, yelped as it pushed ahead, and Zalba let it go, picking up his own tentative gait. That puma, he reasoned, could it be doubling back to get at the sheep? That he must not get too far away from the band also occurred to him as the moon came out full to hover over the center of the basin.

Whistling the dog back, Zalba realized the big cat was an old hand at this game. His best chance to protect the sheep was to be back with them, and with the reappearance of his dog, he swung about and gazed anxiously at the night-enshrouded terrain.

The long days of tending the sheep—from before sunup to dusk and beyond—and the fact he had to put up with his own cooking, had thinned Zalba out. He walked for long stretches instead of riding his horse, and his muscles had firmed up. He liked the solitude, which was snatched away from him when he set his mind on Angelita. To win her hand, Zalba knew he could no longer be a herder.

"But she has so much. And I have nothing."

Suddenly the dog broke toward the camp site even as streaks of gunfire began cutting toward the scattering sheep. Breaking into a startled run, Zalba tripped over sagebrush and sprawled forward and his rifle spilled off to one side. Scrambling to his feet, he ran on and up a short rise and over it to encounter two horsemen breaking out of the night with blazing guns.

One of them snapped a wild shot at the Basque. The bullet ripped across Zalba's upper face, and he reeled in shock and pain. Everything spun around and blood streamed into his eyes. *Pow-Pow!* The first lead slug missed and punched another hole in the exploding night; the other bullet found Zalba's thigh, and he went down.

One of the marauders shouted, "There's one Basque won't mess with a ewe again."

His companion laughed sardonically as he kept on urging his horse into the midst of the confusion of other riders and sheep, punching out more bullets with reckless abandon.

An instinct to survive brought Zalba rolling over and over and into a scattering of sagebrush. Dimly he could make out the faraway glow of his campfire, knowing that he had to get away from it and these killers. Back home there had always been the haven of the mountains, and a homing instinct brought him upright. He sagged into a limping walk, not realizing that the bullet lodged in his thigh had cracked his hip bone. What mattered to Zalba, and threw a deep fear into him, was his diminishing ability to see, and he rubbed at his eyes to rid them of blood. He staggered on and into the yielding branches of a limber pine. He sank down to crawl in under the branches, and it was here that Zalba Goyeneche broke out sobbing.

Not only had he failed to protect his sheep, but there was every chance this night would be his last. He had failed the other Basque herders, and more importantly, no longer could he ask for Angelita's hand in marriage. For she would not want a whimpering coward.

Shifting his legs, he cried out at the intense pain that suddenly radiated from his hip wound. "Think," he muttered through his pain, "you must stop the bleeding." His probing fingers went down along his thigh to find to his relief that there was only a trickle of blood. Somehow he tied his bandanna around his leg, then fumbled on the ground until he found a short piece of wood, which he tied into the bandanna as a tourniquet. Gingerly he brought his left hand up to feel along his forehead. His fingers eased along the long welt left by the bullet and found that some skin had been peeled away and lay just above his eyes. He did not know if his eyes had been damaged all that severely, as the pain coming from his face seemed to be shrilling out of every part of it.

The marauders had moved well away from the Basque's beckoning campfire in pursuit of still more sheep to kill. With the moon out and the sheep in more open ground, Harge Yardley and his brothers merely kept reloading their guns and going at it again. Harge recollected the herder's dog had gone down, and now he reined his bronc at a canter over to Treech Rincon holding alongside Eli.

"You sure you hit that herder?"

"Hit him twice, Harge," said Rincon. "He's dead, as he went down hard."

"Okay," said Harge, and then he whistled shrilly to call in the others, and as they broke toward him, Harge gestured they were pulling out. He led them due west at a fast canter, pleased at the way it had gone, but going sullen in the eyes when he thought about the miles still separating them from that road ranch.

Still under the pine tree, Zalba stirred and in rising bumped his head against a low branch. Only then did he realize he'd passed out. With awakening came more pain than he'd ever felt before, while around him everything seemed merged in a deep blackness. He lay there for a while, gathering his strength and thoughts, and above all, listening for the sounds of danger, of roaring guns. The one sound not penetrating the night was the bleating of sheep, and Zalba's anxiety grew through his pain.

Groaning, he became aware of a hard object lodged against his lower back, and he groped a hand there to touch the butt of his holstered gun. At least he had that if they came looking for him. His tongue flicked out to touch his fevered lips and encountered some dried blood. Then he felt himself going under again, and he simply let himself and the pain go.

"Right over there some three, four miles," remarked Zach Lankford, "is where a Crow war party almost took this here child's scalplock."

"The Crow haven't been in these parts for a heap of years," ventured Moses Quinta.

"An' I ain't got no hair to speak of no more either. We should be gettin' in close to where we seen that fire. Reckon like you said, Moses, it was one of them Basque sheep wagons."

The moon had swung to the western limits of the basin. It had been at least three hours since they'd pulled out of Lankford's mountain retreat. For Moses there was the hard realization that had he kept his mouth shut right now he'd be sharing that big cozy feather bed with Celia, and not getting sore to the saddle as they scoured the terrain ahead for dead sheep and the sheep wagon. He'd run out of cigars and sorely could use one right now.

Reining up, Lankford swept the old brimmed hat from his balding head and gummed his teeth as he checked their present whereabouts. "Kirby Creek angles back thataway. Up yonder, to the right some, there's natural springs. Speakin' of springs, Moses, d'ya ever soak yer skin in them thermal springs over to Old Thermopolis . . . ?"

"Yup, and I aim to do so again mighty soon. You smell that?"

Zach Lankford replied ominously, "More than wood burning." He put his hat on adding, "Over yonder ridge is a long draw running westerly and more open land beyond that."

It struck Moses as he loped his horse ahead that someplace around here he and Josh Medran had run into herder Martin Iturri. Now what Lankford had just uttered took on a chilling meaning as Moses followed the plainsman up the sloping ridge. Night still lay heavy on the land, and the sky was thick with stars. They let their tiredness slip away as they crested the ridge and viewed the darker reaches of the draw below, where a few flames still licked at the charred remains of a sheep wagon. Strewn about were the dead bodies of sheep. They came down slowly into the level reaches of the draw and rode on toward the camp site.

From their saddles they took in the wheels and metal axle, the blackened remains of wood sunken down on the ground, and a few metal pieces that had been bolted to the wagon tongue. "Do you see that herder's hoss?"

"Probably killed it, too," said Moses as he nudged his bronc around the wagon, where he drew up abruptly, took off his Stetson, and began cursing the cruelty of what he saw.

Lankford rode up and he, too, gazed down at what the flames hadn't devoured: a part of the back wagon steps and the boots still hugging a dead man's legs. Lankford spat out, "It just don't make no sense, Moses."

"Cattlemen doing this?"

"Yup. This is out-and-out murder."

His mind tied up in angry knots, Moses slid down from the saddle. "No sense trying to pick up on where these marauders went. At first light we'll find some rocks to cover the body with. This could be Iturri, a Basque we run into a few days back." He looked for a place to make camp. "Zach, you don't have to go any farther. I'm bein' paid to do this."

"Quinta, you never was much of a tracker as I recollect. What I just seen pisses me off, too, dammit. I've been here longer than most in this basin. So I'm claimin' my right to find these killin' hombres."

"Or could it be, Zach, you just want to get some aging cobwebs out of your mind? It'll be a long haul finding them, and you're no spring chicken."

"We're both ornery old roosters, Quinta. No sense keeping a night watch, as these bastards are long gone. We'll camp upwind from here."

"Not all that long until sunup."

"Don't need much sleep. You know what Napoleon said . . ."

"You mean the great Bonaparte?"

"Said that only a moron needs more than five hours sleep a night."

Moses smiled. "Guess I'll have to cut down on my sacktime. Didn't know you was so well versed in world history."

"Seen the Great Wall of China once . . . and some pretty concubines in Hong Kong, too."

"I reckon, Zach, we can table that until tomorrow."

Under the protective mantle of night, Zalba Goyeneche made his tortuous way up a rock shelf. To his dismay he'd discovered he couldn't discern anything out of his left eye nor all that much out of his right, but he kept pressing on guided by his will to survive the horrors of this night.

"Uphill . . . away from them . . ."

Sometime later he realized the sky was brightening, and that he had scaled the upthrust of a rocky hill and was on a high plateau stretching northeasterly where it hooked up with the Bighorns. Around him were screening pines, but even so he kept to the shadows as he moved on in a crabbing walk. Painfully he leaned forward to lower himself to a sitting position on a flat rock. He set down the short piece of stout branch he was using as a crutch and ever so slowly tried stretching out his wounded leg. Zalba gasped in pain—for he knew the slug was still in there.

What he needed was water—to drink and to flush out his wounds. Still pounding at Zalba was his fear that the men who tried to kill him were close by. Blinded as he was, he could stumble into them. What he could see out of his right eye was limited—the trees fuzzy green shapes holding on this rugged terrain. He'd torn pieces from his shirt and wrapped them around the wound on his forehead. Now he judged by gazing skyward in the direction of the sun that it was midmorning.

Stretching out on the rock, he let the weariness take over again, and his eyes closed, and a darkness began forming in his mind. "No—" he gasped out, "you will not die up here . . . not give up, Zalba Goyeneche."

By sheer force of will he pushed to a sitting position and from there used the crutch to come erect. He held there for a moment, swaying, choking down the pain and strange feeling of vertigo. Zalba knew he was getting weaker, having lost some blood, but he knew the moment of shock had passed. If he could find water and food, he might survive this day . . . and the next.

"Angelita . . . if only you were here . . ."

Many times during the day Zalba forced himself to go on, but he found that when he did stop for a breather, it was even harder to hobble back to his feet, as the wound to his hip was stiffening and starting to swell. What he feared most was that the bullet would cause lead poisoning.

Dimly, as he struggled on, he could make out the mountain ahead seeming to flee away from him. He had worked his way off the ridge to come down along its eastern slope, some instinct fetching him this way. He was in deep shadow now, barely able to place one boot in front of the other, when the life-giving sound of falling water penetrated his senses.

Frantically he looked around out of his right eye, a thicker copse of brush signaling to him that behind this lay a natural spring. "Come on . . . must have water . . . must rest . . ."

Pressing on, he lost his footing to sprawl forward, where he went tumbling through the clutching fingers of thorny brush. The fall stunned him, and it took a moment for him to realize that within the reaching span of his hand lay a shimmering pool of clear water. Under him the soft belly of sand hemming the pool yielded to his hands. He dragged his body forward like a man trying to scale a sheer cliff face. He managed to crawl into the water despite its chilling impact, forgetting everything but his need to slake his terrible thirst.

As some sanity returned to Zalba, he realized the water had taken away some of the pain. But he kept his body submerged— and there near the shallow edge of the pool he forced himself, through his mind's eye, back to the terribleness of last night. It came to Zalba that though he hadn't seen the men who'd tried to kill him, he'd heard at least one of their voices before. It had been higher pitched than the others, sort of like the upper keys of a piano in tone and filled with scornful malice.

"It . . . of course"—he muttered, fighting the blackness starting to take hold of his mind and body—"it was one of those . . . who came to the hotel. When Angelita and I were—"

Without warning, remembrance came full-bloom, and horror gaped Zalba Goyeneche's eyes.

"The man who hit me, the gunfighter . . . the one lusting after my Angelita . . . this *Rincon* . . ."

Remembering sucked the remaining strength out of Zalba, and he gave himself over to the blackness, even as a golden eagle chanced to soar overhead in search of sheep or smaller game.

Ten

"They sure killed a lot of sheep."

Moses Quinta kept looking about. Noon was approaching, a day warming into the seventies. Beyond a scrub tree lay a dead dog and more dead sheep. The sheepherder's dead horse was still hobbled and was beginning to swell up. His eyes went back to the fire-blackened remains of the campfire, and he finally said, "Could be that herder got away . . ."

"If he did, Moses, he won't show himself to us. Don't blame him none. This was the same bunch that hit that other band of sheep. They've headed westerly for the Bighorn."

As soon as Moses climbed back into the saddle, he fell in alongside Zach Lankford astride his rangy cayuse. Once they got beyond ground chewed up by the stampeding sheep, it was to pick up on the bold trail left by the marauders. These men hadn't bothered to hide their trail back toward the river, and Moses knew it was getting to him. He could understand why cattlemen hated sheepgrowers, as to them it was like mixing tar and water. Even so, they were responsible for their actions. Killing Martin Iturri went beyond the pale and he couldn't fault that sheep outfit over at Elkhorn for wanting to hit back.

"Dammit, Zach, they're flaunting the law in my face."

"For sure they don't respect that badge. I expect once they cross the river, they'll scatter back to their ranches."

"Like before," said Moses. "I just want to get my hands on one of them. I'll guarantee he won't do any more sheep killing."

"Kind of worries me, you talking like the Quinta of old."

He grinned. "I reckon that old rep of mine will eliminate the need for gunplay."

"Carsey Kemmerer, I don't suppose he came along—"

"Especially, Zach, since he likes to have others do his dirty work."

"Celia, she's still a handsome woman. I still remember how you two used to go at it hammer and tong. Sure surprised me when you got married."

"It still shocks me a little," said Moses. "Me a married man, that is. Seems they cut into that draw."

"Yup, and the way those hoofprints are spaced, they were really pushing their horses. The only thing we gotta worry about is if they cross over at Tucker Crossing, as it gets a lot of traffic."

This proved out much to Sheriff Quinta's dismay when around midafternoon the wide-spanned Bighorn appeared when they cleared a high hump of land. On both sides of the river, cattle were spread out with cowhands pushing them across from west to east. Tight-jawed, he rode with Lankford down onto the floodplain, while wondering if any of these cowpokes had glimpsed the men they were chasing.

When Moses got in closer, he recognized Lafe Prescott's Circle LP brand and some of the 'pokes working the cattle. Pushing on through the milling cattle with Lankford holding behind, his probing eyes cut through the rising dust to the rancher and his *segundo* holding on a high bank while taking in how the tail end of the herd was faring in the brackish river waters.

"Quinta? I heard they conned you into pinning on that badge. An' Lankford, good to see you, too."

"Yup, Lafe, this badge only proves wisdom has passed me by. Ozzie."

The *segundo* nodded back around the tailormade he was smoking.

"Me'n Zach here have been tracking five men since late last night. They didn't just kill sheep this time, Lafe, but a sheepherder, maybe another."

"They could have used the crossing, Moses. But if they did, it was before we pushed in here."

"You own land on both sides of the river."

"On this side as far east as the south fork of No Water Creek. Why'd you ask?"

"Could be after what happened that sheep outfit will strike back. And you being closest, Lafe, it could mean some of your cattle being taken out."

Lafe Prescott had big hands, thick shoulders, and a large head—and he was shrewdly amiable when it came to dealing with his basin neighbors. "We can handle trouble if it comes. But I'm hopin' it won't."

"You weren't at that meeting over at Worland."

"No, Moses, as I don't cotton to Kemmerer's high-minded ways. There's nothing he'd like better than a range war. If I was you, Sheriff, I'd check out the deeds over at the courthouse. It might only be a rumor, but what I hear is that Kemmerer is taking deed to a lot of land east of here."

"I'll do that, though it seems to me Carsey has his hands full with what he owns now."

Lafe Prescott shrugged. "Man gets ambitious, he always wants the whole loaf. Take care, boys."

Once they were west of the river, they clattered their horses onto the stagecoach road, and here they drew up to take stock of what to do next. North along the road some twelve miles lay Worland. Celia would be there, at her daughter's, celebrating her birthday. One year, Moses recalled, he'd given his wife a single red rose, which to her had been about the best present she'd ever received. She had preserved it in one of her books,

100

and now here he was about back at Worland, coming in empty-handed.

"Some'll go south keeping to the road," said Moses. "The others'll head north the same way. They may have gotten away this time, Zach, but dammit, I'm gonna track those killers down. That Basque Iturri, deserved better than to be burned to death."

"They probably shot him, then heaved him into his wagon. He could have been alive until the fire got to him."

"Could have been," Moses agreed around a weary inhaling of hot summery air. "What about you, you fixin' to head back to your place?"

"I could tag along just to say howdy to Celia."

"I need a tracker."

"What you payin'?"

"Same as my deputies get."

"Which ain't a helluva lot, when you consider this basin is a powder keg ready to explode. Okay, ain't got much else to do for amusement. There is one thing—"

Quinta brought his horse to a lope while reaching for his last cigar.

"How come you've never seen the Yardley brothers out yonder ridin' herd over them Basque sheepherders?"

"Could be they're gettin' paid to hold back," pondered Moses as he exhaled cigar smoke. "By that sheep outfit, maybe. I've seen that look in your eye before, Zach, so spell it out . . ."

"You head back to Worland and do right by Celia. Me, I aim to head riverward and track along it, as just maybe these killin' rascals recrossed the river."

The words of Zach Lankford hung heavy in the air for a moment, with Moses chewing over their dire meaning in his mind. "Could be Treech Rincon and his dirty-assed cousins are workin' both sides of this thing. But who'd be the joker in the deck? Some cattleman . . . ?"

"Sheriff get paid more than a deputy?"

"I guess so," snorted Moses Quinta.

Wheeling his cayuse off the road, the plainsman shot back, "Then, Sheriff, you figure it out."

Chuckling, Moses watched the old plainsman pull away and until Lankford had slipped down onto the floodplain abutting close to the Bighorn. "You cranky old bastard," he muttered, "just don't get yo'self killed."

As he rode down close to the riverbank in search of fresh hoofprints, Zach Lankford mulled it all over. What he knew about the Yardleys from the not-too-distant past, and the other things told to him by Quinta, painted a grim picture of impending violence. And of treachery, if his hunch was right about the Yardleys drawing a Judas's wages.

Zach Lankford had been in the Bighorn Basin a heap of years before most. When he had first come in through the narrow recesses of the Wind River Canyon it was to find a handful of ranchers battling the harsh elements and the Crow and Shoshone and Blackfoot. Sometimes he would leave, either to head down to places in the Great Divide Basin or try the mountains just for a change of pace. But he'd always been drawn back, the last time when 77 Ranch owner Celia Farnsworth had hired on gunfighter Moses Quinta. "She sure the hell took the wind out of his sails," he muttered.

Still ghosting along the riverbank, Lankford began to center his thoughts on the task ahead. He knew that any track was a will-o'-the-wisp, sometimes vanishing as quickly as it was laid down. Tracks existed briefly at the interface where the sky dragged along the surface of the earth; out here on the plains, eroded by wind, the weather moved across them, and they quickly perished.

But tracks were made by creatures of habit, either man or animal, each track as different as snowflakes. Lankford figured a man was no different than, say, a mule deer, in that their tracks brought them to a food cache or to water, to a resting place, or to rut with the female of the species. Mule deer would hole up during the day, high in a treed cul-de-sac on the side of a rise, with its back to a rock wall, and facing downslope. Many a time Lankford could recall leaving the track of a deer to swing around a hill and come angling onto its crest. From there he could look down on a mule deer snugged down no more'n a few yards away. Neither deer nor elk ever looked upslope, since danger for them came not from the sky but from hunters like Zach Lankford.

"Creatures of habit," he muttered to his cayuse. Habits—if one knew them—that could lead to a successful hunt. For even animals as wary as elk survived by adhering to strict habits in that an elk herd was bossed by a cow elk. The cow dictated when they would slink off during the day into a thick stand of mountain pines to rest and chew their cuds and head for a watering hole near dusk. The best time to hunt them, mused Zach Lankford, was just after sunup. He recalled when him and Moses Quinta had done just that up in the Bighorns, bagging not one but three bull elk three mornings running.

They'd shot the first bull just after the cow had brought the herd out in a meadow to graze, when dew was still glistening on the grass. But instead of showing themselves, the pair had held in concealment as the rest of the herd puzzled for a while over what had happened before settling in to graze again. Soon the cow elk had led the herd out to find water, and only then had they slipped out to gut and skin their kill and carry their prize away. Had they made a kill near sundown, as many were wont to do, they would have been forced to leave the dead bull lying there overnight, the scent carrying to the herd, which would vanish into higher mountain timber. As it was, the following morning Lankford and Quinta watched the herd graze in the same meadow. This time Lankford had the honors of downing a bull adorned with a prime rack of horn.

The memory of that hunt brought a rueful grin to Zach Lankford as he kept on pushing through more brush. Even if he found where some horsemen had crossed the river, he couldn't be sure they were marauders. And even as he pressed on, he could feel a body change as he shred thoughts that he was washed up, just stoved-up with rheumatism and a relic of by-gone times. "Me and you, cayuse, who the hell gives a damn if we just drop dead one day? As this world keeps a spinning and them Chinawomen keep dropping babies faster'n jackrab-bits. Shitfire, cayuse, them's fresh tracks—"

He'd just cleared another thicket of willows, and was swatting at mosquitos, when he spotted them—the hoofmarkings of at least half a dozen horses etched plain in soft riverbank sand. Happily he reined up. Cannily he shifted his glance easterly and along the opposite bank, the only movement that of a golden eagle staring boldly back at the plainsman from the upper limbs of a cottonwood.

Lankford could feel the excitement beginning to take hold. He knew it was them, the sheep killers. Wisdom honed by a thousand days following a like number of tracks told him that. In his younger years he would'a let out a Pawnee yell or worse. Now he just let the cayuse dip its head to drink as he studied the marks left by exactly five shod horses.

"East of the river . . . nothin' but empty tracts of prairie split by creeks and draws—unless . . . ?"

Unless, he drew it out silently, they're beelining for that dumb Swede's place. They'd be no different than miners after shovel-ing out a ton or so of crude copper ore in a Butte mine, leaving to slake their thirst at a saloon. Just like a lawyer after screwing somebody in a court of law, they wanted their just reward, and Lankford judged for the men he was trying to find it was Erik-sen's road ranch.

"Dammit, this is their track. Which'll take me to where they'll be rutting an' foulin' the air with whiskey talk."

Crossing over grudgingly, as the swift current was sweeping him wetly downstream, he eased his grip on the reins to let the

104

cayuse have its head. And then he came out of the river and rode on until he found a suitable place to build a campfire.

Crafty logic had long ago told Zach Lankford that haste was a tool of the foolish. The tracks he'd found this side of the river were spilling out northeasterly—to that road ranch. But why? Could be there were other reasons than just to bed with a whore and get snorting drunk? He wished Quinta had come along.

When Lankford pushed on after drying out, he gauged he'd reach Eriksen's place after sundown, which set well in his mind. The road ranch squatted on a rise where some trails crossed, coming out of scattered ranches. There was a tower stacked above the second floor of the main building, which had been used to keep watch during Indian days. Now the many outlaws frequenting Eriksen's liked to keep watch from up there, sipping whiskey as they did and cuddling up to one of the whores.

Sometimes on hard ground Lankford would lose sight of the tracks. But he kept riding northeasterly. And pretty soon they'd appear again, the same spacing between them of men pushing their hosses damned hard.

The daylight hours pushed on, too, and now when Lankford decided to ride down to a small rile of water he wheeled his horse sharply toward some brush. Concealing himself in the brushy thickets, he recentered his eyes on three riders coming in from the west. The two flanking the man in the middle wore nondescript clothing, but their six-guns were thonged down low. He let them come closer, angling as they were to plunge their horses across the thin stream of creek water. The way shadows were coming in, he wasn't sure about the other rider, but Lankford waited stoically, the cayuse aware, too, that these men might bring trouble.

"Should I know that gent?" Lankford ran his eyes over the expensive saddle and rigging and the man clad in a dark brown leather coat and low-cut cattleman's hat. And he knew it was some bigshot cattle baron on his way to the road ranch.

"Hellfire, if that ain't Carsey Kemmerer I've been gelded!

105

Yup, it sure enough is Kemmerer." Other memories came back to Lankford of rancher Kemmerer—of how the man liked to sneak off to some distant place and wallow amongst the whores even though he was married to a proper woman.

He waited until the trio of riders had loped over a distant hillock. Pushing out of the thicket, Lankford drawled ponderingly, "Quinta, you should be here. As it ain't whores Kemmerer's after this time. Yup, Kemmerer is paymaster for the Yardleys. What do you say to that, cayuse . . . ?"

Promptly the aging cayuse swung its head back to cast a wild cerulean eye at the plainsman while trying to sink its teeth into Lankford's boot.

Cackling, Lankford said, "Don't worry, cayuse, if somethin' goes haywire the pair of us'll see plenty of action."

Upon arriving in Worland that same evening around six o'clock, Moses Quinta bypassed the county jail in favor of a haberdashery store frequented by his wife, Celia. One of the women clerks peeled away from a counter and came smiling up to Moses.

"Sheriff, we were just about to close."

"Has Celia been in here?"

"Just to look at some dresses and things."

"Did she mention anything in particular that she liked, ma'am?"

"Oh, yes, Sheriff Quinta. Over here, this outfit in our display window."

He followed the clerk and glanced at the tweed riding outfit and the black boots that went with it and said, "Wrap it up and put it on my bill."

"Or, Sheriff, she did like this woolen sweater over here. We just got it in from Canada—isn't it darling?"

"Wrap that, too. Those flowers in that fancy vase . . ."

"Those are just to dress up the place."

"Roses are Celia's favorite. Especially long-stemmed roses; just one will do, so name your price."

A quarter of an hour later Moses rode through the spreading darkness down a dusty lane. From houses came cheery lights, and he passed an apple tree that had just come into fragrant bloom. Other trees rose darkly in front of more houses and sheds and a few picket fences. Turning onto another side street, he stared over the upper edges of a hedge at people milling about in a back yard. A long table was there, too, covered with a lacy white tablecloth, and Chinese lanterns hung from poles spread along a back walkway. He knew most everyone helping Celia Quinta celebrate her birthday, as they were ranch folk with a sprinkling of townspeople. He reined up, laden with presents and the single long-stemmed rose wrapped in white paper, hoping for a glimpse of Celia. When she came out of the back door carrying a platter of fried chicken, he spurred his bronc toward the opening in the hedge, where he nudged the gate open with the toe of his boot. One thing Beth, Celia's daughter, prided herself on was this neat lawn encircling the big rambling house.

"Beth and her never-be-late-for-chow-or-you-go-hungry bit," Moses muttered around a teasing smile, as he brought the bronc off the walkway and onto the lawn. As he rode along the side wall, much to his delight the bronc decided it was time to dump a load of fertilizer. "This should really get her dander up."

Clearing the wall, he threw a smile at a rancher acquaintance, and then he drew up as Celia spotted him. Their eyes locked; silent questions went out and were answered. He swung down from the saddle to groundhitch the reins. At Celia's quick approach, he held out the red rose, and she took it with misting eyes.

"You made it."

"You didn't think I wouldn't?"

"Not for a minute. I love you, Quinta."

"That's what you told me away back at Buffalo, when you stacked that deck of cards so's I'd marry you, Celia Farnsworth.

Here, these presents are wearing on my arm. Tanner Bledsoe, glad you could make it."

"I'd say my wife dragged me in here. But I'd'a come anyway just to help honor your wife's birthday. Your thirty-fifth, Celia . . ."

"At least," she laughed back. "Go stable your horse, Moses . . . and what the hell is that smell . . . ?"

"It ain't aftershave lotion," Moses threw at her as he ambled back toward his bronc. "My hoss just figured Beth's lawn needed more minerals and such."

Tanner Bledsoe said, "I'll keep you company, Moses."

In the stable, as Moses tended to the process of unsaddling his horse, they exchanged small talk. Bledsoe had land adjoining the 77, though the bigger share of his acreage lay farther to the west. "I've been wondering, Tanner, why you didn't join forces with Kemmerer?"

"Man's a fool, in my opinion. You know, Moses, in my day I expect I've seen it all: fights, drought, 'pokes gettin' struck by lightning or dying in some stampede. We don't need the kind of medicine that Kemmerer wants to hand out."

"No, Tanner, a ranch war will just keep things simmering for years. But we might have one. Down southeast of here, some twenty miles, you know around Kirby Creek, a Basque herder was killed, maybe another. By cattlemen, I figure."

"That damned Kemmerer."

"Or others," sighed Moses. "There *are* other hotheads in the basin. I was hoping Marty Graham would show up tonight. You seen him of late . . . ?"

"Nope. I've been stickin' close to home."

"No need to burden you with my problems, Tanner."

"Tell me, neighbor, just why in tarnation did you take on this sheriffing job?"

"Maybe during puberty I wasn't fed enough milk. Just don't know, a number of reasons. I was with Jim Graham the night he was killed. If anything, that's it, Tanner."

Around nine-thirty everyone began leaving for their homes or local places of lodging. During the course of the evening, Beth had exacted a promise from her stepfather, Moses Quinta, that he either remove that equine fertilizer from her lawn or he could find another place to stay tonight. And Moses had just come out of the stable, shovel and bucket in hand, when all three of his deputy sheriffs loomed out of the darkness of a back alley. He held there as they swung in to dismount.

"Kenny spotted you uptown, Moses."

Josh Medran went on, "From what I hear there's going to be another raidin' party tomorrow night."

"Killing two herders isn't enough for them," Moses flared out angrily. "That Basque, Iturri, was one of them."

Confusion screwed pensive lines in Medran's ruddy face, and he said, "It couldn't have been those associated with Carsey Kemmerer. Can't be, Moses, because of what Corvin Baugh told me."

"Baugh went along before when they hit some bands of sheep?"

"He more or less said that, Moses."

"I want Corvin Baugh in my office by tomorrow noon."

"Shouldn't be any problem, as Corvin's still in town. I can't believe that Martin Iturri is dead. Man who can handle a rifle like he can . . ."

"It was Iturri against half a dozen. They hit his camp at night. I don't know if he was still alive when they set fire to his sheep wagon with him in it." His steely gaze took in the three lawmen he'd inherited when he became sheriff. Like Medran, they were capable, but the way it was beginning to stack up, Moses knew he'd have to deputize a couple more men and be damned to what the county commissioners had to say about it. This didn't include Zach Lankford, whom he figured was his ace in the hole, out there by his lonesome tracking down the men who'd taken out those herders.

"Josh, I figure if Corvin Baugh spent a night in jail he might see things differently."

"You're callin' it, Moses."

He watched them swing about and climb into their saddles. Kenny Tuttle was the oldest of them at thirty-two, a jug-eared man with sandy hair. The youngest of the bunch was John Kornkven, a man for whom Moses was still reserving judgment. John would fill out to the size of his rancher father if a slug didn't take him out first. But they were what he had to work with and depend on, and he'd back their play to the hilt.

Before reining out, Josh Medran paused and called back, "Be sure to give my birthday greetings to Celia."

"Yup, and I'll see you boys at first light."

Hefting the implements he carried, Moses headed on toward the house, as his mind filtered thoughts of how Lankford was faring, until he finally decided, "The old fart can take care of hisself."

Then, and somewhat reluctantly, he began shoveling hoss droppings into the bucket, mindful of both Celia and Beth watching him from the house.

To which Moses grumbled, "Next I'll wager they'll come out with a toothbrush and make me get right down to the roots of this here chore—"

Eleven

A prowling wolverine scurried away from the iron-shod hooves of Zach Lankford's cayuse, loping closer to the few brightly lit buildings making up Eriksen's road ranch. Lankford had held out, watching the place after rancher Carsey Kemmerer had pulled in, wanting the rancher to get settled in with those he'd come to see.

Late as it was, and with no moon out, nobody was keeping lookout from the tower on the main building. But even if someone had been, the route Lankford was taking kept him following a shallow draw. He doubted either the Yardleys or Carsey Kemmerer would remember him, as all he'd been for the 77 was a cook—someone far below the rancher's station in life.

"Awful snobbish back then," Lankford snorted. "Probably still the same."

Tonight he would play the role of recluse plainsman come out of his den to swill down some corn whiskey and eye the girls. Coming past a ramshackle shed, he took in the horses tethered in front of and along a side wall of the main building. He passed behind the building and came up the opposite side wall, where he eased out of the saddle and dropped the reins, knowing the cayuse wouldn't budge from the spot. Farther out came the sound of crickets, the distant wail of a coyote—

111

through the three windows on the wall spilled the familiar sounds of men drinking.

Glancing upward, he checked to see there was nobody standing on the balcony running around this wall and the facade. A long time ago one of those English lords had put up this place, and some of the fancy woodwork remained. But it had been a moon of Sundays since Tule Eriksen had slapped on a coat of paint, and empty bottles and trash littered the ground. Lankford eased over to one of the open windows, nearly choking on the overwhelming stench of stale beer and tobacco smoke.

"If that ain't an old flame of mine! I thought Thelma up and passed away a couple of hunnerd years ago," he muttered.

The woman he was eying was seated at a table with a couple of gents who were sagged in their chairs. One of them could barely raise up his head to lap his tongue at a shot glass, though he was damn-well trying. The other's eyes had a glazed look as if he'd just been poleaxed in the head, and Lankford reckoned it wouldn't be too much longer before the man would pass out. Thelma—and Zach Lankford was sure it was her—had probably been matching drinks with the two hombres at her table. Back a ways was the bar, composed of some old planking taken when one of the hip-roofed barns had been demolished. The barroom had once been the main living room, and when that English lord had suddenly pulled up stakes, he'd left behind framed pictures, some of which were still hanging along the walls. Then a miner out of Butte, Montana, came in and turned this into a road ranch. Afterward there was a succession of owners until the Swede showed up, with some cash and a nasty disposition.

At a back table a man sat alone nursing a bottle, and farther along was another stony-faced gent, neither talking to the other, and both with the look of gunhands. At the bar was, Lankford knew, a man Moses Quinta would dearly love to run into— Treech Rincon. Standing with Rincon, who was swaying some, had to be one of the Yardley brothers. Behind the bar was a former railroad man named Eckersly, and when he wasn't tending bar, he was the Swede's odd-job man. Two other whores were sitting at a front table where they could keep watch on Rincon.

"Only three of them Yardley brothers," mused Lankford. "Which means Harge Yardley must be upstairs someplace with rancher Kemmerer." Part of the answer came to Lankford when the hardcases who'd accompanied Kemmerer here appeared at the top of the staircase, with two more girls of the line hanging on to their every word. Now all of them came down laughing as Zach Lankford pondered over the whereabouts of Tule Eriksen. He didn't want the Swede sneaking in from behind and coldcocking him.

His eyes flicked to Thelma, who pushed up from her chair and came directly toward the window. He figured she'd veer within the next few feet and go in to one of the downstairs washrooms to count the greenbacks she'd just lifted from the pockets of the pair of snoozing Yardley brothers. As she turned, he thrust his upper body through the window, grabbed one of her arms, and used his other hand to wrap around one of Thelma's plump breasts.

Zach Lankford hissed threateningly as he pulled her in close to the window, "You scream, Thelma, an' I'll rip this tit right off your chest."

"Zach, you bastard," she hissed back. "I thought you were dead."

"The feeling is mutual."

"Well?" she glared.

"Where's the Swede?"

"Went to the kitchen to cut up some steaks."

"Tule always did have a fondness for knives."

"You outta know that."

"Tule missed, as I still got a pair of testicles. I owe you, Thelma, for not screaming your ass off. Which is a helluva lot bigger than when I viewed it last."

She threw Lankford a snaggily toothed grin. "As I recollect, Zach, you was sweet on me."

"Don't get your hopes up." He let go of her and drew back into shadow. But through the window came a double eagle, which she clutched on to. And he added, "I see you still haven't lost your grip. Look, Thelma, I ain't here for socializing; at least not tonight." He mused: Don't burn your bridges just yet.

"You after one of them back there? Or the Yardley brothers?"

"What you don't know can't hurt you, Thelma. Go powder your nose, an' later tonight, maybe we'll go out and yowl with the coyotes."

He slipped away, but only around to the back door, and once he was inside, Zach cut to his left and went up a back staircase. He knew the layout on the second floor, having vacationed here, as he called it, on numerous occasions, until him and Tule Eriksen had taken a dislike to one another.

"Just because I wouldn't pay that whore," grumbled Zach as he slipped down the upstairs hallway. Opening the second to last door, he eased into a dark bedroom. There was a connecting door to a large room used as a suite for big spenders such as Carsey Kemmerer, and to this door crept Zach Lankford. Hunkering down, he found he could clearly hear the voices of two men.

"Harge, that five thousand I just paid you is part of a war chest we've got up."

"You mean them other ranchers, Mr. Kemmerer, are dead serious about drivin' sheep out of the basin."

"Exactly that. Getting back to what we were discussing, Harge. You took out one herder. But . . ."

"That other one, he was hit bad. If he wasn't killed outright, he damn-sure bled to death. It was darker'n all getout, so he sure didn't know who it was out there."

"Okay, Harge, but you must understand, I don't want the finger of suspicion pointing at you."

"I damn-well second that motion. Here's mud in your eye."

"Pull back for a while, Harge. The next move has to be up to sheepman Burt Taggart. I want him to get angry enough to try pushing sheep across the Bighorn."

"My brothers and I could be a part of that." Harge Yardley's worried tone of voice carried to the plainsman starting to cramp some in the legs where he was crouching.

Again Yardley spoke. "What about this pain in the ass sheriff over at Worland?"

"Moses Quinta doesn't scare easily. What worries me more, Harge, is that he sees things other people miss."

"What's that supposed to mean . . . ?"

"Let me worry about that."

Zach heard the sound of a chair scraping away from a table, and he came erect and moved to the only window, which he eased open. Crouching through the window, he slipped onto the balcony, and from there slipped over the railing to hang down and then let go and fall a few feet to the ground. Grimacing, he tugged his gunbelt back into place as the cayuse rippled its nose in a suspicious sniff.

To which Zach replied, "You outta know my stink by now."

Mounting up, he reined into the darkness, while resisting the temptation to go on a real bender with Thelma. He knew she wouldn't tell anyone he'd been there, but he had plans to come back, not only to slop down drinks with Thelma, but to straighten out the set of Tule Eriksen's mind.

"Cheap bastard should have bought hisself a funeral home. As he just might need one."

"Where were the Yardleys?"

Burt Taggart's anger struck the walls of his office and reverberated back to him. Just this morning a camptender had returned with news that two of his herds had been hit. Not only that, the Basques tending them had been gunned down. He didn't know their names, nor did it matter all that much.

"I'll tell you where," he went on, "lazing around some saloon when they should have been out there." Taggart's scornful eyes went to the four men scattered about his office. Three more were hanging around Elkhorn waiting for orders from the sheepman, and more were on the way. Notable among them was Chuck Dacy, out of the Indian Nations. Now it was to Dacy that Taggart directed his words.

"The ranchers have started this thing."

"A lot of them are against you, Mr. Taggart, which is what it comes down to. Just how much backing can you expect from the Varney sheep interests?"

"Out here I have free rein and enough money to back me up. You've worked for me before, Chuck, so you know what to expect."

"Reckon I do." Dacy shrugged. He had a long bony face that registered little emotion. He hadn't bothered to tell Taggart that he'd just broken out of jail down in Salina, Kansas. He considered himself more a highwayman than gunslinger, though if occasion demanded he'd unlimber his .44 Peacemaker, and when he did, it was to kill. Through lazy eyes he took in the men he'd be leading against the ranch element. Except for Stacy Watt, with whom he'd worked before, the bonafides of the others were open to debate. But it didn't matter if Taggart lived up to his promise to hire on at least twenty more hardcases. He decided to plumb the waters about this. "Burt?"

"Yeah," said Taggart as he looked up from a map spread over his desk.

"You're paying us a lot of hard cash——out of which you expect results, which you won't get if this isn't done right. I expect you remember that bloodbath down in Nevada."

"In which we were almost driven out," said Burt Taggart. "The lesson we learned is that if you gamble for high stakes, you'd better be able to back up your play. I know what you're driving at, Dacy. I'll get you those additional gunhands."

"Until then?"

"About quitting time," Taggart said, looking through a window at the activity on Main Street. "Until then, we hold back. We do nothing against any rancher. What we want is to lull them into a false sense of security, let them believe they've won. But, Dacy, take out some men tomorrow and check out my herders. If you run into Harge Yardley, tell him to get back here pronto."

"And if we encounter some cowmen attacking some of your bands—"

"Take out after them. Now here, when the time is ripe"—he waited until the gunhands had risen to close around his desk and take in the map—"here is where I intend to drive at least five thousand head of sheep across the Bighorn River."

"That'll really make this a full-fledged ranch war."

"A war I intend to win. No matter what the cost."

"In blood and killing."

"There'll be that," Taggart said bluntly. "On both sides. So if any of you have any kin, I suggest you make out a will."

Gunhand Chuck Dacy grinned and said nonchalantly, "I make it, I spend it just as quickly. I expect when I cash in my chips one of my pards will divest me of my boots and guns and saddle."

"What about your hoss?" said Stacy Watt.

"Stole it. Come on, there's some poker tables over at the Ornery Bull that need some action. I want to relieve you boys of some of that hard cash before you blow it on the whores."

"Remember," Taggart said as the hardcases began crowding out the door, "you'll be leaving early tomorrow morning."

To which Dacy shot back, "Don't need any shut-eye as I lost my cherry before I was even weaned. But come sunup, we'll be humping outta here."

That some Basques had been killed *did* matter to the owner of the Navarre Hotel. A day after one of the camptenders had

117

returned to tell of the double tragedy, Javier Dominquez had locked the doors to his place of lodging. With his wife and daughter, and accompanied by other Basques, Dominquez had gone out to the final resting place of Martin Iturri. There he had spoken words from his Bible, a short but solemn service.

Afterward they had gone farther to the southwest in search of Zalba Goyeneche's grave site. All the while Angelita had held on to a stoical silence. They found the remnants of Zalba's last campfire, the rotting carcasses of sheep, and as the sky darkened into night, a camp was made, as it was over thirty miles back to Elkhorn.

As they sat around a campfire after supper the talk was about all of the good things Iturri had been known for. They sipped whiskey from cups and spoke softly—all except for Angelita holding out by a rocky crag overlooking their camp.

Elena Dominquez, whose eyes were filled with sadness, said, "She truly loved this Zalba. For I have never seen her like this before."

"She has taken it badly."

A solemn nod from Javier Dominquez told them he agreed. "What is happening now is like a cold Arctic wind hitting a wind out of the Tropics. A storm breaks out, and from it all kinds of bad things happen. We all know the risk of being a herder out here. You, Santiago, you herded sheep over in Utah same as me."

"Si, a storm broke out between this sheep company and some ranchers. We were lucky that time."

Dominquez held up his glass. "Let us drink to the memory of Iturri and Zalba Goyeneche—both good men."

Up on the rocky outthrusting, Angelita Dominquez knew that she was drained of tears. Never had she been so shocked as when word was brought to her that Zalba Goyeneche had been murdered. At that moment her heart seemed to shatter into meaningless pieces. But late that night in the sanctity of her bedroom Angelita felt a presence, as if Zalba were calling out

118

to her. It was then she realized that he could very well be alive. The next morning she had confronted her father with this, only to receive a few words of condolence.

Out here the feeling Zalba was still alive came even stronger to her. There was no grave, and they had searched a considerable distance during the day. Now as Angelita stood there, gazing at where the starry sky hugged against the Bighorn Mountains, something that Zalba had told her burst into her thoughts.

"When in trouble," she murmured, "he would always go to some high place. To the mountains. Those men came at night. Perhaps he was only wounded . . . and if so, he would follow his instincts . . . go seeking the high places . . ."

Shifting her glance to the campfire, Angelita now knew what she must do. Most of them had come on horseback; her parents had trekked out in a buggy, in which some of their supplies had been loaded, with the rest of the supplies aboard a packhorse. Tonight, she deliberated, long after everyone was asleep, she must take the packhorse and go in search of the man she loved.

"I have no other choice!" she cried softly.

In the morning the first Basque to rise took on the chore of making a campfire. False dawn still lay upon the basin, as did the chill of night. Dew sparkled upon prairie grass, and gray clouds held captive the upper reaches of the Bighorns. It was such a morning the Basques enjoyed above all other things: the quietness, a time to say to oneself, *Osagarria*.

As the flames leaped higher, one of the Basques turned away from the campfire and ambled over to the back of the buggy in search of food to prepare for breakfast. To his surprise he discovered most of the sacks were empty, and he removed his beret and scratched at his hairline, troubled by all of this. His name was Beltram, and last night he had removed the packs from the packhorse and placed the packs under the buggy. He leaned over; panic clutched in his throat when he suddenly realized the packs were also missing.

"The horses, what about them—could a renegade Indian have snuck in here while we slept?"

Quickly he swung away and hurried toward the horses; out a little and with hobbles on their legs. A head count revealed the packhorse and another horse were missing. His shout back toward the camp site shattered the quietness of early morning.

Everyone threw aside bedrolls. Javier Dominquez slapped a felt hat over his head as he scrambled to his feet. For this one night of camping he'd left his trousers and shirt on but had removed his boots, and in his stocking feet he pushed toward the horses. "Bertram, you say some horses are missing? How many?"

Before the Basque could reply, Elena Dominquez's fright-filled voice pushed the night farther away.

"Angelita—she is *gone!*"

The small party of seven Basques turned anxious eyes to where Angelita had bedded down, only there was just some grass pressed down to mark where her bedroll had been. Elena began weeping, turning away to have Dominquez place comforting arms around her.

"Why . . . Javier . . . I don't understand . . ."

"I know why," he said through his concern. "She has gone in search of Zalba."

"But he's dead."

Bertram said, "But there is no grave."

"What do we do?"

Dominquez said, "She must have left during the middle of the night to try and find Zalba. We will saddle up and go after her." The pain in his eyes told how he felt, but Dominquez also knew his daughter could handle a horse as well as the cowhands of this basin. The dark hulk of the mountains held his attention. "If Zalba is alive, there's where he would go. Come now, to your horses."

The middle of the day came and went, and still there was no sign of Angelita Dominquez, though one of the Basques came

120

across her trail—a trail that brought them ever higher on the lower reaches of a spiny ridge hooked to the mountain range. Rock outcroppings and the profusion of pine trees made riding difficult. Dominquez had been forced to leave his buggy behind, with Elena waiting in it and one horse still hitched to the buggy. He'd unstrapped the harness from the horse he was riding, and he was tiring rapidly, as were some of the others.

When they reached the narrow crown of the ridge, to their dismay more ridges appeared to the east, with low draws in between where antelope and a few cattle grazed. The sun beat down at them through the oppressive silence of the high elevations—and in their haste to pull out in search of Angelita some had left their canteens behind.

A Basque nodded toward Cloud Peak pushing into the steely blue sky. "Those mountains hold many secrets."

"So, Javier, shall we go on?"

"To do so would endanger our lives. My daughter, she's a stubborn woman . . . when she sets her mind to something . . ." A weary hand brought a bandanna swiping across his face. "She will either find Zalba or perish. Is that not the way of the Basque . . . ?"

"So we go back to Elkhorn?"

"Si, Bertram. We'll get word to the sheriff and then get together some supplies and fresh horses and come back in search of my Angelita."

"Do you suppose Zalba is really alive?"

"If he is, she will find him. Probably he's badly wounded, or worse. At least we know one thing." Dominquez swung his horse around and brought it at a slow walk between two boulders encrusted with green moss. "She loves this Zalba Dominquez."

"Si, a love that could cause her to lose her own life. Si, this Zalba Goyeneche is a very lucky man."

Twelve

Moses Quinta knew he was hearing the truth from the other man in the cell, longtime basin rancher Corvin Baugh. The cell door stood ajar, and they were sipping coffee from tin cups, though uncertainty still rode between them.

"Now I regret siding with Kemmerer," said Corvin Baugh. "Moses, I was part of every foray we made to kill a few sheep. But only sheep. These Basques, they're just innocent men caught in a web of violence. And me a part of it."

"Look, Corvin, if I wasn't wearing this badge I just might have been in your shoes. We're cattlemen. At least you've been one a heap longer than me."

"What you mentioned before about keeping sheep out of certain countys—that's one solution. But after this . . ."

"So far all you've told me is that Kemmerer has been calling the play. What about Marty Graham—he ever ride with you?"

"Marty? No. He stays tight to his ranch nowadays. He took it awful bad when his pa was gunned down."

"You still haven't told me the names of the others involved in these night raids."

The rancher dropped his eyes to his big workworn hands holding the cup, as his jawline grew taut from the strain he was under of having been arrested. "You said I'll be needin' a lawyer."

"You and the others," Moses said tiredly. "Don't worry, I'll find out their names. Corvin, I'm going to let you go. I'm hoping from here on you'll confine your night riding to your ranch."

"I appreciate this, Sheriff. You know I'll pay for my share of what sheep were killed, you know that. But look at this from a cattleman's viewpoint. This sheep outfit hiring on the Yardleys . . . an' from what I hear, Treech Rincon. And maybe more gunhands."

"This is my job, Corvin, upholding the law. You also know there's rumors flyin' about that this sheep outfit plans to drive sheep this side of the Bighorn."

"A big mistake if they do."

"Be a bigger mistake on your part if you get involved again," Moses said tautly, as he came out of the cell followed by the rancher.

After the rancher had picked up his personal belongings and was gone, Moses left to head upstreet, where as he expected he found Washakie County Judge Thurman Springbuck in the dining room of the Antler Hotel. A former schoolteacher, Springbuck had for a half dozen years operated a hardware store before folks asked him to run for office. And like Moses he'd had to learn judicial matters on the job. He was tall and gaunted out, with Lincolnesque features along with a mole on his lower jawline. He was in the midst of eating a breakfast of biscuits and gravy and side pork and nodded at Moses easing down at the table.

A waitress came over with a cup of coffee, and to her Moses said, "Clara, that looks good. But add some fried potatoes to my order."

"You sure you can eat all of that, Sheriff."

"Been out on the trail." He patted his upper belly and grinned up at her before she headed away. Plopping a couple of cubes of sugar into his cup, he set his Stetson on an empty chair and picked up a spoon to stir his coffee.

"How long have we known each other, Moses?"

"Well, reckon long enough."

"Then you know we have to do the right thing."

"I took a step in that direction, Thurman, when I locked up Corvin Baugh. Then I let him go with the understanding there'll be a trial."

"Corvin and I were pretty thick in our younger years. Like so many others, he feels obligated to side with Kemmerer. Even when he knows he's wrong."

"I didn't pry much out of Corvin."

Washing his food down with coffee, Judge Springbuck said, "Didn't think you would. Something else brought you here . . ."

Moses gazed back into the judge's pondering eyes, and he said, "Two more killings—Basque herders."

Sadly the judge said, "I knew it would come to this. Are you absolutely certain Baugh wasn't involved?"

"Somehow I know he was telling the truth about him and the others only taking out some sheep. On the other hand, there's Carsey Kemmerer and the off-chance he could be involved in these killings."

"Just because Kemmerer has taken on some gunhands? I know the man—bullheaded as they come, Moses."

Sheriff Quinta, with a look taking in others clustered around a few tables, narrated in a low voice his running into rancher Lafe Prescott pushing some cattle across the Bighorn. ". . . so, Kemmerer is buying land east of the river. We know he's got the money to do it. But why now, when he's pushing into his late fifties?"

"No crime for a man to put his money to use."

Moses nodded as the waitress set his plate on the table, and a pot of coffee. He reached for the pepper shaker, a speculating twist to his mouth. "No, nothin' wrong with that, Thurman. But he's reachin' out for some reason. And I aim to look into it. We tracked the men who killed those herders westerly to Tucker Crossing."

Shoving his cup away, Springbuck said firmly, "I want these men in my courtroom. If it's Kemmerer . . ." He placed both hands palm-down on the table and leaned in closer to fix his steely gaze on Moses. "I ran for this judgeship because I felt I could handle it. You are my sheriff, and Moses, we cannot have Carsey Kemmerer or anyone else throw the law in our faces. Ever since you pinned on that badge, men have been coming to me to rekindle your past misdeeds. But you do what you have to do. You have my full backing. Yup, friends of ours might go to prison, but nobody forced them into this poker game."

"I appreciate this, Thurman."

"I've got some papers to shuffle."

"By the way, I'll need at least two more deputies."

"You've got them."

"What about the county commissioners?"

"What else do you need?"

"Well, there isn't a better tracker in these parts than Zach Lankford. Last I saw of Zach he was trying to pick up on those tracks south along the Bighorn. So, just between us, Thurman, I deputized Lankford."

"I expect you want this kept quiet, Moses."

"I do. And I can pay Zach out of my salary, too."

"No, not now, not when three men have been killed. We can always get money to run this county. We can never replace men like Jim Graham . . . or those Basques . . ."

To mind for Moses came thoughts of herder Martin Iturri. "Yup, Thurman, certain men are irreplaceable."

Before riding out of Worland, Sheriff Quinta and his deputies went over the names of some men they figured could be taken on—though he refrained from telling them of Zach Lankford's involvement in helping to track down the killers. When he did pull out, it was in the company of Deputy John Kornkven, forking a rangy bay gelding. It was a good day's ride out to Carsey Kemmerer's Flying K Ranch, one that Moses knew had to be made.

One of the chores he'd assigned to Josh Medran was to head over to the courthouse, and from there the land office, to pour over records telling of recent land sales. If this didn't pan out, he would dispatch his deputies to other county courthouses in the basin. As they cut away from the main road to canter along a trail gouging off to the southwest, it made no sense to Moses that Kemmerer wanted to buy land where sheep were being grazed. When sheep had come in, some ranchers had sold out rather than wait to be boxed in by bands of sheep.

"I was going to head out here alone, John. But we needed to talk."

"Fire away, Moses."

"Your pa wants more for you than just bein' an underpaid lawman."

"He talk to you about this?" Kornkven said testily.

"Oh, he didn't put it in words. An' don't get your dander up either. Education you've got—you could go on to some of them fancy colleges."

"Could," John Kornkven admitted. "Could become a doctor or something. But the basin suits me just dandy, Moses. You could fire me . . ."

He smiled back, and then with a resigned sigh Moses reached to his shirt pocket for a cigar, as a gentle breeze began fluttering and rustled the short prairie grass and shrub brush. "Could do that, John, if I wasn't so doggoned shorthanded as is." Through cigar smoke he added, "When we get out there, just for spite Kemmerer might sic those hired guns on us."

"We can oblige them."

"But we won't. From what I hear from Kemmerer's foreman is that these hombres are packin' notched guns. Men like this are generally fast with a gun but not all that swift when it comes to sizin' up a situation. Just let me sweet-talk these hombres if their trigger fingers get to itchin'."

Later that afternoon a ridgeline falling behind told them they were on Flying K land. Eventually they began sighting cattle, and along with them, a few antelope. The terrain was rugged and the grass thick, as Kemmerer's ranch contained a lot of watery rivulets. Spring water gushed out of a low elevation and brought them reining over to where a water tank had been installed. The ground was muddied around the tank but dried out hard. Dismounting, they let their horses drink sparingly, while Moses gazed to the west and into a wide draw spilling out a little dust.

He drawled, "We're about two miles from the home buildings."

"Is this a reception committee?"

"More like some hands hazing up cattle from all that dust. Just remember, Mr. Kornkven, keep a damper on your temper if anyone starts hurrahin' us. An' just where in tarnation did you' get that checkered shirt? You look like a peacock in that thing."

His face reddening, Kornkven swung into the saddle, and then he spurred after Moses reining toward the draw. When he got alongside, he said, "My girlfriend gave it to me for my birthday."

"Forgot about your birthday, John." Moses' eyes squinted to hide their smile. "If you up and marry this filly, you just might wind up wearin' a matchin' pair of longjohns or worse. Anyway, when we get back I'll treat you to a sarsaparilla."

"I'm of legal age now," John retorted.

"Maybe so, and I don't reckon it'll be the first time you sucked down some corn whiskey either. I believe that's Kemmerer's *segundo* in charge of those cattle . . ."

Out of the draw surged a mixture of around two hundred baldys and red Hereford cattle, the 'pokes hazing them shrouded in dust except for foreman Lavin Roach raising a lazy hand as he headed for the lawmen aboard a roan cutting horse. He was string-beany and slatfaced, and it had been a week of Sundays since Moses had seen Roach sporting a gunbelt as he was doing

127

now. He came on at a lope, his slate-gray eyes holding silent questions.

As for Sheriff Moses Quinta, he knew and respected Lavin Roach as being a square-shooter, though it took some effort for the man to open up into any kind of conversation. Moses knew he wouldn't get much out of Roach in the way of what Carsey Kemmerer had been up to lately. Moses wondered, too, why a man with Roach's credentials would stay on with a man like Kemmerer. Way back when Moses had first gotten hitched to Celia, Lavin Roach had been one of the first to offer the hand of friendship, something that had stayed constant in the passing years.

Pulling a cigar out of his pocket, Moses flipped it to Roach just as the man eased in close, which provoked from Roach an appreciative grin. "Sheriff, by golly, this is mighty generous of you. Howdy, John."

"G'day, Mr. Roach. Those are some fine cattle."

"Movin' them out to a fresh pasture. Good day for it, too." Lavin Roach leaned in closer to draw flame to his cigar from the match cupped in Moses' hand.

"Is the bossman home?"

"I expect he is, Moses."

"These are troubled times," Moses said bluntly. "As a lawman I've got to ask, Lavin, just how your 'pokes figure into these raids against sheepmen—"

"So far none of my men have been involved. I know, Moses, you're just doin' your job. I respect that."

"What about those two hired guns of Kemmerer's?"

Steadily Lavin Roach returned Moses' questioning stare. "I'd be lying if I said they weren't involved in those raids. They've kept their distance, as I do."

"Thanks, Lavin. One more thing, is Carsey fixin' on hiring some more hardcases . . . ?"

"That you'll have to ask the bossman. See you, boys." He reined away to catch up to the small herd of cattle.

"Why didn't you tell Roach that two Basque herders were killed?"

"No reason to, John. I expect Lavin and everyone else workin' here will learn about that soon enough. As it is, Lavin spilled out a lot more words than he's accustomed to. Let's ride on in."

Beyond the draw a wide meadow spilled away to a tidy collection of buildings and corrals and holding pens. There was the main house, and a few older buildings, and the bunkhouse, coated with white paint and red roofing. In the background they could make out two barns facing one another—Moses figured they were put there to help ward off wintry winds spilling out of the northwest. From what he'd heard, Kemmerer's wife rarely came out to greet visitors. Perhaps she knew that her husband had tried to make a play for Jim Graham's wife, the shame of this turning Mrs. Kemmerer into an aging recluse.

A heavy anviling sound announced their arrival. The smithy hammered for a while, and then the sound died away. Now there was a low word from Moses to his deputy, and John Kornkven turned the slant of his gaze to the south wall of the main house, along which was stepping a man wearing a gunbelt. Moses said, "Got to be one of Kemmerer's scummy watchdogs. If Kemmerer's in there, he won't come out to put down no welcome mat, as that ain't his style."

"Far enough, Sheriff!"

Moses just kept on walking his horse closer, and rankled at what he was viewing; this cold-faced man wearing a fawning sneer. Now up from a hammock on the front porch rose the other gunhand, but he just stood there next to one of the stone support posts, with the low stone wall of the porch cutting just above his knees. Farther to the left were the porch steps, and Moses reined on toward them as if he were a man with nothing more on his mind than getting in out of the sun.

"Dammit, Quinta, you old fart, you deaf or what?" flared out the gunhand holding by the wall. "You ain't welcome out here."

Something jogged in Moses Quinta's memory. Maybe it was the way the man kept jerking his head as though suffering from a nervous tic. Or it could have been the man's big round bulging eyes and short beak of a nose—and now with remembrance came Moses' response, "You're a far piece from the Dakotas, Owl Head Johnson."

"So what," he spat back.

"So," muttered Moses upon slackening his reins and easing a leg over his saddle as he swung down. "I reckon if Seth Bullock over at Deadwood learns of your present whereabouts, this old fart could collect some reward money."

"I ain't wanted noplace."

Snorting, Moses kept a watchful eye on the gunslick as he tied his reins to the hitching post. "John, you keep your eyes peeled on Owl Head. As I recollect, the son'bitch does a little skippin' dance when he's got up enough nerve to unlimber his pistola. You—!"

The man on the porch blinked at the shout coming from Sheriff Moses Quinta. He glanced at Owl Head Johnson for support, and some kind of signal.

"I figure you got a long gun stashed behind that support post," said Moses. "Just sidle away easy like. Or any sudden move you make'll be your last." The next instant Moses' right hand blurred, the Colt cleared its holster, and a snap shot from it stirred the gunhand's mop of stringy brown hair and shattered an upper windowpane. Grimly Moses watched as the man tippytoed away from the support post as he elevated his arms.

"Easy, Sheriff, I ain't committin' suicide for nobody."

Then Carsey Kemmerer exploded out of the front door, yelling at Moses, "You shot a hole in my window!"

"Your man owes me, Kemmerer, for givin' him a haircut." Moses slapped the Colt back into his holster. "We can talk out here, Carsey, or back in my jail."

Through a scowl the rancher ordered his hired guns to vamoose. Tautly he said, "Okay, Sheriff, I'll hear what you have

130

to say." Then he presented his back to the lawmen as he trudged angrily back into the house.

On the porch Moses picked up the rifle leaning against the support post. Instead of ejecting the shells from the Winchester, he yanked the lever back hard until it snapped. Gazing at Kornkven standing below the steps, he said, "I sure hate bushwhackers, son. Keep watch out here. An' I'll send out some cookies and milk."

Moses found the rancher waiting for him in a smaller room just off the front living room, a room in which there was a small fireplace and a few gun racks hooked to the dark wood-paneled walls. In one corner stood a rolltop desk, and there was a small table and four chairs, but it seemed Kemmerer preferred standing with an elbow hooked on the fireplace mantel. Anger was still etched on his stony face.

Bluntly Moses began, "I'll cut right to the bone. Two sheepherders were gunned down. An' Carsey, you're my prime suspect."

"The hell you say," snapped Kemmerer. "You have a lot of gall accusing me of something like that."

"Another thing, you're so damned anxious to start a range war. Why? So you can keep buyin' up more land?" Just for a split second he saw behind the angry glitter in Kemmerer's eyes to the ugly soul of the man and to part of the truth of what he sought.

"Quinta, the people aligned with me can drum you out of office. We are respectable cattlemen, determined to protect what is ours."

"Cut the bullshit, Carsey. You ordered these raids. For all I know"—and to Moses Quinta this was a shot in the dark—"you could have been behind Jim Graham's killing."

"Damn you—" Kemmerer reached out to a nearby gun rack, barely controlling himself, then he lowered his arm. He forced a toothy smile. "I won't forget you said that, Quinta, ever. Now I want you off my ranch—and don't ever come back."

131

Levelly Moses replied, "After I threw Corvin Baugh in jail, he opened up to his part in these raids. I expect I'll be arresting more involved in this." Part of his reason for coming out here was to push Kemmerer in an attempt to force the man into making a pivotal mistake. He stood there taking in this prideful and arrogant man, and then one stride brought Moses closer, to launch a backhanded slap, the force of which snapped Kemmerer's head to one side and drew blood from the man's nose.

"I was a gunfighter once, remember! I was paid once to punch out the lights of men like you, and the scum you hired. You like to use the word, *ever.* Kemmerer, don't you ever, ever threaten this old fart again, *comprende?* As it won't bother me a tinker's damn to kill again. So just hold back on the cookies and milk as we're leavin'. An' give my best to Mrs. Kemmerer."

Only when they were out of rifle range of the buildings did Moses Quinta begin to relax. He was still tensed up, and if one of those gunhands would have been near him right now—especially the one referring to him as an old fart—there's no telling what he might do. Slapping a hand on the saddle horn, he said to Kornkven, "It just might be Kemmerer might show up in Worland sportin' a coupl'a black eyes."

"I heard that slap clear outside."

"Man's got a hard head—I bruised my knuckles."

"You handled that pretty good back there."

"You mean Owl Head Johnson?" grunted Moses. "Him and his partner are in way over their heads. Kemmerer now, he's goin' loco in wantin' a range war."

"You have a reason for hitting Kemmerer?"

"Reckon I wanted his undivided attention." But the truthful reason, mused Moses, was that he had injured the man's pride. Out here this was a bigger sin than rustling a man's cattle. Now he knew that Kemmerer wouldn't rest until he'd evened the score, either by getting back at him, or taking his vengeful anger out on the sheepmen. In either case Kemmerer would act quickly and not all that rationally.

"Once we get back, I just hope we got some men wanting to be deputies—we'll need them. You still could head out, John, for some institute of higher learning . . ."

"Nope—sheriffing is what I want to do."

"Then you just keep your eyes peeled to your backtrail from here on in."

The rage in Carsey Kemmerer spilled over onto his hired guns summoned to his office in the main house. Though he'd stemmed the flow of blood which had spilled from his nose, the pain was still there. "I thought you two knew how to handle a situation like this. He'll pay, damn him, for what he did."

"He . . . he got the draw on us, Mr. Kemmerer."

"No matter now," muttered the rancher. "Pour some more whiskey into my glass." His lidded eyes stared across the desk at them as he went over the exchange of words that had taken place between him and Quinta—that he was buying land as part of his overall plan, but let Quinta, or anybody else, find anything illegal about that.

If anyone knew, Carsey Kemmerer voiced silently, that I've committed murder, same as Moses Quinta, or probably these hired guns, not once, but twice . . . It had not been the act of a desperate man, either. The crimes had been carried out two years ago when a cold autumn wind had brought to his doorstep prospectors weighed down with gold nuggets. They'd appeared at night, spectral creatures wrapped in tattered but serviceable clothing, and despite his misgivings, he had let them share the larder at his table. Even at this precise moment he could bring to mind every detail, all that had been said that night.

"Ring Claibourne—that is a strange name."

"Not to my father, sir," said the prospector as he tried to make himself comfortable in the sanctity of all this western splendor spread about the dining room. "As the story goes, the

133

night my father proposed marriage to the woman who became his wife, he had to cross a river swollen with flood waters. In crossing over he became dislodged from his saddle, but somehow survived to find that the river had claimed the ring he was carrying."

"A delightful story," smiled Kemmerer. "So as it turned out, you were that ring. We haven't heard much from your partner."

"Blakely has his moments," said Claibourne, "but it seems not tonight. We are somewhat bewhiskered and seedy, Mr. Kemmerer."

"Gold in the Bighorns? There was talk of that, oh, five years ago. But nothing came of it. Yet according to the little you told me, gentlemen, it is more than a rumor after all."

Ring Claibourne dipped a hand under his tattered coat and came out with a leather pouch, out of which he produced a small gold nugget. He offered this to the rancher, saying, "You have been a gracious host. Please, take this for your troubles."

As Carsey Kemmerer placed the nugget in the palm of his hand, he managed to repress his growing excitement. If they, he wondered, could give him this nugget, surely they must have a considerable fortune in their packs. They were heading back to Provo, Utah, as disclosed to him by Claibourne. But they most certainly had plans to return in the spring. Kemmerer was having money problems, caused by a drought that had gripped the basin for the last three years. He would go under—unless . . .

"This is most gracious of you, Ring. But I cannot accept it—out here we never turn anyone away."

"I understand, Mr. Kemmerer. That you took us in despite our grubby attire is . . . admirable."

"Hunting for gold—seems to me that's speculation at its most daring." He handed the nugget back to the prospector around an engaging smile.

"Others went into the Bighorns before us, I have to say truthfully. But not all that far." Ring Claibourne looked at his partner

134

starting to doze off over by the fireplace. "This was during the Indian days."

"When men lost their scalps."

"Between us, Mr. Kemmerer, we drew some maps of the general area where our mine is located, just in case something happens to us on our way home. To wind this up, I have to say that we have amassed a small fortune."

The prospectors remained overnight and on into the following week, all because of Carsey Kemmerer's persuasive powers. Slowly he gleaned more about the location of their gold mine. One thing in Kemmerer's favor was that his wife was off visiting relatives in Cheyenne. And then—exactly a week after they had appeared at his doorstep—the owner of the Flying K crept into the bedroom occupied by Ring Claibourne and slit the man's throat, then went on and killed the man's partner, Blakely. Kemmerer's worse moments came when he had to dispose of the bodies. But later that evening, with this accomplished, he found some maps and a fortune in gold nuggets in their packs.

Carsey Kemmerer brought the gold out of Wyoming to cache in a Montana bank. Carefully, with an innate caution, he used it to stave off his creditors. But it was the maps which continued to intrigue him, all of them pointing to land pushing up onto the western flanks of the Bighorn Mountains—land that he realized he must own title to at any cost. Hunkered in the middle of this land was Elkhorn—a slumbering little settlement until the one day sheep interests came in and shattered all of what he planned to do.

"Uh, Mr. Kemmerer," piped up hardcase Owl Head Johnson. "We was talkin' about you paying out cold cash to hire some more gunhands."

"So we were," he answered as the past dimmed away from Carsey Kemmerer. "And we shall. Tonight we hit some more bands of sheep."

"Those herders make awful nice targets."

135

"No," said the rancher. "Just kill a few sheep. We keep this up and it won't be too much longer before that sheep outfit either pulls out of the basin or strikes back. Then we'll wipe them out."

Thirteen

Zalba Goyeneche kept holding in by the waterhole, as this was the only lifeline open to him—to leave it would see him perish. Oftentimes he would remove the bandage encircling his forehead, soak it in water, and then tie it in place again. The wet bit of cloth eased some of the pain, though Zalba's vision was still limited to his right eye.

Nightfall was lowering upon him once again. But he had managed to scrounge around for wood to make a campfire. He had done this many times back in the Pyrenees of Spain. And but for his wounds, he would have felt right at home, even though hunger pangs were erupting from his empty stomach. He had used his knife to slit away his trouser leg, exposing the wound at his hip. Now the blade of the knife was embedded in flames.

"If I survive . . ."

The rest of it fell away, but not the harsh determination Zalba kept contained within himself—that he would find those who'd killed his sheep. This gunman—he threw out to the silent heights around him, the massive rock walls and pine trees holding him captive—will have returned to Elkhorn, secure in the knowledge that he had murdered this Basque.

Reaching for the knife, he brought it down to where the fingers of his other hand were touching the lump under the skin. As long as the bullet remained in his thigh, he couldn't flush out his wound, and it was sure to cause blood poisoning. Shifting a little so as to use the flickering light coming from his fire, he quickly made an incision along the bump. Zalba gritted his teeth, then fumbled through the blood seeping out of the incision for the leaden slug. To his surprise, it came out somewhat easily. Even though the air was cooling down with the approach of night, sweat dampened his face as he thrust the blade of the knife back into the fire to reheat it. From his wound the blood flowed freely, flushing it out. When the blade started to redden from the heat of the fire, he wrapped a hand around the handle and brought the knife down to cauterize both wound openings.

"Aahhhh . . . !" He screamed at the intense pain, which held briefly, then throbbed away.

Zalba sank back onto the bed of pine branches he'd fastened as he let go of the knife. His vision had cleared but it was still blurry, more so now as tears spilled out of his eyes. Now all he wanted to do was to drift off into sleep. And if morning found him still alive, Zalba Goyeneche knew he must struggle on in the hope of finding a trapper's cabin or line shack, where there might be food and people.

He could feel himself going under, and though he knew it would get a lot colder up here, that was of little concern, for he could do nothing about the cold nor fend off an attack if a grizzly bear or puma found him.

Distantly came the echoing reverberation of rifle shots, three shots evenly spaced, and in Zalba surged sudden panic that it was the killers of his sheep.

"Sleep . . . sleep . . ."

The night became darker as he slipped into a tired sleep, and as he did, the tip of the moon slipped impishly over a ridge of the Bighorns to beam upon the dying flames of the campfire.

Lowering the rifle, Angelita Dominquez stared passively at the dark hulk of the mountain. Unlike the man she was seeking, she had the comforts of a bedroll and warm clothing and food—along with a growing concern for Zalba, for how could anyone survive these cold mountain nights unless that person was properly outfitted.

During the day, her second out here, she was coming to realize the difficulties of the task she'd undertaken. First of all she had to find a trail for her horses where none existed, and she could make only a few miles a day. The terrain was mostly up and down, and in this altitude, rest stops were more frequent. On a height, what she viewed revealed to Angelita the awesome depth to the Bighorns, the endless miles of ridges and pine trees. Still, she couldn't shake the feeling that Zalba was out here.

With a field glass she had found in one of the packs, she had scoped in on her father and the other Basques a long way back. After a while they had turned back, with Angelita pushing on deeper after the man she loved.

Returning to her campfire, she crouched down and lowered the rifle beside her bedroll. The horses were tethered nearby to the low branch of a limber pine; the horse she was riding whickered softly in greeting. With her back braced against his side, she lifted her eyes to the gathering darkness and whispered, "My darling, if you were within sound of my rifle, please blow me a kiss."

Angelita clutched that thought as she slipped into the bedroll and stretched out. For a long time sleep eluded her. The moon, a welcome friend, came fully in view. Night sounds stirred the air: a sudden rustling of leaves caused by the wind, the yip-yapping of a coyote on the prowl, and then her own voice murmured, "If only I could stumble across his trail." Her last thoughts before sleep were of Zalba. If he had been wounded, there'd be some trickles of blood, and of course his footprints down where the ground was softer. Before Angelita realized it, sleep claimed her, and it seemed but a moment that she awoke to the awareness that the sky was graying into dawn.

Rising, she rebuilt the campfire and put a coffeepot on to heat. Then she turned to the task of saddling her horse and putting the packs back in place, a chore she found a little easier on this third morning of her search. The horses had grown accustomed to her presence, and soon she was leading them through a jumble of huge rocks to a mountain rivulet, where they drank.

A half-hour later she was in the saddle, reining the horse along the shoulder of a ridge tapering southwesterly. It took Angelita another hour to search the summit, and holding to the saddle, she fumbled in the saddlebag for the field glass. Through the glass she found deep ravines to either side choked with trees and underbrush—any one of which could reveal the tracks left by Zalba.

"Perhaps if I signal with the rifle again?"

And when she'd unsheathed the Winchester, she simply held the barrel skyward and triggered off three evenly spaced shots. The horse under her pranced in short, nervous steps that brought it closer to the lip of the cliff. Reining it back, she replaced the rifle, with a sudden impulse taking her down the western slope of the high ridge, pushing farther up into the side of the mountain.

"I hope and pray I've made the right choice," she uttered.

This time the sound of gunfire was a lot closer, forcing Zalba into a decision. He must leave this spring and find another place of refuge. He was still gripped with the deep cold of night, and it seemed even his bones were aching. Somehow he forced himself away from his bed of piney branches, the gunbelt slung over his shoulder, and limped along with the help of a branch he'd stripped of bark.

"So, morning is here . . . and it seems I'm still alive. But why? To endure more suffering?" Inwardly he scolded himself for succumbing to self-pity. He limped out of tree covering and toward some bushes heavy with dangling clusters of red chokeberry fruit. Hungrily he began plopping the tiny red beads into his mouth, as he sank down onto short green-velvety grass strewn with mountain flowers.

After a while he could feel a little strength returning to his weary body. He stuffed some chokeberry clusters inside his shirt, and mindful of those rifle shots, he began pressing on, but more to the northwest, as if drawn that way for some unexplainable reason. When he came to a stream, he eased down and drank his fill and ate some more berries. Now Zalba gazed over the lay of these elevations, the mountain a lot closer, beckoning.

"No, I could never climb there . . . not with my leg stiffening up . . ."

And he realized, too, that more vision was coming back to his right eye, and with this realization, renewed hope bucked up his spirits. Going on, he crossed a small meadow and came upon a game track punching into the pine forest of the mountain. Here he found there were very few low branches obstructing his passage, the mantle of trees cutting sunlight away. Tortuously he moved on, knowing that if he stopped for any length of time he might never have the will to get up.

Under the trees the ground was fairly uniform, strewn with pine cones and carpeted with needles shaken down by windstorms. As he labored on, a shaft of sunlight just ahead told Zalba he was coming to an opening. Then he found himself standing at a dropoff and gazing down at a wider pathway disappearing into—or so it seemed to Zalba—sheer rock. Turning, he managed to work his way down the sloping wall of shale to the path.

Joy and hope, erupted in Zalba as he discovered marks left by someone wearing hobnail boots. There were other footprints, too, made by shod horses. Going to his knees, he could discern that the prints were old, that someone had passed this way during a rainstorm, leaving the prints etched in dried clay.

"But someone has passed through here," he said hopefully. "And might again."

141

The sound of water roaring around rocks drew him, limping down the path, and where it bent to pass into a narrow opening going deeper into the mountain was a stream gushing down into the basin. Zalba wondered if this path led to an abandoned mine. Slowly he moved deeper into the rocky draw—the path twisting, disappearing—and as he followed it Zalba discovered a small log cabin and a shed and brush concealing what could be the opening to a mine.

Questions danced in Zalba's mind, but his first concern was to find something to eat, and he stumbled toward the cabin door. Once inside the cabin, he found that it was filled with the musty scent that came from being shuttered up and not occupied for some time. And there, on the cupboard shelves, were cans of food. Grabbing one, he used his knife to slice it open. Then he simply let the beans gush into his mouth, chomping them quickly and gulping them down until the can was empty. Hungrily he cut open another can, this time moving out to the front porch, where he sagged down and propped his back against the log wall.

As he ate from the can, he looked about, and as he did, it occurred to Zalba that men with considerable skill had put up these buildings—perhaps in the last five years or so. Wood cut with a cross saw was stacked along one wall of the shed to just below the eaves. Like the cabin, the shed had a peaked roof, which he knew would help keep snow from piling up and breaking roof boards.

He began to doze off, secure in the knowledge that now he would survive this terrible ordeal. When he roused himself, late afternoon shadows were there, and so was a burning thirst. Slowly he pushed up and entered the cabin in search of something that would hold water. Armed with a small galvanized pail, he left the cabin and hobbled down the narrow path that punched silently through the secluded draw.

Coming out of the draw, Zalba soon found a side trail curling down toward a stream foaming over mossy-green rocks. Close to the bank were some flat rocks, and gratefully he eased down onto a rock, where he thrust the pail into the water and brought it out to drink thirstily of the icy cold water. Breathing heavily from the exertion of walking, he rested for a while, reaching as he did to remove the bandage from around his head.

"Perhaps I might find some liniment in the cabin."

There was a moment of dizziness, and he let it pass. Overhead the sun, though lowering, was still casting out a lot of light. Across the stream and in the pine trees a pair of blue jays flitted. Back at the cabin he had decided to strap on his gunbelt, recalling those shots he had heard, and its heavy weight now caused him to unbuckle it again and set it on a nearby rock. Scooting around on the rock, and going onto his belly, he brought the bandage into the water and let it soak.

Suddenly Zalba realized something other than his reflection was staring back at him, something that lay twinkling dully on the stream bottom. Reaching deeper into the water, his fingers closed around what appeared to be a rock. But when Zalba brought it out of the cold water, he knew that what he held was a gold nugget.

"So big . . . ? I don't believe this . . . !"

To him it seemed as if it weighed a pound or more, and he knew most assuredly it was gold. For back in the Pyrenees he had come across gold nuggets, but never one this size. Perhaps it had washed down from higher up during a gullywasher of a rainstorm.

Ruefully he murmured, "I came not seeking gold but a haven. Perhaps there will be a good life—*Osagarria*—after all."

Wedging the nugget in a trouser pocket, he squeezed most of the water out of the bandage before retying it around his forehead. He would return now with a pailful of water, and after cleansing his wounds and body, and perhaps having some more food, crawl into one of the bunks.

Questions layered in Zalba's mind as he retraced his steps into the draw. Laboring along, he pushed those questions aside and thought instead of Angelita. "At least she is safe back in Elkhorn. But he will return, this Rincon. And so must I."

Angelita couldn't tear her eyes away from the tracks she'd found along the ravine floor. Companion to the bootprints were holes punched into the ground, one after another, made, she knew, by someone limping along with the help of a crutch.

She'd tied a longer rope to the halter of the packhorse, the other end of which was looped around her saddle horn, and she was afoot at the moment and holding on to the reins of her horse. A day in the saddle had taken its toll, but with the discovery of these prints she shrugged her tiredness aside. Of more concern to her was that the day was coming to an end. Still she kept following the trail in the hope she'd come upon Zalba.

She wore riding boots and a worn pair of Levi's, a thick woolen shirt, and a low-crowned hat drawn down over her forehead, with her raven hair pinned up to keep it out of the way. Her eyes flared with the intensity of her search.

There was something gnawing at Angelita Dominquez, an alien feeling—this hatred that had sprung up toward the Bighorn Basin cattlemen. What had her father often said?—that hatred could tear someone apart. To her it was more than mere human emotion, it was as if most basin ranchers considered the Basque herders inferior beings. For them killing a herder was the same as taking out a sheep. She knew this must change—otherwise there would be no end to the violence.

Riding around a high hump of ridge, she found herself taking in a small pond screened by trees, and she rode on in to dismount with an eager anticipation upon finding the remnants of a campfire.

She swung down, gazed about, and murmured, "My darling, I can feel your presence. Please, Zalba, do not die on me."

The day was ending, and indecision danced in her eyes, whether to hold up here or go on. Before her were the rising

144

heights of the mountain, and in sunken places shadows had already taken hold. It would not help either of them, she realized, if she continued her search only to have a mishap in the dark.

So, much against her will, Angelita Dominquez turned to the task of making camp. Long after night had claimed the mountain she sat hunkered close to her campfire, unwilling to seek her bedroll. Angelita knew all she'd do was toss and turn in her fears for Zalba. But tomorrow—tomorrow she knew her search would end.

Fourteen

Plainsman Zach Lankford splashed across the river crossing under a noonday sun. He loped past a high-wheeled freight wagon pulled by mules and followed the scoria-covered road into the business section of Worland. His first stop was at the sheriff's office, where he was told by Deputy Medran that Moses Quinta was out of town.

Lankford merely grunted as he swung about and left. Reclaiming the saddle cinched to his cayuse, he hunted up a livery stable. The hostler was wary about giving oats to such a mangy-looking critter as the cayuse, so he let Zach have the honor of doing it.

"I'm trusting you'll keep watch over my belongings," he glared at the hostler. Then Zach ambled through the open front door, drawn downstreet by his hunger pangs.

Instead of heading for the cafe beckoning just across the street, he shouldered through the batwings of the Red Garter Saloon, as he recalled that its owner, Maggie Gillian, put out a fine spread of cold cooked meats and cheeses to entice customers. Before the building had been turned into a saloon, it housed a stagecoach line that had gone out of business. Maggie had slapped a coat of varnish on the log walls and had a local carpenter redo the woodwork around the doors and windows. She was prideful of her bar, as it curled around an L-shaped wall,

146

and on a busy day such as now three bartenders were waiting on customers.

Easing up to the bar, Lankford knew by the presence of at least twelve cowhands that something was in the wind. Back at a table Maggie Gillian was dealing out cards, the usual cigar wedged between her thick lips, and she was exchanging sass with another player. Maggie was no fashion plate, as she had on a woolen shirt with the sleeves rolled up to her elbows—this over a flowery dress—and shards of gray streaked her brown hair. Lankford was willing to wager that under the shirt you could find a .32 revolver.

"Tough old bitch," he muttered, as a bartender he knew replaced a bottle on the back bar and came to wait on him. "Hans, I thought you worked over at Riley's place . . ."

The bartender shrugged and said, "I am a widely traveled man. Been a spell, Zach." Hans Ulrich was only in his middle forties, a big-boned man with knobby wrists and a deadpan expression, his black hair slicked back thick against his skull. His face told the story of a man held captive by hard liquor. He'd work for a while in some saloon, and then Ulrich would go on a bender. When he came out of it, Ulrich would simply go looking for another job tending bar. His wife had left him years ago, and his son, now grown, despised Ulrich. But he could be counted on to pour a stiff drink, which he did now for Lankford, this into a double-shot whiskey glass.

And Zach downed it just as promptly, shuddering the hard whiskey down, to have Ulrich refill his glass. "That was damned good, Hans. Been out on the trail drinkin' warm water and piss-poor coffee. The place is crowded today."

"Been this way ever since the sheep trouble started."

"That so." Zach fingered out a silver dollar, and he picked up the whiskey bottle as he turned toward a side table laden with food. He gobbled down several hunks of venison sausage and some cheese and washed this away with a swig from the whiskey bottle, even as his wary eyes picked out certain cow-

147

hands. They were in here, he pondered, even though this was a busy time of year for ranchers. He set his eyes on Rives Portolo, a once-upon-a-time 77 hand.

Be just like Portolo, he mused inwardly, to be one of those raiders Moses told me about. As I recollect, Rives had a little mean streak. But until Moses does get in, that poker game looks mighty invitin'.

He eased around the crowd at the roulette wheel, where one of Maggie's bargirls was hammering away at a piano, to slip onto the empty chair to Maggie Gillian's left. She wrinkled her nose, then her head swiveled and she stared at Zach and sourly, "You bring in some trailkill or what?"

"It's just me, honey doll."

"I thought you was dead."

"Had some close calls of late, but dead this tom turkey ain't. What's the stakes?"

"Same as usual. You pay for that bottle?"

"Why, honey doll, you just cut me to the quick." As he gazed back at her through a snaggle-toothed grin, Zach fumbled around in a coat pocket, and when he removed his hand it held a crumbled greenback, which he smoothed out on the table. "This government note should be enough to buy me this place."

"Don't you wish. What the hell, Lankford, about a third of that greenback is torn away."

"Three-quarters is better than half a note."

"I just hope my lard-ass banker lets me deposit this thing," Maggie grumbled, as she slid some chips in front of Zach. To show her displeasure, she blew smoke into his face.

"Ain't she the darling one," grinned Zach to the other players.

One of them, from the cut to his western-style clothing, was a cattleman, who drawled, "Lankford, is it? I'm Gil Harney."

Now the three others players chipped in with their names, a pair of them locals, and the pudgy man a lumber salesman from Cheyenne. Now to Harney, Zach said, "Yup, when I started

148

working for the 77, you were a ranch foreman. Now you own your own place. I guess grit is what it takes."

"To hell with grit," Maggie said. "Just ante up before you boys forget how to play this game."

After a few hands Zach got into the flow of the game, as he'd pushed his reasons for being here in Worland to the dark edges of his mind. He had the capacity to push aside any worries and just enjoy the moment. As the afternoon wore on, the smoke got thicker, forming a wispy cloud that hung just above the hats of those standing at the roulette wheel. And more 'pokes and ranchers drifted in.

There was a sudden commotion, and when everyone at the table shifted in their chairs to look, it was just a cowhand trying to lift the heavyset piano player off the stool that was sizes too small for her plump posterior. More laughter erupted around the smoky interior when he fell over backward with her spilling on top and cursing hellfire at him.

"I just hope," Zach said philosophically, "that the magic hasn't gone out of that relationship. I'll buck that raise, Mr. Harney . . . to the tune of two silver dollars."

The lumber salesman twicked his nose—a giveaway sign that he was bluffing. And Zach sighed as if he'd just been handed a birthday present when lumber salesman bumped his raise. Zach's eyes slid to the bar owner peering sourly at her cards, and when she discarded them, he chuckled.

"Long's you ain't playin', honey bunch, why don'cha fetch me another bottle—for that matter, drinks all around."

Maggie Gillian flared out, "I bet you've never taken a bath, Lankford. And you're so old that if you did your carrot would probably fall off."

"Drinks all around, Maggie dear," he teased her.

"Aw, shit, I'll go tell Hans to bring 'em. Harney, raise him again as he's bluffing." Heaving to her feet, she headed for the bar.

Now a louder voice cut through the late afternoon chatter,

the words directed at Zach Lankford. "It ain't just any stink. It's sheep stink. Ain't that right, Lankford?"

Zach laid down his hand to reveal a full house. His eyes darting about, he honed in on Rives Portolo pushing closer to the table. Portolo was short but blocky, and he always seemed to wear a smirk and two guns thonged down low. The other players began easing their chairs away from the table and otherwise ducking out of the way. But Zach held there, boredom glinting in his eyes, as he knew someone had put Portolo up to this.

"Rives, that was a real pretty speech. But it lacks imagination. You could'a said, 'Hey there, you bloated old pussgut, you been laying up with sheep again. Or—' "

"Come on," Portolo taunted, making a beckoning gesture with his left hand. "You and that damned Quinta are cut from the same coat of wool."

Grinned Zach, "You still carry that pigsticker, Rives? You do? Ain't that just peachy. So happens"—Zach eased the big Green River knife out of its doeskin sheath and rose ever so slowly—"I brung mine along, too. That is, unless you ain't man enough, Portolo, for a little knifeplay . . ."

Rives Portolo decided to go for his gun. He had it all going for him: the nasty grin of a man knowing he was about to gun somebody down, the draw smooth and swift and now the six-gun clearing leather. To the shock of most everyone in the saloon, Zach's knife sliced deep into Portolo's arm, the throw about as accurate as Lankford had ever made. Rives Portolo screamed. The gun fell from his nerveless fingers and he dropped to his knees. All Rives could do was stare in disbelief at Zach's big Green River knife hilted into his arm.

"Whoever set Portolo up ought to back up his play," Lankford said loudly into the hushed silence.

"Enough!"

The man who'd spoken was the sheriff of Washakie County. The batwings sagged behind Moses Quinta as he came on through the press. He was dusty and looked trail weary, and everyone could see anger stamped plainly on his face. "Someone else could have gotten killed here."

"What do you mean, Sheriff?"

"Within the last week two Basque herders were killed. You'll read about it in tomorrow's paper. Someone get that slobbering cowpoke over to the sawbones. You, Lankford, are under arrest."

"Huh?"

"From what I saw you took advantage of Portolo."

"But, Moses, he was goin' for his hogleg."

"Yeah, yeah. And the rest of you, go about your business. The fun's over."

He brought Lankford out the front door, and only when they were a couple of blocks upstreet from the saloon did Moses say, "I'll go over to the sawbones and retrieve your knife, Zach. I just got back from Kemmerer's place."

"The man gets around." First, Zach told about finding the Yardley brothers and Treech Rincon boozing it up at Eriksen's road ranch. "So who comes in to join them but Carsey Kemmerer and a couple of hardcases—along as bodyguards, I reckon."

"Kemmerer and the Yardleys?"

"It gets better, Moses. They not only killed those herders, but it was Harge Yardley taking out Jim Graham."

"I know Kemmerer is buying land east of here. But him aligned with those deadbeats? Just what kind of a killing game is Kemmerer playing?" He paused under a roof overhang and looked back at the saloon. "A lot of cattlemen in town, and here it is the middle of the week."

"They're up to something."

"Zach, we need more evidence than you overhearing Kemmerer talking to Harge Yardley. Kemmerer's lawyers would laugh us out of court. I reckon the Yardleys headed back to Elkhorn. I want you to go over there, Zach, and find out what they're up to."

"You ain't gonna throw me in the calaboose . . ."

"That was just to simmer things down back there. Rives Portolo—he's as slow a thinker now as back when he worked for me."

"You know they're in town for only one reason, Moses."

"Here to form another raiding party. Watch yourself over there."

"You, too, Quinta, as I ain't got paid yet."

"When you're over at Elkhorn, drop in and see the owner of the Navarre Hotel."

"Yeah, you told me about this Dominquez."

"Zach, is that really you?"

Both of them turned toward Celia Quinta and her daughter, Beth, just coming up, and Celia held her smile as she embraced the plainsman. "Oh, Zach, you look wonderful."

"That ain't what yer husband's been throwin' at me, Miz Quinta. Doggone, you're still about the handsomest filly I ever laid these peepers on."

"You remember Beth . . ."

"Yup. Asked her to marry me one time. Now she broke my heart by marryin' another."

"Well, Zach, you have to have supper with us."

"Would, but I'm a wage-earner now, Miz Quinta."

"Ah, Celia," said Moses. "Zach's one of my deputies. But he doesn't have to pull out until tomorrow morning." He drew his wife aside as Zach carried on an animated conversation with Celia's daughter.

"Did you have any trouble out at Kemmerer's place?"

"Nope," Moses smiled.

"But there *is* going to be more trouble. I hear the talk around town."

"Judge Springbuck is allowing me to hire more deputies. I'm using Zach to do some tracking. Just between us, honey, I'm on the verge of breaking this thing wide open. Hopefully there won't be any range war."

"Two Basque herders getting murdered," she threw at him worriedly, "means one has already begun. Moses, I knew what you were when I married you—not just a gunhand but a kind and decent man. It took real grit to pin on that badge. Whatever you do . . . just be careful, my darling husband. I don't want to spend my retirement years by my lonesome in our big four-poster."

He drew Celia close, and they kissed. He said, "Got some papers to shuffle. An' probably some'll be dropping in to ask about those deputy sheriff jobs. Maybe we could ask Zach to move back to the ranch when all of this has run its course."

"Maybe."

During the afternoon Moses hired on one deputy, and just before he was going to call it a day, a county commissioner dropped by. "Sheriff, I can understand why you need more deputies. But why do you need this tracker, Lankford? You have to understand, Quinta, there isn't too much money in the county fund."

"Judge Springbuck has the final say in this. You boys want a safe town and law and order, which don't come cheap. Maybe you want this badge back?"

"No," the commissioner said quickly.

And when he made a hasty exit, so did Moses, taking that ambling walk over to his daughter-in-law's house. Lankford was there, taking haven out in the back yard, where he sat talking to Raoul Dixon, Beth's ranchhand husband.

During the evening meal partaken in the dining room, they exchanged light talk while washing the beef stew down with a vintage wine. They steered clear of the present troubles in the basin, their talk drifting back to the earlier years, some bad, but mostly a lot of good ones.

"Zach, isn't it awfully lonesome up there?"

"Why, child, I've got squirrels and birds and other small game for company. Me move back to the 77? Celia, I 'preciate the kind offer. But—"

153

The glass exploded out of the big lead-glass window facing onto the south lawn. Moses shouted, "Get down!" The thud behind him told Moses the slug had embedded high into the living room wall. He didn't know what to expect, as he wormed belly down over to the front door and to his gunbelt hanging from the coat rack. Behind him came Lankford and Raoul Dixon.

"I don't reckon that was somebody out turkey hunting?"

Moses nodded, as he gazed back at the light still pouring out of the lamps and the women crouched low. "Hold in here."

He stood erect and slipped out through the front door to come along the wall and take in what lay beyond the south lawn. All he could see through screening trees was light coming from other houses, and he dropped his six-gun low to his side. It had been a warning shot. A message from Carsey Kemmerer.

Moses let his anger slip away. This was neither the time for that nor for snap decisions. He knew this sheriffing job required a cool head . . . and just a little luck.

"But Kemmerer . . . you just made a big mistake. As that bullet could just as easily have killed Beth . . . or Celia . . ."

"He's gone."

Glancing over his shoulder, Moses said, "Yeah, Zach, he slipped away. Kemmerer is a bigger fool than I thought."

"Next time he'll go for the kill."

"And so will we."

"Harsh talk for a lawman."

Moses chewed this over as he gazed back at Lankford, then he said, "First I despoil Beth's lawn with horse manure. Now this—just could be I've worn out my welcome."

Fifteen

On the outskirts of Elkhorn, the holding pens owned by the Varney Sheep Company were being used to hold horses owned by recent newcomers to these parts. Camptenders had driven out wagons loaded with supplies. Some of the Basques were working on the wagons, greasing axles and replacing wooden wheel spokes. They worked with the uneasy knowledge that danger lurked out in the basin. All of them knew it was more than rumor that sheep would be sent across the Bighorn River into cattle country—where they and the sheep and the herders would be fair game for marauding cattlemen. Now with the arrival of more men packing guns, the order to move out would be given any day.

Uptown, Burt Taggart was going over last-minute plans with Harge Yardley and three gunhands including Chuck Dacy, the man Taggart had picked to be his second-in-command—though he hadn't bothered to inform Harge Yardley about this as he was still angry over some of his herders and sheep being killed. What he figured was that Harge should have had brains enough to send his brothers out, to have at least one gunhand with each band of sheep. No, the damned fools had stuck together.

He should have let the Yardleys and Treech Rincon go. But he needed every gun he could muster, especially when the big push came across the Bighorn. A big wall map before which

Taggart stood was marked to show the location of each band. And jabbing a finger at the map, he said, "We'll keep bunching them in along these low draws. But not all the sheep. We'll hold these bands over here in reserve."

"You contracted with some landowners to bring in your sheep. But to get there we have to funnel the sheep between these two ranches." Chuck Dacy, a tailormade dangling from his lips, scratched at the stubble of beard thickening on his face. "To get even that far, we'll have to use Tucker Crossing."

"I see no problem," chipped in Harge Yardley. "With me ramrodding this operation—"

"No, Harge, I might as well tell you the way it's going to be. I'm going along, too. Out there I'll have Dacy relaying my orders to the men."

"After all the risks we took," Harge muttered resentfully.

"Nothing personal, Harge," said Burt Taggart, the taut smile flicking away. "You'll still get paid the same."

"Yeah, well, I don't know as how I'll cotton to takin' orders from Mr. Chuck Dacy, if that's his real name . . ."

"Pull out, then."

His eyes shifting to Taggart, Harge chewed this over as he hooked a hand in his gunbelt. He knew he couldn't quit, not when things were heating into a range war. Not when he could still make a lot of money. They had thirty men, while the ranchers could get together in short order at least a hundred.

"You know we'll be outgunned out there."

"Perhaps," said Taggart. "I'm expecting some more men this week sometime. The difference is, my men aren't just working cowhands."

"I've strung along with you this far, Mr. Taggart. Have you ever thought about asking that some U.S. marshals be sent into the basin?"

"What could they have done to prevent my sheep from getting killed? And, Harge, what about the law over at Worland?

156

Sheriff Quinta's a cattleman—when the chips are down, he'll side with his own kind."

"If my cousin Treech don't kill Quinta, I aim doing so, as I owe him plenty. We still got some wages comin'."

"Yes, we'll settle up right now. I guess that's all for now, Dacy."

"What if those men don't show up?"

"Then we'll leave without them."

Out in back of the Navarre Hotel Javier Dominquez and two other Basques were gathered. A somber mood had hung over everything ever since Angelita had taken the packhorse and gone off into the wilderness in search of Zalba Goyeneche. Some of the camptenders staying at the hotel, and the few Basques, were all for going along with Dominquez in search of his daughter, only to have Burt Taggart put in an appearance at the hotel with orders for them to get ready and move out.

The Basques with Dominquez were no longer herders, and now they made a living by doing odd-job chores around town. But gray-haired Pedro and Carlos Abaurrea were determined to help their friend find his daughter. Dominquez said, "One day I had a search party. The next, well, they cannot go. It is as simple as that."

"Now here it is, almost four o'clock," said Pedro. "Our packs are ready. We can still pull out today. At least get under way, as tomorrow we will be that much closer."

"Si," said Carlos. "We must do what we must do. I know your Angelita, she is very capable. But, Javier, I know of many men who have succumbed to what these mountains can throw at them."

"We go, then," said Dominquez. "I will tell Elena."

"And we will tend to the horses."

Dominquez found his wife tending bar. He hesitated in the doorway, waiting until the customer she was serving was settled at a table, then he went into the barroom. Dominquez was wearing heavier clothing and a wool-lined coat under which he had on a gunbelt. Elena came down to the back end of the bar to her husband.

"You don't have to tell me you are going."

"Si, we should have pulled out before this."

"That couldn't be helped, Javier. You know, like our Angelita, I have this feeling Zalba is alive."

"I don't know what to think. Especially now that Taggart has brought in more evil-eyed men. Zalba, si, there was no grave—"

"And if Zalba Goyeneche is alive and you find him, he had better marry Angelita after all this." She held back her tears as they embraced. "Go with God, my heart."

When Dominquez and his two Basque friends and the pair of packhorses they were taking along moved downstreet past business places, they took note of the many strangers using the boardwalks. Their fear—as they had expressed earlier at the hotel—was for their Basque friends working for this sheep outfit.

Pedro said, "This Taggart hasn't learned that guns are simply for killing if they are in the wrong hands. And why should he even consider bringing sheep across the Bighorn."

"Si, he has enough grazing land as is," said Carlos.

Clearing the last buildings, they set their horses into a lope on a road angling to the southwest. What they intended doing was to keep to the road until it cut past a long ridgeline knifing out of the Bighorn Mountains. Then they would chart a course across the rugged terrain.

"We are not as young as we want to be," said Dominquez. "So, I expect, this will be hard on us."

"We will endure."

"So we shall, God willing."

Now that he had paid his brothers, they had gone on to spend it in the saloons, leaving Harge Yardley and Treech Rincon at a side-street cafe. "You know," said Rincon, "Jake ain't so bad. But Dyson and Eli don't have brains enough to come in out of a lightning storm when it comes to throwing away money. This job, Harge, is petering out, I know that."

"A sweet deal while it lasted. Montana, it don't appeal to me no more. So I'm open to suggestions."

"Yeah, don't worry, we'll think of something, as we always do, Cousin." Rincon shoved out of the booth and spun a silver dollar onto the counter in passing to pay for their meal. Out on the boardwalk, they held, sizing up the action on the street.

"Taggart now," said Harge, "has got the balls of a brass monkey. Even I've got to admit that. Still it rankles me him picking this Chuck Dacy to be second-in-command."

"You thinkin' of bracing Dacy?"

"I might, dammit, Treech."

"Don't" Rincon stepped out into the street and so did his companion. "Like you got planned, Harge, we still have to get word to Kemmerer as to when these woolie-lovers pull out of here. Then you know what'll happen—Kemmerer'll turn Tucker Crossing into a shootin' gallery. But, old buddy, us'ns won't be there."

"But Taggart and that damned Chuck Dacy will, and not a damned thing they can do about it."

"Except die," laughed Harge.

"Okay, here we are in this one-hoss town, and just what in hell we gonna do for excitement tonight?"

"There's them whores just stagecoached in over at Tatum's Saloon . . ."

"Reckon we can give them a gander. What I'm really wantin' to do, Harge, is lay my hands on that hotel owner's daughter."

"She's Basque."

"An' got it in all the right places. So after I'm whiskey-soaked, reckon that's what I'll do."

* * *

The two-day ride went uneventfully for Zach Lankford. Along the way he'd slipped past bands of sheep grazing on high places in the basin. There were fewer cattle here than west across the Bighorn. By his remembered reckonings he had another fives miles to go to reach Elkhorn. And if he held the cayuse to its present gait, he should pull in around sundown.

But he'd sighted some mule deer bucks adorned with the biggest racks he'd seen in some time. Upon spotting him, they'd pulled out fast for the higher ridges, pushing up into the mountains. "Stringy beef don't cut it for this child. I need me some venison." He thought about the Basque hotel owner over at Elkhorn. "I don't reckon this Dominquez would pass up some free meat either. Okay, cayuse, we're goin' hunting."

He left the stagecoach road behind, picking out as he rode brushy pockets high on ridgelines. Riding into a hollow, he loped along to finally reach the southern end of a ridge and from there let the cayuse pick its way up the sloping ridge covered with pine trees. The ridge pushed on for at least five miles, rising slowly. Atop the ridge he could see below him the brushy pockets he'd viewed from the road. He dismounted and tied the reins to a tree branch. Hefting his rifle, he walked along the edge of a drop-off following the flow of the ridge.

Finally in the shadows cast by the few pines standing guard over a brushy pocket, he made out the rack of horns belonging to a tawny-coated buck. The buck was lying down, with its head low to the ground, surveying everything below. Clacking the hammer back, Zach brought the rifle up—and he didn't even have to aim, as the buck was no more than twenty yards downslope of where he stood. The rifle bucked against his shoulder. The slug penetrated just at the base of the skull and the deer shuddered for just a moment before it went limp.

"Like stealin' candy from a baby," he muttered.

Later on, after having gutted the buck, he tied the carcass back of the saddle, despite the misgivings of the cayuse, and continued on his way. The last mile he whistled his way into town, an off-key rendition of an old riverboat song.

But here Zack stuck to back streets and alleyways when he could, as he hunted up the Navarre Hotel. For in passing the holding pens owned by that sheep outfit, he'd taken in some hosses that looked like they could eat up the miles without working up too much of a sweat. The kind of hosses used by men on the dodge.

"These sheepmen are building up a small army. Good thing I came over here, as it isn't just the Yardley brothers that Moses Quinta needs to be worried about."

If local merchant Clyde Burdick had gone straight home from his store, he wouldn't be confronting gunslick Treech Rincon across the poker table. As it happened, Burdick and his wife had argued over some trivial matters when he'd gone home for his noon meal. He'd been determined that neither his wife nor any other woman would handle the family finances. His displeasure over that was the reason he was here in Tatum's Saloon.

"Did I hear right, farmer, you're accusin' me of double-dealin'?"

The merchant spread his arms apart to show to Rincon he wasn't armed. "I didn't say that . . . just that you've—"

"See," Rincon snarled, "this farmer's a damned poor loser. What the hell, nobody asked you to set in here."

"I'm leaving," the merchant announced to the other players. And he started to rise, only to have Rincon lurch up and hit him flush in the face. The merchant tumbled over backward.

Quickly Treech Rincon came around the table, where he drunkenly began stomping the downed man with his boots—in the rib cage and belly and face. Rincon felt a hand clutch onto his shoulder and spin him sideways. He caught a brief glimpse of Chuck Dacy's face before his vision was blocked by the fist pounding into his cheekbone. Rincon sagged, but somehow kept

161

from falling down. The next thing he knew, Dacy had plucked away his six-gun, and Dacy and another gunhand had hustled him out through the batwings. A shove in Rincon's back sent him sprawling into the street, and with his gun landing nearby.

"Rincon, we don't need your kind of poison around here."

He lay there as Dacy and his companion reentered the saloon, wondering why Harge Yardley and his brothers hadn't stepped in to help him. Then he remembered they'd peeled out for another bar. Through his lips came an empty threat, "I'm coming back in to gun you down, damn you, Dacy."

Struggling to his feet, the drunken gunhand realized that his gun was on the street, and he bent down to pick it up. He jammed it into his holster and swept an angry hand across his cheekbone to wipe away the trickle of blood. Now he spat out street dust, as he swayed into a downstreet turn. Without the Yardleys to back his play, he wouldn't brace Chuck Dacy.

He shuffled on for another block, seeking a saloon, then he sighted the Navarre Hotel, and veered that way, dragging along his anger, rekindling the lust he felt for the Basque woman. A side door carried him into the barroom, which at the hour of eleven was empty of customers. The sight of the bottles behind the bar brought Rincon around the front end of it, and he plucked a bottle of imported Spanish whiskey off a shelf and with an ugly grin twisted out the cork. He gurgled down the whiskey as he reeled to the back end of the bar and drew up to get his bearings.

"What's her name, yup . . . Angelita . . . get her here and we'll make . . . make sweet music together." Piercing to him was the fact that lights were still on in the dining room. He headed there, passing through the open doorway, the rattle of pots coming from the kitchen pushing Rincon on.

As he cleared the last table in the dining room to the chink-chinking of his spurs, Elena Dominquez appeared in the doorway, blocking his progress. "What do you want?"

"Well, if it ain't some old bag. I want her . . . want Angelita."

Rincon stepped forward to have the woman retreat into the kitchen.

Elena Dominquez had recognized the drunk as the man who'd invaded the privacy of their dance, the one who had hit Zalba Goyeneche. Controlling her fear, she went swiftly behind the chopping block table and picked up a butcher knife only to have Rincon laugh drunkenly. Sucking down more whiskey, he drew his six-gun. An offhand shot punched a hole in a large enamel pot. "The next one, you old bag, will pluck away an ear unless you tell . . . tell me where your daughter is. You got that?"

"Please, you leave! I do not fear one such as you! You are an animal—"

"Why you—"

Neither Treech Rincon nor Elena were aware of the back screen door being pushed open and Zach Lankford silently easing into the kitchen just behind Rincon. The deer carcass was draped over Zach's shoulders. He hefted the deer with both hands and slammed the carcass at the gunhand. Suddenly Rincon found himself attacked by legs and hooves and the bloody remains of a dead animal. The heavy weight of the deer slammed into his upper body and threw him against a cupboard filled with chinaware.

Elena screamed at the sight of this barbaric newcomer clad in buckskins and screamed again as Zach lunged toward the downed Rincon, who was trying to struggle to his feet. He grabbed Rincon by the front of his shirt and vest and struck him a vicious blow square between the eyes, the sound of it like the flat of a hand striking a table top.

"Who are you?" Elena gasped.

Zach gaped at the woman gaping back. "Sheriff Quinta"— still holding onto Rincon's shirtfront, he hit the man again— "sent me here."

"Are you a lawman?" Still not convinced, Elena would not relinquish her hold on the butcher knife.

"Kind of, Mrs. Dominquez. Me and Quinta go back a long

163

ways. This deer is a present for you folks. Now you just hold in here whilst I remove this human vermin. Just touching him I could get the scabbies."

He picked up the unconscious gunhand, slung Rincon over a shoulder, and threw back as he went out the screen door, "I'll be back to take care of that carcass, ma'am."

And Zach was back—within fifteen minutes—after having dumped erstwhile gunfighter Treech Rincon in the water trough out front of a saloon. When he came in, it was to find the hotel owner's wife sitting down at a table in the kitchen, two cups of coffee poured along with a plateful of cold cooked meats. At her right hand was a revolver. "So," she said, "let me see your badge."

Dipping a hand into his coat, Zach produced a badge, as he said, "I thought all this ruckus I caused would turn up your husband."

"Please . . . what was your name . . . ?"

"Zach Lankford, ma'am." He claimed the other chair and removed his hat. "Left Worland two days ago with orders from the sheriff to keep an eye on the Yardley brothers."

"This man's name was Rincon—the worst of the lot."

"Treech—reckon he came into the basin after I'd left the 77. I'm, what you'd say, retired."

"Then you haven't heard about my daughter, Mr. Lankford." She told of the trip to pay last respects to the two Basques killed by the marauders. Only as it turned out, one of them could still be alive. "So this bullheaded daughter of mine takes off into the wilderness in search of Zalba. And just today my husband and two of his friends left in search of Angelita."

"Those mountains cover a lot of territory, Mrs. Dominquez. Not that I want to alarm you. By those holding pens, I saw some horses and wagons, men camping out."

"The pens belong to the sheep company. Sometime this week, the rumor is, everybody will leave."

As Zach took up her invitation to partake of the food, he

164

knew this meant that Burt Taggart was going to carry out his threat to move sheep across the Bighorn. And if Rincon was here, so were his cousins. He pondered over the fact that it would take a week or two just to herd bands of sheep into one large band, more days to get them over to the river. Come tomorrow morning, after scouting around town tonight to catch a glimpse of the Yardleys, he'd have to fire off a telegram to Moses Quinta.

Now he said, "Mrs. Dominquez, I'm one of a dying breed known as a tracker. After I take care of a little business tomorrow morning, I'll take off after your husband."

"You will help us?"

"You betcha, ma'am. There's just a chance that if this Basque, Zalba, got away, he could identity those who attacked him and killed his sheep. Asides, ma'am, I was weaned up in them Bighorns. Now, I'd better get to carving up this mule deer. See that rack; bet it would look just dandy out in your barroom."

Sixteen

"Quinta, I'm not the only one who feels you've sold out to that sheep outfit over at Elkhorn! Everyone here has got the same notion." Carsey Kemmerer sat at the head of the long banquet table, smug in the knowledge that he had the backing of everyone there.

Moses Quinta had come in alone, as he'd sent his deputies out to watch some of the crossings along the Bighorn River. Big brassy lamps lit up the hotel meeting room, and for the most part the ranchers were drinking coffee, though a few whiskey bottles were in evidence.

Moses started out by asking the ranchers to hold back on raiding any more bands of sheep—stating that if they did, he'd be making wholesale arrests. So what happened was that a raid scheduled for two nights ago hadn't come off, and this had gotten to Carsey Kemmerer.

Moses said, "Under the law everyone has equal representation. At least the law I'm gonna hand out. Carsey, once again you're dead wrong as to my personal beliefs. You spout off to me again, I damn well will toss you in jail." Their eyes bored holes in one another, with Moses barely holding back on accusing Kemmerer of being responsible for busting out a window in his daughter-in-law's house. At the moment Moses had a strong urge to call Kemmerer outside, where they'd settle this thing gun against gun.

"The rest of you," Moses said through his controlled anger, "had better listen up. I'm tired of being called this and that . . . and having some son'bitch punch out my windows. What you're gonna do is send a delegation over to Elkhorn and palaver with this sheep outfit. Otherwise—an' you can make book on this— Judge Springbuck is turning this whole mess over to the federal boys. You know gettin' rid of them is worse'n bein' plagued by locusts. So you think on that."

A rancher pushed to his feet—Wayford Clark, owner of the Double D—to say, "Quinta, you're right. You kill something, it's dead forever. Especially a man's self-respect. Much as I hate sheep, well, more 'n that I hate having a ring put through my nose."

Nodding at what the rancher had said, Sheriff Moses Quinta left the meeting room. He could have accused Carsey Kemmerer, in front of his peers, as being the man responsible for the deaths of those Basque herders. He could have said that Kemmerer's only reason for wanting a range war was personal gain. But Moses said to himself as he found a saloon, Way things are going, Kemmerer'll find a way to hang himself.

Somehow the persuasive powers of Carsey Kemmerer managed to hold the coalition of ranchers together. His ace in the hole, which he hadn't revealed, was of the Yardleys getting word to him when and if the Varney Sheep Company made good on their promise to bring their sheep westerly. But even after the meeting broke up—a lot earlier because of Sheriff Quinta's threats to bring in some U.S. marshals—rancher Kemmerer clutched his worries tightly to his chest. Despite this, he went along with some ranchers planning to make a tour of the saloons and gaming joints.

Carsey Kemmerer had an inner sense of wanting to obtain

more than what he had—more land—certainly a wife that could satisfy his lust for the flesh, but he could never have enough money. He knew, though he pushed it aside, that once he'd killed those two Mormon prospectors and stolen their gold, he could never go back to being just a rancher. For a new world had opened up to him—one in which he could control the destiny of others to suit his greedy purposes. It was so simple, really, just how gleaming gold nuggets in sufficient quantity could empower a man. The fellow ranchers he was walking with down Main Street were content with their lot. He reckoned they'd die contented but poor.

Coming to a saloon, he saw—under the deeper shadows of an overhanging porch hooked to the next building—one of the gunhands he'd hired lolling on a rough-sawed bench.

"Hey, Carsey, you've been awful quiet."

"Got a lot on my mind, I reckon." Kemmerer let his teeth flash through the collecting darkness of night in a reckless smile. "I'm buying drinks around . . . and the biggest steak in town afterward."

"The hell you say, Carsey," said another rancher. "We'll just shake dice to see who buys. Damn, ain't this the saloon where Millie O'Toole dispenses her favors?"

"Tillman, you outta get out more."

"Ever since the missus got back to goin' to church, she's been crimpin' my style."

The ranchers filed into the saloon, and a short time later gunhand Owl Head Johnson entered. He went directly to the bar, where Johnson hooked a boot on the brass railing and ordered a cold beer. He'd been hanging around town, waiting for Kemmerer to show. And he was still puzzling over being told to fire a warning shot at Sheriff Moses Quinta, as men in his line of work preferred to go for the kill.

Through the back mirror he watched the ranchers hunkered in close around a table. They were plotting something, as these were the men closely aligned with Carsey Kemmerer. They knew him as a gun for hire and kept their distance, which didn't faze him a tinker's damn. When Kemmerer had ridden in, Wade Beechum had come along. Wade was Owl Head Johnson's high-line partner. Johnson liked to hang around the night spots, but Beechum had an aversion to bright lights and local lawmen—and like now, Johnson figured his partner was out fishing some-place along the river.

Draining his glass, he beckoned for a refill as Carsey Kemmerer left the table and came up to the bar. The rancher slipped a hand inside his coat and withdrew a bulky envelope. "I want you and Beechum to head over to Tule Eriksen's. Wait there until Harge Yardley shows up, which might be a few days. Then give him this envelope. Harge will have a message for me. Soon's you hear him out, hightail it back here to Worland."

"That Tule charges plenty for his rotgut and whores."

Kemmerer took out his wallet, and he peeled out some paper money. "This should take care of your expenses. One more thing. It could be that Harge'll ride in alone. If he does, you hear him out. Then, Owl Head, you'll earn another five hundred if you gun down Harge Yardley."

"If he's alone, as me an' Beechum ain't buckin' all of them Yardleys and that Treech Rincon."

"Saddle up and pull out right away. You hang around town, you might run into the sheriff. That money in the envelope I gave you is for Yardley; but if you kill Harge, I want the enve-lope back. Make no mistake about that."

"You're callin' it," he said uneasily. Ever since hiring on, the outlaw knew what kind of rages the rancher could fly into. Sometimes at night he'd spot Kemmerer pacing along the front porch, a drink in hand, his eyes filled with the strange craziness of a man torn by inner demons. Him and Beechum, he'd gotten to thinking, needed to avail themselves of the Outlaw Trail a'fore long, because to hang on here would see Kemmerer scrawl them on his hit list—as it stood to reason that along with Harge, the other Yardleys and Rincon had to be taken out.

"Well?"

"Okay, we'll head out right away."

The rancher held by the bar until the hardcase was gone, pondering over whether or not he should hold back on killing Harge Yardley. Either now or later, he told himself. All of them must die. The gold makes it all worthwhile.

The first order of business for Moses Quinta was to get a long overdue haircut. Afterward, and with cloud cover shielding the early morning sun, Moses had returned to his office at the jail to await the return of his deputies and catch up on some paperwork. Like the haircut, this was a chore he likened to a man being forced to attend a quilting bee. Yesterday the clerk of court had brought over some writs that it was Moses' duty to deliver.

He grumbled, "Let my deputies handle them writs" Somehow he just couldn't hold behind his desk—rising to make a pot of coffee, going back to check on the one prisoner he was holding in the cell block—for his thoughts lay elsewhere.

First of all, it hadn't set all that well with him when he'd sent Zach Lankford over to Elkhorn. But logically who'd suspect an old renegade like Zach as being a lawman? His deputies were closer, keeping watch last night at crossings along the Bighorn River—the reason being the marauders led by Kemmerer had been riding high, wide, and handsome. Each of them, including the two he'd just hired as deputies, were equipped with field glasses—another expense he was certain would be challenged by the county commissioners.

"Come this autumn I will be one happy cowpoke. Then no more tinny little badge to wear. Yup, come in . . ."

He smiled at the messenger boy following his knock into the room, and Moses dug out a dime. "Aren't you Jug McHale's younker?"

"Yessir, Sheriff." He handed Moses a telegram, caught the flipped dime in midair, and wheeled about to go.

Easing onto the edge of the desk, Moses muttered, "Reflexes like that, that younker might turn out to be a gunfighter. Now, what do we have—"

Quickly he scanned the contents of the telegram sent to him by Zach Lankford. It detailed the buildup of gunhands in Elkhorn, and wagons being prepared and loaded with supplies. And the sheep outfit's plans to make that push across the Bighorn River. The door opened as he came to the last sentence; a flicking glance by Moses found it was Deputy Josh Medran, and behind him, Kornkven. "Am going to help in search for Dominquez's daughter and a Basque herder."

"Trouble, Moses?"

"They're gonna do it," he said flatly to his deputies. "Shove woolies across the Bighorn. Anything happen out there?"

"Night was quiet as a graveyard," replied Medran.

"Same here," said John Kornkven, as he picked up a cup from a side table and went to the stove to claim the coffeepot.

"Might as well tell you now as later," Moses said. "I hired Lankford to do some tracking. He sent this telegram from Elkhorn. A Basque herder . . . I wonder? Could be only one herder got killed. Maybe the other one got away—and if he did, this Basque might be able to identify some of these marauders." On a wall between two gunracks was a map showing the Bighorn Basin. Going up to it, uncertainty flared in Moses' eyes.

He said, "They could cross those sheep over most anyplace. Doesn't make any difference which crossing they use, as Kemmerer will get wind of it."

"Yup, from the Yardley brothers."

"And Zach Lankford right out there in the middle of it. But he's a wily old codger. Kemmerer now, him and his gobbling up all this land east of the river is still a puzzler. Sooner or later, though, Kemmerer'll have to cut ties with the Yardleys, and you know what that means . . ."

171

"So, Sheriff, just how do we play this?"

"My first order of business is to fire off a telegram to Lankford. Tell him that we're heading his way. 'Cause if they find this Basque herder, this is one hombre the cattlemen don't want kept alive."

Moses Quinta left to step out into the dusty street and allow a freight wagon to pass as he took a quick squint at the morning sun beginning to push away from clouds. His patrol of Worland last night had revealed that Carsey Kemmerer and other ranchers were overnighting. What he wanted most last night was to run into Owl Head Johnson and that other hardcase.

"Damn, big lead-glass windows like that are expensive. Especially when my daughter-in-law is stickin' me with the repair bill."

He brushed by a woman exiting from the telegraph office, which was also used to hold freight and where the stagecoach pulled in. Going to the counter, he reached for a yellow pad of paper and a stub of pencil. "Hey, Mulligan, this place gettin' so hard up it can't afford a decent pencil . . . ?"

"Oh, howdy, Sheriff Quinta. Got a box of pencils right here. How you been?"

"Mostly pissed-off of late. Here, take a gander at this message I want sent over to Elkhorn."

"Hmmm, to Zach Lankford." Placing the paper before him, the operator began tapping the telegraph key. He kept at it for a few moments, then he lifted his hand away from the key and turned concerned eyes upon the sheriff of Washakie County.

"Line appears down," he said.

"You sure?"

"Yessir, just to Elkhorn. Now, there I can reach Old Thermopolis and north up to Manderson. But easterly, 'fraid the line is down."

"Keep trying," Moses said. He turned away and drifted out to the boardwalk, moving briskly along it. Common sense took

172

hold, telling him the Varney Sheep Company was on the move. And if so, they had cut the telegraph line.

"Got more to worry about now than a broken window."

Seventeen

The face peering back at Zalba Goyeneche in a broken shard of mirror was gaunt and covered with black stubble. But at least he'd had a hot bath and applied a clean bandage over his facial wound and blind left eye. The last few days had sapped his strength, but he knew he was healing.

"I suppose a man can live with only one eye," Zalba said, as he set the mirror by the washbasin.

The door and windows were open to air out the cabin, and late yesterday afternoon a mule deer had come within pistol range. In the cabin he'd found a few staples, salt and canned food. All he knew of his whereabouts was that he was high along the western slopes of the Bighorns, as the mountain forest concealed what lay below.

Moving to the table, he picked up the gold nugget he'd found in the stream. Of equal interest was the location of these buildings, hidden way back in this sheer-walled canyon gouging deep into the mountain. Only blind luck—and he smiled at the phrase—saw him stumbling in here. In the shed Zalba had come across equipment used to mine gold. To him this meant those who'd been here before would return. When he'd prowled about yesterday, he had found the concealed mouth of a mine, and with some difficulty—getting in there meant easing through a

174

narrow fissure that sprang up from the floor of the canyon, as the mine opening was covered up with large rocks and brush.

Armed with his gunbelt and a canteen, and clad in a heavy woolen shirt he'd found in the bedroom, he cradled his hat over his head and left the cabin. He detoured by the shed to enter and select one of the pickaxes, and from here Zalba went deeper into the narrow canyon, which soon took an angling turn. There was no sound other than an occasional release of thin mountain air through his lips, which came out hoarfrosty white. Here the sun never penetrated, and Zalba was grateful for the heavier shirt. From the shed he'd also taken a lantern to use when he got into the mine.

A short angling turn and he was there. He stopped for a breather and flexed his leg, only to have pain radiate from his wound. Setting the lantern on a nearby rock, he went closer and began to pull brush that had been placed there in an effort to conceal the opening. He formed a narrow aperture without too much trouble, and going back for the lantern, he slipped into the rounded mine opening, the roof barely a foot above his head. Using what light there was, he went in as far as he could, then he used a sulphur match to light the coal oil lantern.

Instantly more of the mine revealed itself to Zalba Goyeneche. What caused a trilling of excitement in the young Basque were the tiny pinpricks of gold glittering in the mine walls. He kept moving along, the tunnel widening into an inner cavern composed of eerie rocky formations. Then he held up, puzzled, a tinge of fear keening his ears to a nearby roaring of water cascading over rocks. He held the lantern more before him, not wanting to drop into some treacherous void.

He sensed rather than saw the mine was edging away, rather than flowing up higher into the face of the mountain. The coloration of the rock formations reminded him of a Spanish cathedral. Then he came to where the mine forked into a pair of dark passageways, and again he hesitated. Here and there under

175

lamplight he could see gold shining dully, just traces of it, or perhaps it was pyrite, fool's gold.

Zalba wasn't certain at first, but in the passageway off to his left came a vague light and the sound of a waterfall. The other passageway seemed darker, threatening.

Look for a track, he scolded himself, or are you like fool's gold, a stupid oaf?

Lowering the lantern a little, he could make out a worn path, and there, too, markings left by someone wearing hobnail boots. He didn't hesitate now, but continued on, the slight ache from his wounds forgotten in the anticipation of what he might find: perhaps the mate to the nugget he'd left in the cabin. In the passageway he was forced to crouch, reaching out with his free hand to touch the cold stone wall. More light came at him, an uncertain glowing, but it told Zalba there was an opening to the outside. Impishly the passageway took a sharp jog to his left and got narrower before it turned again to slope downward. All Zalba could do was pull up suddenly at the sight of a stream pushing in from someplace in the mountain to boil its waters out through a slotted opening, forming a waterfall.

A ledge projected out on either side of the stream—which could be no more than four feet across—and Zalba stepped onto the ledge before he realized that the ceiling and wall to his right were literally paved with streaks of dull-gleaming gold bands. He had heard of gold sometimes being found in pockets—still he was awed by what he was viewing. Across the stream he saw a small wheelbarrow and stacked there, too, some shovels and pickaxes.

"So much gold?" he murmured in disbelief.

It came to Zalba how they had gotten gold ore out of here, slowly and back through the tortuous length of the small passageway. Holding the lantern up before him, he knelt by the narrow rivulet of clear water, to have it blink back at him with tiny gold pebbles strewn on the streambed. He came erect and went along the ledge to look out of the opening, down at the waterfall to the stream below and the wide carpeting of pine trees extending to the floor of the Bighorn Basin.

Perhaps, he mused, the pocket of gold extended deeper into the mountain, and the stream had washed out gold nuggets over the eons. "Why," he gushed wonderingly, "just with a pocketful of nuggets I am no longer a poor Basque herder. And I'll be wealthy enough to ask for Angelita's hand in marriage. If she'll still have me . . ." For now his face was marred with a scar, and he was blind in one eye.

Taking a last look at the spreading reach of all that lay below and beyond—the Absarokas—he made his way back along the ledge. Dropping down, he set the lantern by his side and pulled up his shirtsleeve. He reached into the cold waters and groped for a gold nugget before he realized the stream was much deeper than it appeared.

"No matter, there is no need to hurry."

Pushing to a sitting position, he craned his head upward to lay an entranced eye on something that men throughout the world had searched for, and killed for, he guessed since the dawn of civilization. And as he did, Zalba found himself somewhat detached from all of this untold wealth—which he could now have a part of. For those who'd been mining here had first claim and were coming back. "But just a small part . . . enough to live comfortably . . . my Angelita and I . . ."

It took a while for Zalba to work his way out of the mine and back to the cabin. In the aftermath of his excitement over finding all of that gold came a weariness. He claimed one of the bunks, the lower one, putting to use the practical side of his nature as he rested. He would have to walk out of here, laden down with food instead of sackfuls of gold. He'd take just a few nuggets—which he'd show only to Javier Dominquez, a man whose word he could trust, and of course, Angelita.

And so he nodded away, dreaming of the moment when he would once again return to Elkhorn. When he awoke, early afternoon sunlight pierced against a bedroom wall. And refreshed,

Zalba went out to satisfy the empty growling in his stomach. Then arming himself with a small gunnysack and a gold pan and shovel, the strap of a canteen slung over a shoulder, he began the slow walk which would take him out of the canyon to the stream to where he'd found that gold nugget.

A flipping of a mental coin had brought Zalba upstream from where a path angled in from the main trail leading to the cabin. In the trees around him, birds flitted and sang and the wind moaned, and every so often a deer or elk would ghost by. This was the serenity he'd always enjoyed, and he whistled softly as he went along the stream to find the occasional gold nugget. A week of this, he figured, and also time to let his body heal, and he would pull out of here.

The stream curled and eddied around big mossy boulders and fallen trees. Farther along was the waterfall, and he glanced at it from time to time, reminded of the riches that were up there. Coming to a quiet pocket of water protected by encircling rocks, he stood on the bank staring down at gold nuggets strewn on the graveled streambed, and he began removing his shoes and stockings. Rolling up the legs of the work trousers he'd found in the cabin, he thrust a tentative foot into the water and grimaced.

"Cold as ice." He stood gazing down into the pool of quiet water, then rolled up his shirtsleeves as out of the pine forest ambled a bull elk. He watched it come to the stream to drink, and when he whistled softly, the elk sprang about and was gone.

Gingerly he reached into the stream, adapting to the numbing feeling of the cold water, and moved out to knee-depth. He began reaping gold nuggets, some as small as the nail on his little finger, while down on the bed of the pool gleamed still more gold dust.

He had brought along hunks of venison he'd charred back at the cabin, but prowling about in the cold water was tiring him rapidly. There, he told himself, he could always come back tomorrow. He wrapped the nuggets he'd gathered in a torn piece of shirt, which he tucked into a small gunnysack.

After putting his shoes on, Zalba wandered back along the stream bank to find the path. He worked his way up to the main trail pushing into the canyon mouth. Idly he was musing over what the gold could do, setting one foot in front of another as he went along the trail.

Zalba spotted fresh horse droppings ahead on the trail, and a cold chill washed over him. He struck for the screening brush at a limping and pain-racked lope. From the brush he took in prints made by at least two horses, and some of his fear went away.

"Maybe these miners have returned?" he muttered.

The miners would discover, once they entered the cabin, that gold nugget Zalba had left on the table and other signs of recent use. Most certainly the miners would kill him to keep the location of the mine secret. But what was he to do, out here in the midst of this mountain wilderness? Zalba lay aside his canteen and the shovel, but kept a firm grip on the gunnysack as he unlimbered his six-gun. Cautiously he kept to the fringe of the brush and trees lining the trail pushing along the canyon floor, expecting at any second to be fired upon and even killed.

A blue jay cut through the darker shadows in the canyon, but Zalba failed to see the bird, his right eye poking ahead for danger. Coming around a bend beyond which lay the cabin, he drew the hammer back on his revolver. As the cabin came into view, there by the front porch stood a horse, and beside it a horse bearing a pack.

"There is only one miner," he exclaimed. And Zalba paused as he deliberated over his next move. "If I can get one of those horses . . . I can ride out of here . . ."

That hope brought him skulking across to the cabin side of the trail just as someone stepped out onto the front porch. The way the afternoon shadows were piercing about in distorting waves, caused by clouds cutting by the sun, he couldn't make out if the miner was wearing a gunbelt; most certainly he had a hideout gun.

Zalba pressed on, to within twenty or so yards, then he shouted, "You there, stay where you are! Now, raise your arms about your head where I can see them!"

"Zalba?"

Stunned into silence, all he could do was freeze as Angelita Dominquez stepped down from the porch. She stopped, staring back at him, and she called out again, "Zalba, my heart . . . you're alive?"

The revolver dropped to his side, and he began stumbling to meet her as she ran toward him, hot salt tears running down her cheeks. He sagged suddenly, and went to his knees, drained of strength but filled with the joy of her presence. Dropping down, she threw her arms about him, raining kisses upon his face, mingling her tears with the young Basque's. Slowly she became aware of the bandage, and she cried out, "Oh, my darling, you're hurt . . ."

"Not anymore," he said softly. "You're here? Out in this wilderness? How did you find me?"

"I found you—that's all that matters."

He'd dropped his revolver, momentarily forgetting about the gunnysack—the gold paling because Angelita was here. "My leg," he said, "I must stretch it out." He tried hiding the grimace of pain from her.

And she said, "They did that to you, too, Zalba. Come, let us go into the cabin."

"You won't believe what I have in this sack, Angelita," he stammered, abruptly remembering the treasure. "I can't believe it either." With her arm to steady him, he held on to the sack and his revolver, and they entered the cabin, where he nodded at the table. "See that gold nugget—there are more like it in this sack."

"Gold—it seems so . . . unreal."

"But that nugget is proof." Opening the gunnysack, he pulled out the small bundle and spilled a cascade of gold nuggets onto the crude wooden table top. "Back of the shed and where the canyon ends, there is a mine."

"It must be true," she murmured. "All this gold? But now, what is important is you. I must tell you, Zalba, they killed Martin Iturri."

"I know who they are, these awful men, Angelita. They work for Mr. Taggart. The one who came to the hotel that night and hit me—he is one of them."

"Is this true?"

"As true and real as these gold nuggets."

"If they find out you're alive . . ." She kept standing as Zalba sank onto a chair, uncertainties dancing in her eyes.

He looked up at her and shrugged, saying, "Sooner or later this bandage must come off. I must tell you, Angelita, I have been blinded in my left eye. Another bullet struck me here, in the hip." He reached to the side of his head to untie the knot holding the bandage in place. And removing it, he sat there as Angelita took in the healing scar lancing across his lower forehead and along part of his left eye. He smiled at the new flow of tears and said buoyantly, "But my right eye tells me you're as beautiful as ever."

"Oh, Zalba, my heart—I fell in love with you the first day you came to Elkhorn. Nothing will ever change that."

"So, enough tears." He kissed her hand touching along his cheek. "We have venison, other food—and each other."

"Yes, one another, always."

They pulled out two days later, allowing their horses to plunge downslope in an attempt to reach the basin floor and find a road that would take them to Elkhorn. Lower on the mountain, they stopped again to rest their horses and to scan the reach of the mountain above them. It was as if the canyon and the cabin and the mine had never existed. Though Zalba knew that he could find his way up there again.

But for the moment, his mind was set on getting home, as

181

was Angelita's. Zalba reassured her when he stated, "The bands of sheep are way out in the basin. Here, there is only the pine forest and the wind."

"But once we reach Elkhorn—"

"I was thinking about this sheriff, Quinta, I believe his name is, over at Worland. We must get word to him about these treacheries done by Rincon." They resumed their homeward trek, and after a while, Zalba said offhandedly, "Will you marry a one-eyed Basque?"

"Are you asking for my hand in marriage? Si, si, as long as we're together."

"Hold up!"

"What is it?"

"I thought I saw something. Way below along that ridgeline. Just to be on the safe side, we'll keep to these trees."

"What if it is those killers . . . ?"

"We have guns, too, Angelita. And plenty of cover. I tell you, if it is them, Rincon will be the first to die."

Zach Lankford stared up at ridges passing into the mountains like the corrugated riffles on a scrub-board. It hadn't taken him long to catch up with Javier Dominquez and his companions. Then Zach had convinced them to angle into high country where Killdeer Creek flowed into the basin. The Basques had been more than glad, not only to have the tracker help them, but also to more or less take charge of the search.

Zach had passed along to Dominquez the concern of Sheriff Quinta over this outbreak of violence against the herders. "If I was a herder, I'd pull out of here," said Lankford.

"There aren't all that many jobs for Basque herders, Mr. Lankford," said Dominquez, as he pulled out his neckerchief and wiped the dampness from his forehead. It told on him that his saddle was becoming mighty uncomfortable—but not the other Basques, as they'd spent a lot of years out in places like this herding sheep.

Carlos Abaurrea had coal-black hair dusted with gray but youthful eyes hemmed in by age lines. He rode erect, with a light touch on the reins, and he'd brought along an old Henry rifle. Up through these trees stippling a long ridge, they were single-filing it, Abaurrea holding in behind Lankford slouched aboard the cayuse. Coming behind with the packhorses was Pedro, grinding his teeth around a briar pipe, and instead of a beret he had on a floppy black felt hat. Even Javier Dominquez felt a kinship toward the plainsman, and they'd been talking freely as they rode. Now with the going getting tougher, each man lapsed into silence.

Zach was the first to rein out on the crest of the ridge, which was fairly level, and he gave a tug on his reins. When Carlos came alongside, he said in broken English, "So you know this country pretty well. As I used to know all about Nevada."

"When the Crow and Blackfoot roamed here, I knew it a lot better—had to in order to keep this scalplock. So, way down below is Killdeer Creek." He glanced at Dominquez coming in on the opposite side. "A couple of ridges over is where you trailed after your daughter."

"They all look the same to me."

"As does every limber pine. A wounded man has got to find water and vittles."

"I don't know if Zalba was hurt. But we must assume so. It's a wonder he wasn't killed the same as Iturri."

"Farther up, gents, are spiny canyons pushing out of the mountains. That big hunk of rock yonder is Cloud Peak. A way to go to get to that. What you told me about your daughter, she's roughed it before, which should help. But the Bighorns— tough place even for a man."

Pedro called out, "By the sun it is around three; like the horses I am growing weary."

"Me, too," said Zach, as he put his eye to his field glass.

"I've found that if you just keep on in the saddle you miss a lot. Got a nice view from up here. So if we was to hold for a spell, somethin' might show itself."

"Si," said Dominquez as he swung his horse away and rode it under a pine tree close to where Pedro was easing out of his saddle.

"We could use some whiskey?"

"Si, Pedro, and coffee."

Carlos Abaurrea, as Zach handed him the field glass, inquired quietly, "What do you think?"

"Their chances? Truthfully, if they're still alive, fair, as it's a long way out of here. Trouble is, if this Zalba is hurt bad, even if we do find them he could die before we get him to a sawbones. Just between us."

"Si, Zach, I comprehend."

They dismounted, with Zach saying, "You keep watch through that glass while I get your horse into shade and loosen its saddle cinch. The mountain, Carlos, you've got to let it speak to you."

"How well I know. Sometimes you see something that shouldn't be there—like smoke from a campfire." Propping a boot on a rock, Carlos began scanning a distant ridgeline.

Under the trees, burning pinion needles wafted to Zach as he tended to the horses. One thing about these Basques, he commented silently, it didn't take them long to whip up a campfire and a prime tasty meal. He especially admired the way they packed along some prime whiskey, too. Moving over to where Dominquez was sitting by the growing flames of the fire, Zach lowered to sit cross-legged, to which Javier Dominquez said, "I sit like that, I'd be bedridden for a week. How old are you, Zach?"

"Me an' these mountains grew up together. Only I've got more bumps and bruises." He watched, with growing anticipation, as Pedro poured a generous amount of whiskey into four tin cups, and when the coffee came to a boil, he poured coffee into the cups. With tired but appreciative smiles, those at the fire sipped the brew as Pedro went over to hand a cup to Carlos.

"How pridefully stupid," began Dominquez, "of the plans of this sheep outfit to buck the cattlemen. That is all it is—pride. I want what you have. In Spain or Europe or here, it is all the same."

"The Chinese would drive bamboo shoots under your toenails before cutting off some vital body parts. A man's pride sure left him in a hurry."

"Last night, Zach, I prayed for the safety of my daughter and for Zalba . . . for all of us."

"Zach," Carlos called excitedly from out in the open. "I might have seen something—"

Everyone left the campfire to congregate around Carlos Abaurrea, who handed the field glass to Lankford. "Whereabouts?"

"Way to the east and up along the flank of that rise; just left of that red barren spot."

"If it's them," Zach said dryly, "they made better time than I thought. Nope, nothin' there now. An' from here to there, gents, is a two-, three-hour ride. You'd best hold in here, as my cayuse and this child are just warming up to a good day's ride."

"We could go along?"

"Nope, Javier, if it's them, most likely we'll be needin' fresh hosses. So hang in here. An' keep the campfire burnin' as I'll be late in gettin' back tonight. One thing—yonder is within sound of my bear-killin' rifle. If it sounds, you'll know I've found your daughter."

For the rest of the afternoon, Zalba Goyeneche held them in the lowering shelter of pine trees. Rather than lope the horses, he held them to a walk, pausing at times to scan distant heights. And it was now in stopping to rest that Angelita picked up a distant tendril of smoke spilling away from a flat but high ridge

185

off to the southwest. She pointed this out to Zalba, and he said grimly, "I knew I had seen something." He broke off what else he was going to say, as it had suddenly dawned on him that the vision in his right eye was as good as before—all traces of fuzziness having ebbed away.

"We still have a long way to go to get out of these high ridges," she said. "They are just as far from us as we are from them, Zalba."

"Wisely said," he smiled. "We will push on for a little while longer, then make camp. You know, Angelita, how lucky I am." Reaching up, he felt along his bandage. "Even though this has happened, just a shade closer and . . . but why talk about that."

"I'm happy that you want to give up being a herder."

"In a way, so am I. The gold I found will give us a new life. Perhaps we can make a trip back to the old country."

"Whatever, my heart. My mother still hasn't made up her mind about you, Mr. Goyeneche."

He gestured with his hand; a kind of stabbing motion. "She frightens me, the way she handles that butcher knife. As if I were a turkey she was about to carve."

Angelita's laughter touched upon passing tree limbs. She reined in closer and punched him lightly on the forearm. "I will tell her this."

"Only it will be Zalba Goyeneche," he said manfully, "who will ask your father for your hand in marriage."

The rest of the day passed quickly, while westerly the sun had reddened to cast an alpenglow over the lowering sky and the distant peaks across the basin. They made camp down where velvety grass grew along a stream—a spot well chosen by Zalba, as thickets would conceal their campfire.

Later under starlight they sat side by side, Angelita using her saddle as a backrest, and as for Zalba, he had put down one of the pack racks, over which he'd draped a saddle blanket. He was far more weary than he cared to admit and worried, too, that sight wouldn't return to his injured eye.

"Tomorrow should see us coming out of these ridges and down by the foothills."

"We don't have much food left," she said. "So we won't be needing the packs. You'll ride easier using my saddle. Riding bareback won't be all that bad. How does your leg feel?"

"Truthfully, it's awful sore. Tonight, when it gets colder, it'll stiffen up again. Oh, for one of those hot baths I enjoyed back at the hotel." He reached up and lifted the bandage away from his left eye and blinked a few times. Then he exclaimed, "I saw flashes of light, Angelita. Maybe I will see out of my eye again."

"Zalba, put the bandage down and leave it alone. I hope so, too, darling."

"Hello, the fire!"

Zalba spun toward his rifle, and he was levering a shell into the breech when the plainsman called out again, "Easy with that long gun, Zalba. I can see you folks plain. We sighted you earlier this afternoon. Got your pa with me, Angelita. Only thing is him and old Pedro and Carlos are camped back yonder. Me, I'm Deputy Sheriff Zach Lankford out of Worland. An' I'm comin' in peaceable."

"Come on in," Zalba said cautiously, as he motioned Angelita away from her saddle and behind him.

Zach came shuffling out of the darkness, holding the reins of his cayuse and grinning broadly. He'd taken the trouble to pin his badge to his buckskin coat, and even so, both Zalba and Angelita were still wary that such a person could actually be a lawman.

"That coffee I smell?"

"Sure," Zalba said hesitantly.

"Just be careful where you point that rifle. You could fire it though, as I told your pa, Angelita, I'd fire my rifle if I stumbled across you folks."

"Do as he says," Angelita said. "Yes, we have some coffee left, Mr. Lankford." Now the sound of Zalba's rifle pierced the deep silence of the mountain, and he fired two more times before putting the weapon aside.

Early the next morning Zach and the others were saddle-bound. They headed down a long draw filled with dead trees that had been destroyed in a brushfire caused by lightning, though new shoots were springing up in abundance. Zach had drawn from Zalba Goyeneche the startling news that Treech Rincon—and that must include the Yardley brothers—had killed Zalba's sheep.

He let it go at that, as it was fairly evident to Zach that the young Basque was in a bad way, despite the occasional smile he flashed for the benefit of Angelita. Clearing the draw, Zach led them to the west as he pointed out the ridge where the others had camped for the night. And in less than an hour the Basques appeared, walking their horses. Then Angelita jabbed her horse into a gallop and waved as she closed in on her father, who yelled at her through a broad smile, "Glory to our Heavenly Father for saving my daughter."

Back with Zalba, Lankford said, "Son, you're the only witness that can send Treech Rincon to prison. I can't tell you how important it is that I get you over to Worland, to tell what you know to Judge Springbuck. Otherwise, Zalba, a lot of men are going to get killed—good men on both sides."

"Of course I will do it," Zalba said tautly.

"First we'll have the doctor over at Elkhorn tend to your hurts. From there over to Worland it'll be a long and painful ride for you."

"It must be done. There must be peace in the basin. And with peace comes compassion and understanding. Men like Rincon, they must be stopped."

"You could include others in that, son. Howdy, boys. Javier, reckon your future son-in-law didn't get killed after all. So, once all this hugging is over, we'd better peel out of here for Elkhorn. Just hope we're not too late."

188

Eighteen

Sheriff Moses Quinta didn't see any need to leave any of his deputies back in Worland. They'd pulled out at noon, with Moses still unable to fire off a telegram to Elkhorn, as the line was still down. The work of those sheepmen, he figured. His saddle creaked as he snaked a glance back at the river crossing and the cowtown of Worland.

Some of those ranchers were still holding back in Worland, including Carsey Kemmerer. Probably, Moses pondered sarcastically, while I'm keeping my eyes peeled on them—the rest of 'em are gathering intending to make another raid tonight or the next. Back before pulling out, in no uncertain terms he'd informed his deputies that they'd be returning to Worland with the Yardleys and Rincon, either in handcuffs or draped over their saddles. This was, as Judge Springbuck had agreed, the only way to clear up this killing mess.

By midmorning, as it usually happened, the clouds had burned away, and there was no protection from the hot summery sun. Not a blade of grass or sagebrush was fluttering, but this kind of weather was old hat to their horses holding to a fast lope. Now in early afternoon Moses let himself settle in to the feel of the horse under him, his lower back propped against the cantle of his Texas-rig saddle. They were heading cross-country, avoiding the roads whenever possible, and as yet Moses hadn't told his deputies where they were heading. He mused that he was getting so that he was questioning even the judge's motives.

From the distant glimmer in Sheriff Quinta's eyes, Medran knew better than to ask what this was all about, and he let his horse fall back a little. He rode a horse he'd bought from the Box R Ranch, a big bronc sired by an Appaloosa. The bronc had set Medran back three months' wages, which was a bargain as it was the best hoss he'd ever owned. To his right John Kornkven was mounted on a bay. And Kornkven had toned down his choice of shirts to a drab-colored gray. Behind them came the other deputies, their faces etched in anxious lines as was Medran's. In Medran churned a worry that it had gone way beyond the talking stage, that both factions were going to unlimber their guns. What he didn't want was to be caught in the cross fire.

Medran said, "John, it won't be long before we earn our pay."

"Yup," said Kornkven. "But I wouldn't be so jumpy if I knew what this was all about. Maybe we're headin' over to Elkhorn . . . ?"

"What else is thisaway but scattered ranches and some tough riding. You break up with that filly?"

"Why'd you ask . . . ?"

" 'Cause you ain't dressed so flamboyantly."

"Might, as Milly's a pusher."

"Know what you mean, as I don't want anybody turnin' my crank either. See that lobo wolf, just ghosting over that ridge . . ."

"Don't see many of them anymore. Especially down here on the basin." Kornkven tugged irritably at his hat as a grasshopper skimmed by the bridge of his nose. "More of them hopping pests than usual this year. And this gritty dust . . ."

"Tough year on livestock, too."

Moses Quinta brought his men loping past a small bunch of cattle which broke away only to stop just as quickly and stare after the departing horsemen, a few cows mooing as their grazing had been disturbed. Off by his lonesome stood a big red Hereford bull that just kept on chewing its cud. And Moses muttered, "About as bullheaded as this sheepman, Taggart. But maybe with more brains." Entering a long cut knifing between clayey elevations, he kept pressing on until the ground began to get spongy and reeds appeared along the north fork of Brindle Creek, marked by a lonely cottonwood.

Moses headed for the tree to take advantage of its shading branches and dismounted stiffly. Elaborately he pulled out his turnip-shaped watch, though he knew it was shortly past noon, and took a quick gander at the watch face. "Kornkven," he said, "you and Josh mosey up a fire as we'll set in here for a while."

"There's nothing here but this tree—"

"There's water to drink," groused Moses. "We'll chow down now, as later we might not get the chance."

"You're sayin' what, Moses?"

"That I don't want to pull into Tule's road ranch until after dark."

"So that's it," said one of the new deputies. "Tule hates two things—lawmen and getting beat at cards."

"I could arrest him for aidin' and abetting," said Moses. "But it's the Yardleys we're after." He finished uncinching his saddle, and then he lifted it from the back of his bronc. He carried it over to where the shade was thickest and upwind of the fire starting to crackle out heat and flames. "It's another two-hour ride to Tule's place, so we'll pull out of here around five."

Josh Medran said, "Now what makes you think the Yardleys are gonna be at Tule's?"

"Because of the telegram Zach Lankford fired off to me from Elkhorn. I sent Zach over there to snoop things out. That sheep outfit is on the move an' headin' for the Bighorn River. Which means Harge Yardley will try to get word to Kemmerer."

"Yeah, Kemmerer and Harge got together at Tule's. Might do so again."

"It could be a long wait, Moses . . ."

"Only way I can figure to prove Kemmerer is behind these killings. That coffee boiling yet?"

"Gettin' there."

Moses eased his six-gun out of his holster as he drawled, "Check your weapons now. As you don't want any misfires when the shooting starts."

Down on his knees, and so drunk he couldn't hold on to a glass without slopping whiskey out of it, hardcase Owl Head Johnson was trying to get at a nickel wedged in a crack between two floorboards. He wasn't down there alone, as a whore adorned in a silk kimono and Owl Head's Stetson was astride his back and rocking back and forth.

"Kiyeee," she giggled. "I like playin' horsey with ya, Owl Head."

As for Johnson, he was buck-naked and getting more frustrated by the minute. Watching him from the other bed in the upstairs bedroom at Tule's road ranch was another whore and hardcase Wade Beechum.

"Hey, Owl Head," said Beechum, "what the hell—we got plenty of money left. The tight bastard throws nickels around like manhole covers."

"Yeah, it'll keep," Johnson finally muttered. Shaking the woman from his back, he managed to crawl back on the bed, where he snaked a hand to a chair for the bottle of whiskey. "You girls, go and get gussied up, as I want to eat supper down at the bar."

"Whats'a matter, honey?" the whore said. "You all tuckered out already?"

"Get," scowled Owl Head Johnson. "Me and my partner want some privacy. An' leave that money alone or I'll . . ." He held back his blow as the woman left in a huff, as did the other whore. Guzzling down some more whiskey, he jarred the bottle back onto the chair and fumbled amongst the grimy sheets for his skivvies. "Dammit, Wade, I don't like this waitin' game."

"So what you got in mind, partner?"

"Takin' a long ride where we ain't wanted. No sense in letting Harge Yardley or anybody else have what's in this envelope." He tore the envelope open. "A lot more here than what Kemmerer's been payin' us, Wade. Remember you was talkin' about buyin' a spread out in the Panhandle. With this money we could go in as partners."

"A lot there, awright," smiled Beechum. "Maybe five hundred . . ."

"You never could count beyond ten. There's at least . . . at least two thousand, I make it."

"*Kiyeee,* we're rich, Owl Head." He hawked spleen onto the floor from where he sat sagged on the other bed. "What about the Swede? He could be in cahoots with the Yardleys."

"It's coming onto sundown. He won't be expecting two drunks like us to leave, much less be able to straddle our hosses. So we'll play it cool, hike down for some steaks and frys, and a round or two of drinks with our blushin' damsels. Then I'll suggest we take those whores for a walk, to maybe howl at the moon."

Wade Beechum broke out laughing. "In our lifetimes we've howled at everything but that." Thumbing at his nose, a thoughtful grimace screwed up his forehead as Owl Head pushed up from the bed and moved in his skivvies over to the pail of water on the washstand. Beechum added, "Why don't we just and up pump some bullets into Tule Eriksen and make off with his cash?"

"Because"—Owl Head picked up the bucket and spun drunkenly to send the water cascading over Beechum—"I don't want this damned old fart of a Moses Quinta to come looking for us—savvy? He's the kind gets a hair up his ass and never gives up. Come on, let's throw on some clothes as I'm in need of some vittles." Then he threw the bucket in a corner and headed for his clothes draped on a chair.

Sometime later the hardcases were pushing themselves up from a table and a meal shared with their women of the night. In the course of eating, they'd also managed to put away a bottle of whiskey, matching the one downed by the whores. In the barroom were a sprinkling of customers, and tonight Tule Eriksen was manning the bar. He was a big, sad-faced man with deep, penetrating eyes. Later on, when his bartender came in, Tule would deploy himself at a card table, where he generally won—as he was notoriously noted for not only cheating at cards but also for shortchanging his customers. Since most of them were on the dodge, they rarely complained.

Owl Head Johnson wrapped a hand around the whore's forearm and said gruffly, "Why don't we go out and howl at the moon."

To which Beechum added, "Could use some fresh air. Hey, Tule, pass over another bottle and put it on our bill. And some of those cigars, too."

The big Swede was more than happy to oblige, as; he was getting double pay—for the whiskey and part of what the whores raked in. He didn't know why Johnson and his partner were hanging around but knew they worked for Carsey Kemmerer. Mutely he slid a bottle down the bar to Beechum, followed by a handful of cigars. Just as they were going outside, his bartender arrived, and Tule Eriksen turned to scoop some money out of the thin box he used as a cash register.

Once they were around the side of the building, Owl Head Johnson led the way over to the corrals, in which horses owned by the Swede were standing quietly. "Wade, entertain the ladies while I head around the barn and take a leak."

"Want me to come along and see you do it proper, sugah?"

"Dammit, no," Johnson grunted as he headed into the collecting darkness of night. He went around to enter the barn through the back door, where he set about saddling their horses.

When he was done, he moved up to shout out the front door at Beechum, "Hey, Wade, took a look at our hosses. I think yours has got a gimpy leg as it ain't standin' right."

"Ahh," Wade Beechum said in mock disgust. "You gals keep your steam engines runnin' as this won't take long." He whacked the whore he'd been sleeping with across her ample posterior and stalked away in his high-heeled boots, the picture of a man saddled with an unwelcome chore. But once he was inside the barn, he found Owl Head already in his saddle, and Beechum let out a low cackle as he sought his saddle and reined after Johnson riding out the back door.

At a slow walk they brought their horses to the southwest, keeping the barn between themselves and where the whores were waiting at the corral. Quietly they passed through some screening trees they figured Tule had planted a few years back, and here the ground dropped into a long wash. And here, too, they picked up their gait, laughing and with Beechum handing the whiskey bottle to Owl Head.

"Texas, here we come."

"I'll bet'cha," laughed Beechum, "Harge Yardley will figure it out that Kemmerer has pulled a double-cross. Then the shit will hit the fan for sure. I like the looks of that Old Thermopolis town."

"Yup, we can beeline there and enjoy those mineral baths for a few days. Yup, it would suit me just dandy Yardley punching out this rancher."

Eli Yardley didn't like it a helluva lot that two of his brothers were heading with Treech Rincon on a due west course that would take them across the Bighorn River—while Eli was going with Harge, in the quietness of this night, toward Tule Eriksen's road ranch.

As for Harge, splitting up like this couldn't be helped, because if Carsey Kemmerer didn't show up at Tule's, it would save him that long ride out to Kemmerer's ranch. The rancher might not like Rincon showing up there, but to hell with what Kemmerer thought, Harge mused savagely. He'd also told Rincon to steer clear of Worland.

The sheep were on the move, by Harge's estimate at least twenty thousand woolies, herded by the Basques and their dogs and all those hired guns along for protection. "Those clove-hooved locusts are killin' the grass as they go."

"Yeah, sheep are sure miserable critters. How much farther?"

Harge shot a glare at his brother, his thoughts still holding on the sheep and Burt Taggart—taking those sheep and every-one with him to their deaths, as there was no way those cattle-men were going to hold back. Last night they'd pulled out sometime after midnight when everyone was bedded down. They catnapped during the heat of the day just past, and laid plans with Rincon as to where to head when this was over.

"What if this rancher don't show . . . ?"

"The deal was he'd come over to Tule's once a week to pick up any messages I might leave. We get around that big dome of rock, Eli, and there's Tule's. I don't want you gettin' all liquo-red up, as once that happens you just can't keep your mouth shut."

"Sure, Harge," he said sullenly.

"Shut up," Harge Yardley said sharply as he tugged the reins back. "See them, pushin' along that draw; two riders. Headin' away from Tule's."

"Headin' south."

"Yeah, come on, let's push on in."

"It'll take them at least two more days to bring them sheep close to Tucker Crossing."

"Maybe a little longer. But plenty of time for the cattlemen to muster their forces. This is one gun battle I'll enjoy watching. Might even get off a shot at that two-timin' Chuck Dacy—takin' over my ramrodding job like that . . . damn his hide."

"I hope Treech has sense enough to keep out of it."

"Don't worry, brother Eli, he's a heap smarter than you. But he's awful damned reckless . . . just as bullheaded as that sheepman, Taggert. There's Tule's—and I can smell that whiskey away out here. Git up, hoss."

During the latter stages of this Wednesday afternoon, Sheriff Moses Quinta hadn't come in to the road ranch from the northwest; instead he'd taken a circuitous route way around to the south. They were still out a ways and pushing along under a clear sky. On this stretch of sage-dusted prairie, shadows were elongating away from their horses.

With day purpling into dusk, Moses knew they'd come in on Tule's sometime around nine o'clock. It would be more like Carsey Kemmerer's style to come in before dark. As for Harge Yardley, nighttime was when he liked to prowl.

"Keep your eyes peeled," he warned his deputies and warned John Kornkven, who was lagging behind a little.

"By rights," Josh Medran said to Quinta, "we should have arrested Kemmerer. But like you've been telling me, the other ranchers will back him up."

"Some of them are having second thoughts," said Moses. "That story I had printed in the *Worland Star Journal* will make others hang close to their spreads."

"You didn't mince any words."

"Can't afford to straddle any fence with my words or opinions. Murder's been done. In a way everyone siding with Kemmerer is guilty. Can you picture it, Josh—it would take a carpenter most of the summer to put up a gallows big enough to handle the chore of gettin' 'em hung. But in the end, most of 'em'll be found innocent for one reason or another."

"When you was a gunfighter, Moses, I expect life was a lot simpler—"

"For doggone sure, there wasn't any paperwork. You saw a shady hombre, he handed you some greenbacks to do a job,

197

that was about it. Some that drew against me, you know, Medran, they were just plumb thievin' crooks. It got so you couldn't tell an honest man from a wooden Indian."

All of a sudden it seemed it had gotten a lot darker, and if Moses were sitting at home he'd up and light a lantern. Out here he knew he needn't bother, as this eerie illusion lasted for just a little while to be chased away by starlight, and their eyes would adjust to the deeper blackness draped like black dew over the terrain. One of their horses whickered, and everyone stabbed anxious eyes in the direction they were riding.

Hold up! Moses signaled with his arm. They'd just come up onto an elevation, and below them along a wash bottomed with whitish sand a pair of horsemen were heading directly at them. "Ease back some," warned Moses. "And spread out; could be just some 'pokes out joyridin' but all the same . . ."

Quietly the lawmen pulled away from one another, while hauling out long guns and knowing that from here on they'd take their cue from Sheriff Quinta as to what to do. Moses didn't bother to go for a weapon. Instead he calmly sat his horse in amongst some sagebrush on the rise toward which the horsemen were coming. A glance to either side showed that his deputies had dismounted. One of the riders began cackling drunkenly and waving a whiskey bottle.

And he snickered loudly to his companion, "Yup, Owl Head, we'll stock our place with the best beef money can buy. An' maybe get us a couple of Osage squaws."

In a voice slurred with grim satisfaction, Sheriff Moses Quinta called out as he spurred to the lip of the rise, "Owl Head Johnson, elevate those arms before I punch out your lights! You too, Beechum!"

"What the hell . . . *Quinta?*"

"Me and about twenty deputies."

Drunkenly Owl Head snarled, "Why you old fart . . ." He went for his six-gun.

But Moses Quinta's dipping hand swept out his Colt .44 and

198

it belched flame. The slug from it hit solidly, and Owl Head Johnson flipped out of the saddle so quickly it was a moment before Wade Beechum realized he was gone. Beechum jacked up his arms and stammered, "I give up, Quinta."

"Well," Moses tempted the hardcase, "you could get around to callin' me an old fart, too. Okay, disarm this fugitive and cuff 'em." He nudged his horse downslope as Johnson's horse shied away. "Now why would Carsey Kemmerer send the pair of you away out here?"

"I . . . ah, we ain't done nothing, Sheriff. Just . . . just came over to Tule's for some fun."

"Fun can get a man killed. Is Kemmerer at Tule's?"

"Nossir, Sheriff, like I told you, we was . . ."

"Yeah, yeah. Paw through Johnson's pockets, as he might be carrying a message back to Kemmerer." Moses spun the cylinder to clear it of empties, then he put in fresh loads and holstered his Colt.

"Found this envelope, Moses—filled with a lotta greenbacks." John Kornkven came over and handed the envelope to Sheriff Quinta.

"Did you boys rob a bank?"

"Nossir, Sheriff, we come by that money honest."

"For a fact," grunted Moses. "Now, which one of you scions of the West shot out that window?"

"Window?" gaped Wade Beechum.

"My daughter-in-law's big lead-glass window. I'm still catching it in the shorts about that. Cost me plenty to replace it. Was it you, Beechum?"

"I was there, Sheriff, but it was Owl Head done it."

"You're guilty same as him. Okay, drape Johnson's body over his horse and let's get on to Tule's. When we get there, Kornkven, you hold out a ways with our prisoner."

"What about one of the new deputies?"

"Son, I promised your daddy I'd see that you'd at least get

199

through puberty. And Medran, was Beechum carrying anything of value?"

"About fifty bucks and this bear tooth."

"I'll take thirty of that fifty to pay for that window; let him keep the tooth. It's time to ride."

Along the way Sheriff Quinta kept up a running conversation with his prisoner. They passed through some shrubbery and willows looming out of the night, through trees beyond which they could discern pale light that they assumed came from the road ranch. Once the trees fell behind, they took in the dark silhouettes of buildings. Moses said, "Beechum, you know what I've got against you. Not counting a couple of wanteds. You turn state's evidence, I won't send a telegram down to Colorado citing your present whereabouts."

"Kemmerer, he'll do everything he can to see I don't talk."

"Don't worry about him, as he'll be locked in another cell. Think on it, Beechum." He held there as Kornkven, who'd dismounted, helped Beechum down from his horse, and then Kornkven took a short hunk of rope out of his saddlebag and tied the hardcase to a tree trunk. Moses spurred away, hemmed in by his deputies.

They honed in on the barn, and Medran gestured to some horses tethered in front of the main building. "Always got plenty of customers even though they know Tule is cheatin' them blind."

"They leave blind when they leave Tule's," said Moses. "Awright, Gus and Pilgrim, take off your badges. Me an' Josh'll hold out here while you boys amble in there, as you're new and nobody will make out you're lawmen. Just the same, if the Yardleys are in there, make sure none of them sneak thieves settles in behind you."

"The county payin' for our drinks?"

"Pilgrim, I'll forget you said that," Moses grinned back. "Okay, push on in one at a time. In there you don't know each other."

As Moses Quinta held out by the side of the barn, where he sat slumped in his saddle, he wondered how it would go. The trick was to get the drop on the Yardleys and Rincon, as these gents wanted all the odds in their favor. The stench of the manure pile out back of the barn came strong to him, and through one of the open windows on the side wall came the sound of a stabled horse passing gas, and he commented, "Tule must be feedin' beans to them hosses. Anyway, Josh, Harge dead is no good to us"

"There'll be five of them. Drunk by now or up with the whores."

"And probably broke and waiting for Kemmerer to show up with some blood money. Only Owl Head and Beechum pulled out with that envelope full of swag. But I reckon Tule'll let them drink on the cuff."

"Time to go?"

"Might's well, as that hoss just farted again." He rode alongside Medran, and clear of the barn they shifted their eyes warily about, but everything seemed peaceful. Boldly Moses went in first to tie up his bronc next to some horses. Then he led the way up to a narrow front window, the panes caked with dust, and he brushed some of the dust away and took a gander inside. "I believe there's Eli Yardley at one of the tables, swilling down some whiskey. Means they're here, an' we've got our night's work cut out for us."

Just for a moment Moses eyed his deputy. Medran had hooked on to do law work about a year ago. During that time there hadn't been any bank robberies or crimes to speak of, though from what he'd heard, Josh Medran had handled everything that came his way. Moses said, "Gunfighting—if it taught me anything, Josh—taught me to watch their eyes. Eyes don't lie, unless you come up against a blind man. As for the Yardleys, they probably got it figured they covered their tracks pretty good. So our first move is just to mosey up to the bar and rinse the trail dust out of our mouths."

Taking another squint through the pane of glass to reacquaint himself as to where everybody was in the barroom, Moses strode to the open door and pushed into the din and smoke of Tule's road ranch. It didn't register with anyone until they were coming in on the bar and planting their boots on the railing that it was Quinta and one of his deputies. Just for a shade there was silence, even the bardog keeping clear of where the lawmen stood at the bar, as he wasn't sure if gunfire would break out.

Grinned Moses Quinta through the silence, "Howdy—Eckersley, ain't it? Whiskey around for me and Medran here. How you been?"

"Tol . . . tolerable, Sheriff, just tolerable. What brings you to our neck of the prairie . . . ?"

"Trouble, Eckersley. Or we could just be passing through on our way back to Worland." Moses let himself relax, soaking up an ambience out of his past, a saloon out in the wilds and men on the dodge sneaking glances barward. Gingerly, as if he were lifting a cherry out of a jar, he picked up the shot glass with his thumb and forefinger and saluted his deputy before the whiskey went tumbling into his mouth. "Ah . . . the damn stuff must be cut with turpentine." But Moses' unconcerned smile held.

Nervously Medran said, "Man could go blind drinkin' this donkey piss." But he downed his whiskey, too, and didn't protest when Moses refilled his glass, though he couldn't shake the shuddering grimace away.

A whore gave Quinta a come-hither wink, then from a table rose Tule Eriksen to head up to the bar. He said to bartender Eckersley, "The sheriff's drinks are on the house. So, Quinta, it's been a long time."

Moses had the urge to say not long enough, but he let it go and put away another glass of whiskey before he said, "It pleases me mightily, Tule, being vested with all this new-spangled authority. I could ride roughshod over this road ranch—close it down. But the truth of the matter is, we need a place like this. As even highliners need a place to take a breather from time to time."

"Can't help it any, they pass through here."

"Maybe so many wouldn't if you chanced to get rid of the whores. But I ain't no moralist, Tule. But I'll tell you this"—the smile danced across Moses' face again—"you dodge my next question and I'll put a slug through your left kneecap. I see one Yardley—now where the hell are the others and Treech Rincon?"

"Dammit, Quinta, just two of them rode in." Resentful anger poured out of the Swede's eyes.

"I see Eli Yardley. Could the other one be Harge?"

"Upstairs dilly-dallying with a deck of cards."

"Obliged. Any particular room?"

"Climb the stairs; first door to the left."

"He alone?"

Tule shrugged.

And to his deputy Moses said, "This won't take long." Then he brushed by Eriksen and cut around the bar to the staircase, unaware that Harge had slipped out into the second-floor hallway.

Through his drunken haze Eli Yardley suddenly realized the danger to his brother in the form of Sheriff Quinta just about to start up the staircase. Eli went for his holstered gun and yelled out to Harge—who appeared on the second-floor landing—*"Its Quinta!"*

From behind, Deputy Sheriff Pilgrim Weiss charged in to wrestle the gun away from Eli. As he did, Harge unleashed a bullet to a spot just vacated by Quinta, who had sidestepped away from the staircase and was going for his Colt when a bullet fired by Deputy Gus Hall struck Harge in the pit of his stomach. As Harge clutched at his stomach, he managed to bring up his six-gun.

"Quinta, we'll die together!" he growled.

"No, we won't," returned Moses as he tried to fire at Harge's

203

gun hand, desperately wanting to keep the man alive, at least until he'd wrung a confession out of him. Instead the leaden slug burst into Harge's forearm and he dropped his weapon. He was unarmed now and fear gaped his eyes as he turned to stumble back along a hallway.

Taking the steps two at a time, Moses went after Harge. Yardley reeled toward a window at the end of the hallway. "Give it up, Harge, it's over," Moses shouted.

But the outlaw didn't heed Sheriff Quinta's warning. He took a final lurching step to the window and slammed through the shattering panes. Hurrying forward, Moses grimaced at the outlaw spreadeagled on the ground below. Harge was trying feebly to get to his feet. Heading downstairs, Moses hurried out the front door, accompanied by Josh Medran. They came around to the side wall, and here Moses knelt and placed an arm under Harge Yardley's shoulders. One look into the man's eyes and Moses knew that for Harge death was moments away.

"Harge, can you hear me? Tell me about Kemmerer . . ."

The outlaw coughed out blood and formed a loose-lipped grin. "Quinta, ain't got . . . nothin' to say . . ."

"You mean," Moses said hastily, "you're gonna just die and have Kemmerer go scot free." Then he was gazing anxiously into the sightless eyes of Harge Yardley.

Medran said softly, "We've still got Eli."

"Yup, and Harge's other brothers and Rincon." He straightened up, suddenly bone weary from the strain of what had just happened. He stared off at a grassy knoll and added, "Over there, we'll find a shovel for Eli so's he can dig his brother's grave. Then come sunup we'll try to find sheepman Burt Taggart, who I figure is drivin' his sheep toward Tucker Crossing."

"Moon's coming out full."

"Way it'll be for a while. A killer's moon . . . as when it's full, men do direful things."

Nineteen

Like a wide river of foaming white water, the leading remnants of the band of sheep gorged out of a dry wash, bleating as they fanned out, the dogs of the Basque herders nipping them back into a line about an eighth of a mile wide. They'd been pushed hard, and the lambs were having a tough time of it. But the herders knew better than to voice a protest, either to the gun-packing outriders or to Burt Taggart.

The Basques had been told that the sheep could rest once the Bighorn River fell behind. Though they had horses to ride, every so often the Basques would swing down to check on a lamb which had gotten jostled away from its ewe. The Basques knew their enemies this time weren't a few eagles circling far overhead in the azure sky but the basin ranchers. Innocently they knew it wasn't their fight, and some were of the opinion to pull out. One Basque had done so, going to see Taggart, only to return filled with a helpless dread, spreading the word that none of them would be allowed to leave.

The Basque herders were the least of Burt Taggart's worries. This could be summed up in three words—*those damned Yardleys.* He couldn't shake the feeling it was more than a case of cut and run, and Harge Yardley hadn't mustered up to all of his wild promises. Taggart was astride a thoroughbred horse, and his saddle was hand-tooled at the fancy cost of five hundred dollars. Just before pulling out of Elkhorn, he had passed out special marksman rifles fixed with scopes, and he had one in his scabbard. They had a greater velocity than the standard Henry or Winchester, and along the way the gunhands had readjusted the sights while trying out their new weapons. Even though they'd gone out about a mile, the hammering reverberations of those rifles had carried back to keep the sheep stirred up.

Once again sunlight—enshrouded by a dust cloud raised by the sheep—came low to the west, and the sky began to pale away the opposite way. The supply wagons were up ahead at the camp site they were approaching. The Basques would take turns eating supper at a separate campfire, then return to help keep watch over the band starting to mill up against the wall of a red shaley rise.

Another who'd gone on ahead to get out of the choking dust was Burt Taggart, along with Chuck Dacy. A scouting party had been sent on ahead to get the lay of it at Tucker Crossing; they were due back most anytime. "These new rifles are something, Mr. Taggart."

"They should be, as they're damned expensive." He watched Dacy use his bandanna to wipe the film of dust from the barrel of the rifle, a .50 caliber Mannlicher sharpshooter model.

Hefting the rifle, Dacy grinned as he brought it to his right shoulder and sighted through the scope at a distant target. He muttered, "This sure evens things up."

"You know we'll be outnumbered."

"Too bad those sheep raise so much dust. I expect they've picked up on that and will be there when we hit the river. Now if we could slip across the river, say five of my best shooters, they could come in from behind."

"There's an off-chance if they are at the crossing, they could meet us under a flag of truce."

"After they killed two of your herders—a fat chance at best, Mr. Taggart."

206

"Sometime tomorrow afternoon we'll be coming in on Tucker Crossing," said Taggart through a tired grimace. "Plenty of time to plan our strategy. At least for supper we'll be eating beefsteak."

"A sheepman like you don't like lamb . . . ?"

"I just run this sheep operation," Burt Taggart said through a smile. "I like lamb but not for a steady diet."

"Don't let these Basques hear you say that."

"A strange race, Dacy. Dependable and without too much imagination. How they can stand years of herding?"

Dacy shrugged. "They'll be fair game—like the sheep—once we hit the river."

Stoically Taggart retorted, "I wager they knew the risk when they hired on. Same's you and the other guns I hired. Well, coffee's ready."

Even though Zalba Goyeneche had been advised by an Elkhorn doctor that he should remain in bed to let his wounds heal properly, Zalba was up and around. When they'd first ridden in, even Angelita's mother had not only rejoiced through her tears over seeing them but had hugged Zalba so hard he thought his ribs would crack.

Zalba had given the gold to Javier Dominquez, who'd quietly put it in his safe at the hotel. Then the doctor had set about the business of suturing Zalba's wounds, even as Zach Lankford had gone over to fire off another telegram to Sheriff Moses Quinta. Then he came back to check on Zalba and to tell the young Basque that only his testimony could see the Yardleys and Carsey Kemmerer thrown into jail and an end put to this violence.

Unbeknownst to Angelita, Zalba had left with the plainsman at first light. During the first few miles Lankford had pondered over taking an angling northwest route in the direction of Worland. He'd chewed this over with Zalba, whose sage wisdom about the handling of sheep revealed to Lankford the certainty of the sheepmen and the ranchers colliding at some river crossing.

"The river's low. Even so, you've got to be mighty careful about crossing over due to hidden currents and quicksand. A straight line is what I figure, Zalba. They'll push those sheep plumb on and damned fast."

"When you appeared up there, it was as if by Divine Providence." He opened his outstretched hand.

And Zach Lankford blinked away his surprise when he gazed upon the gold nugget. "Where in tarnation . . . ?"

"It is yours, Senor Lankford."

"Why, son, I just don't know . . ."

"On one hand there is brutality and murder. Yet out of my misfortune came this piece of gold."

"Others, Zalba, have scoured the Bighorns in search of gold. Nothin' came of it." As his horse cantered along, Lankford surveyed the gold nugget he had palmed. "But you need it more'n me, son."

"There is more, if ever I venture back into those mountains. Please, you will take this—really it is a humble reward for all you've done."

Zach Lankford left it at that, as he and Goyeneche kept on the move, expecting to come across a hoof-cloved trail left by a large band of sheep. But his mind was dancing to a different locale, to what Moses Quinta had spouted out about rancher Carsey Kemmerer. Could the gold nugget he'd tucked into a coat pocket be the reason Kemmerer was preaching his brand of sudden death in these parts? Lankford set his thoughts a heap of years back to sink like the teeth of a mastiff into Kemmerer's past. Back then the man hadn't been all that well off, coming with many other ranchers through some lean years. Until up one year when some new buildings and a heap more cattle sprouted out at the man's ranch. Suspicions aside, Lankford still couldn't weave this gold nugget into Kemmerer's adding to his already vast acreage, and he scowled his musings away.

"I savvy a little Spanish."

"La tierra aqui es mala para el cultivo."

"I got that land part?" questioned the plainsman.

Prompted into a lengthy tirade, Zalba's words were a mixture of Basque and Castilian Spanish. After this all that Lankford— who had no notion of what Zalba was talking about—could utter was, "I hope you don't speak Chinese . . ."

Carsey Kemmerer knew he had little choice in the matter— that he had, at least for a little while longer, put his trust in the message brought to him by Treech Rincon. And Kemmerer reckoned that if Rincon knew of his connection to Harge Yardley, so did Harge's brothers. Within half an hour after Rincon had showed up at his ranch, Kemmerer had sent his 'pokes out to warn other members of the cattlemens' confederation that at last the Varney Sheep Company was on the move.

On his way to Tucker Crossing, Kemmerer—accompanied by some of his cowhands and Rincon and the two Yardley brothers—encountered other small groups of cattlemen. By the time they reached the main stagecoach road passing just westerly of the Bighorn River, their number had swelled to sixty horsemen.

"I reckon," Kemmerer smiled at rancher Milt Tyman, "when it comes right down to it, others hate sheep just as much as we do. I thought we might get around seventy to ride with us. Should be well over a hundred or more by the time we hit the crossing."

"What if the sheriff shows up?"

"Makes no difference if those woolgrowers open up first. As a man's got a right to defend himself and his property."

Milt Tyman still couldn't get over the fact that not only had Treech Rincon brought word over from Elkhorn, but here was

209

Rincon in the flesh along with those Yardleys. He said in a lowly aside to Kemmerer, "Still doesn't fit—Rincon coming to warn us."

"You have to fight fire with fire," responded Kemmerer. "I told the other ranchers back on the trail that I've been paying Rincon, under the table so to speak."

"All the same, Carsey, when the shootin' starts, I'm keeping my eyes peeled on Rincon."

"I have to admit I'd do the same, Milt."

As the day wore on, more cattlemen came in from both directions, and then the large cavalcade headed by Carsey Kemmerer reined away from the stagecoach road where a smaller trail forked in between river bluffs Kemmerer's uplifted arm halted them on the trail. Loudly he said, "It's just a matter of spreading out to either side of the crossing up on those bluffs. We've brought supplies; I guess most of you have."

"Day's about spent," said Art Littlejohn. "But you figure they'll be here tomorrow, Carsey?"

"Don't worry, they'll be throwing up a lot of dust. I'd like to have you ranchers join me at my campfire for a council of war. As you know, Sheriff Quinta might get wind of this and come ridin' in. I want to thank you, too, gentlemen, for leaving a lot of ranch work behind just to help out."

"I'd cross the Bighorn in floodstage just to be a part of this. Okay, you Lazy D 'pokes, time to pick out a spot along the bluff to settle in for the night." The rancher left a pleased grin as he added, "And I fetched along a case of whiskey . . . just in case it chills up a mite tonight."

While Kemmerer's calvalcade was settling in for the night, a ways north, on a stretch of basin floor to the southwest of Worland, there rode a cattleman with an entirely different viewpoint than those who'd just pulled in close to Tucker Crossing. This was Lavin Roach, Kemmerer's ranch foreman, who—instead of carrying out the orders given him to alert a few ranchers to the north—was on his way to see the sheriff of Washakie County.

Roach hadn't been able to stomach Kemmerer's decision to hire some hardcases, but he'd gone about his job as *segundo* just the same. Treech Rincon's unexpected appearance out at the ranch had been the breaking point for Lavin Roach. It told Roach it was time to start looking for another job, before he, too, became implicated in this scheme of Kemmerer's—which he'd pieced out had a lot to do with all that land Kemmerer was buying up.

Could this have something to do with those graves he'd stumbled upon earlier this summer? They were smack in the middle of some thick breaks guarding a stream and on the extreme western edges of the ranch. A place a waddy would just come to haze cattle out of the brush during fall roundup. But anyway, Lavin Roach mused, as he sighted in on a windmill marking the approach to Worland, hanging on with Kemmerer could sure sully his reputation.

Roach had been working since first light, and this long ride had tuckered him out some, but loping on into Worland he bypassed the saloons to find the jail. But when he entered, it was to find the jailor with his boots propped on the sheriff's desk.

"Looking for Quinta, are you? Quinta and all of his deputies pulled out of here early yesterday. Nope, got no idea where they was headin', Mr. Roach. Got time for some coffee?"

"Not now." Lavin Roach grimaced. He left to climb back into the saddle and rein away. He knew he had done what he could. And about all he could do now was to hang in here, at least until Sheriff Quinta returned. Afterward it was Roach's plans to head back to the ranch and draw his last paycheck from Carsey Kemmerer.

He rode through shadows elongating away from buildings and elm trees lining a lane, with his worries over all of this stored tight in his mind. "A lot of good men are goin' to die, all because of Kemmerer," he muttered.

* * *

Out where they had shaped a campfire, Treech Rincon was sharing a bottle with Dyson and Jake Yardley, while around them other fires glowed. Sometimes a horseman would ghost by on his way to where most were gathered—at Carsey Kemmerer's camp site. All of the campfires were low on the west side of the river bluffs, just in case those sheepmen had sent out a scouting party.

"It don't make no sense, Treech, our hangin' in here," scolded Jake.

"Yup, Treech, we done Harge's dirty work."

"What I don't like," said Dyson, "is Kemmerer telling you that he sent our money over to Tule's road ranch. Dammit, by now Harge and Eli have probably lost it all at poker."

"Simmer down," smiled Rincon. "That rancher gave us a couple of free bottles of prime whiskey. An' we cadged supper, damned fine beefsteaks to boot. We'll hang in here until three, four in the morning, then sneak out to head for Tule's."

"You still never told us, Treech, where you got them shiners—"

"Go to hell, Jake," he said savagely. "I was blindsided, back at Elkhorn is all. But I'll damn well even the score. Here, suck on this bottle whilst I shape a tailormade."

Somewhere as the night wore on, the plunking sound of a banjo drifted through the darkness. And soon things began quieting down as did the banjo, and campfires were dying out. As he'd promised, Rincon blinked the sleep away around three o'clock, and soon he roused the Yardleys. Ever so carefully they rose and crept away from the others and began saddling their horses.

Treech Rincon had just slung his saddle over the back of his horse when the familiar sound of a hammer being thumbed back froze him where he stood.

The man holding the gun was Carsey Kemmerer, and with him were a few others. Kemmerer said low and taut, "We set out a killpecker guard just for your benefit, Treech. You boys won't be pulling out, as we wouldn't want you to miss watching those sheep come boiling in here—now would we?"

"We—"

"Shut the hell up, Rincon," said a rancher. "I still ain't forgettin' you rustled some of my cattle."

"If what you told us is the truth, Rincon," said Kemmerer, "we just might let you pull out tomorrow. If not—" He stepped closer, the moon flaring down pale yellow beams that lighted up their faces. "You and the Yardleys will be skydancin' from yonder cottonwood."

Twenty

Moses Quinta feared they wouldn't arrive in time, because to the southwest a cloud of dust was spilling awful close to the Bighorn River. At a canter their horses broke across a marshy area spreading around small ponds where teal and sandhill cranes were feeding, and a covey of sharp-tailed grouse flushed out of the bluestem grass. With Quinta out front, they pushed on through tall reeds and went up a sandy cut, where Moses pulled off his sweat-stained hat while reining his bronc to a quick stop.

He didn't have to say anything, as his deputies were staring in disbelief at the largest band of sheep they'd ever seen. The sheep were choking toward the crossing with the main bunch still coming on about a mile away from the river.

"Lord almighty," gaped John Kornkven, "this sheep outfit means business."

"We're still about three miles out," said Moses. "Up there, on those bluffs, I caught sunlight reflecting off something."

Deputy Josh Medran reached back for his field glass. Through it he swept his eyes along the crests of those bluffs and said, "Cattlemen are holding up there."

"Seems a couple of them are crossing under a flag of truce," said Moses. He spurred on, picking up from a canter to just under a full gallop, his bronc stained with sweat but game to still give it a go at this faster gait. Along the way he'd tried to pry out of Eli Yardley the facts of just how deeply Carsey Kemmerer had been involved with Eli's brother, Harge. But Eli had remained tight-lipped, responding to Moses' questions with a goofy kind of glimmer swimming in his eyes. It occurred to Moses that this Yardley, if not the whole clan, wasn't playing with a full deck. Beechum, his other prisoner, had turned out to be jabbier than a passel of women holding an afternoon tea over at the Mission Baptist Church.

Closing in to within a mile, Moses saw that it was Carsey Kemmerer—and he believed rancher Milt Tyman—passing along the edge of the leading elements of sheep, as from the east came Burt Taggart and two gunhands. Easing back to a canter again, he said to Medran, "Take a gander easterly at the way those riders are holding and spaced out—out of Winchester range."

"What about it, Moses?"

"They're gripping rifles. Hand me that field glass."

He grabbed it out of Medran's hand and took in the horsemen through the glass, and then he knew and said angrily, "Some kind of long-range rifle—some foreign make. With them they can pick off those cattlemen framed along those bluffs. I wouldn't doubt either that Taggart has sent some gunhands around to come in from the west to box the ranchers in. The man's no fool."

"And the cattlemen aren't going to back off either, Moses."

"Me an' Medran will head over there," said Sheriff Quinta. "You boys just hold right here. If this whole thing explodes, about all you can do is to head for cover. 'Cause in a gunfight it don't matter what side you're on sometimes, as a stray bullet ain't got no conscience."

On the verge of riding on, a sudden thought came to Moses as he glanced at Eli Yardley. It just might be, he pondered, that when Eli came eyeball to eyeball with Carsey Kemmerer, Eli would crack wide open. Kneeing his horse over, he said to

Kornkven, "Let me have those reins." He swung his horse around and gripped the reins of Yardley's horse. Then Moses cut away from the low river bluffs this side of the Bighorn and onto a wide swath of open prairie. Unlimbering his six-gun, he let it buck in his hand, as he was in close enough now for both sides in this range war to know the sheriff of Washakie County was here.

There was a sudden stirring of cattlemen on the bluffs west of the river, as a lot more had risen out of concealment. Away from the river easterly, the sheep kept flooding in, but a lot slower—the herders using their dogs to bring the main band into a circling movement.

"I figured you'd show your face," Carsey Kemmerer called out to Moses. There was a worried flicking of the rancher's eyes at the man wearing manacles around his wrists. "Isn't that one of the Yardleys?"

Sheepman Burt Taggart broke in with, "Him and his brothers worked for me until a couple of days ago. And I'm glad they're gone."

Drawing up at an angle so that he faced both men, Moses gestured at Yardley. "Well, Eli, do you have any statement to make—"

Sullenly the hardcase muttered, "Like I've been tellin' ya, Quinta, I ain't done nothin' to justify me bein' arrested."

"Some smartass lawyer give you them words, Eli. As I recollect, back at Tule's you and Harge were sure damned willing to use your guns."

Pow! Pow!

The double reverberating echo of a rifle caught their full attention, with everyone stabbing their eyes in a northeasterly direction to locate the distant source of those shots. Now a couple of horsemen pushed over an elevation, vague and hazy figures in the rising heat of day. "Coming from thataway they aren't cattlemen," said Milt Tyman.

"No, but they had good reason to announce their arrival,"

216

said Moses, as he took in the gunhands that Burt Taggart had brought along, and the vast numbers of sheep, and off to his right the men on the river bluffs. He set his eyes back on the pair of riders and picked out that it was Zach Lankford astride that old cayuse of his; the rider with him he identified as a Basque because of the man's red beret.

"I resent your coming here, Sheriff," snapped Kemmerer angrily. And you, Mr. Taggart, you'd better turn your sheep around before this thing gets out of hand."

"Before the pair of you get a war started, I suggest you hear what my deputy has to say."

"Why, that's Lankford!" snorted Kemmerer. "That old fool *can't* be one of your deputies."

As Lankford reined in a couple of yards away, Moses said, "It puts my mind at ease knowin' you're okay. What have you dug up, Zach?"

"I reckon, Mr. Quinta, this young fella can answer that. He's Basque herder Zalba Goyeneche. He sort of mangles his English a little, Zalba does. He—"

Burt Taggart said questioningly, "Goyeneche—it was your band of sheep that was attacked. But . . . you're alive?"

"Si," responded Zalba. "For a while there was some doubt . . . if I would stay alive. That night . . . they tried to kill me. Senor Taggart, they were the men you hired to . . . to watch over us."

"Come again, son?"

"Si, one of them was this Treech Rincon. With Rincon were"—Zalba Goyeneche chopped off his words as he gazed through troubled eyes at Eli Yardley—"are you the one called Harge?"

"The Yardleys—of course they were in on it," blurted Taggart.

An instinct for survival caused Eli Yardley to push taller in the saddle, and like a coyote yelping in fear when it knew it was about to be cornered, Eli pointed his manacled hands directly at cattleman Carsey Kemmerer. Then Eli shouted, *"He paid us to do it—"*

"So you killed Iturri, too!" cut in Moses.

"No, I—" Rage contorted Carsey Kemmerer's face. He wheeled his horse around in a tight circle and savagely sawed on the reins so his horse reared up and smashed into Eli Yardley. A hoof flailed into Eli's chest and swept him from the saddle. Eli's bronc plunged away, dragging the helpless hardcase, whose left boot was caught in the stirrup. Now, while everyone stared in horror at what was happening to Eli, Kemmerer brought his horse breaking back through, scattering sheep, for the riverbank.

Even as this was happening, Moses had brought his horse after Eli's, which was beginning to pull up and circle around and buck away from the thing it was dragging. Another man still retaining presence of mind was Zach Lankford, who calmly pulled out his rifle and fired from the hip. The slug hit the back leg of Kemmerer's horse.

"Hated to do that," commented Lankford, as Kemmerer's horse went tumbling over—and so did its rider—to hit hard and lay there.

Then Taggart exclaimed, "This has got to stop. Tyman, I gave orders to have some of my men swing around to come in from the west. You've got to warn your friends on the bluffs about this. I . . . I'll pull back my sheep."

"Good enough, Taggart." Milt Tyman swung his horse around and brought it hard toward the river.

A short distance away, Moses had managed to calm Eli Yardley's horse, holding on to the reins as he reached back to free Eli's leg from the stirrup. Much to his surprise he saw Eli staring up at him through groggy eyes, and Moses smiled and said, "You had me worried for a while there, Mr. Yardley. Thought I would have to bury you out here instead of taking you back to be hung. Yup, this sure sets my mind at ease."

218

Twenty-one

The chill of an early fall was in the air, and the leaves were already beginning to turn on elm and cedar trees, and tonight out in the street in front of the Navarre Hotel a wedding dance was in progress. It seemed like all of the townspeople were either dancing or clustering along both sides of the street or in the hotel partaking of free drinks and Basque food.

Moses Quinta was neither place but had snuck off to the back patio, a glass of whiskey in his hand. From where he sat at a round white table, Moses took in the dancers. With him were Zach Lankford and Javier Dominquez and Josh Medran. By mutual accord they'd gathered back here.

How quickly it had all ended—out there along the Bighorn River—with the death of Carsey Kemmerer. The fall from his horse had snapped the rancher's neck, and once the cattlemen holding up on the river bluffs were told the truth of Kemmerer's underhanded ways, they'd pulled away to rehash their next move. Which had turned out to be a bunch of the ranchers coming here to Elkhorn to confer with Burt Taggart. Out of this had come a peace arrangement of sorts, though a few cattlemen still wouldn't budge on their hatred for sheep.

Most satisfying to Moses Quinta was the quick trial for the Yardley brothers and Treech Rincon. Next week they were slated to be hung over at Worland, and this was a chore he had mixed feelings about—as soon after, Moses would turn over his badge to the new sheriff. Moses spoke a little about this.

"Figuring it all up, we were lucky."

"Yes," said Dominquez. "Lucky that only a few were killed. You know, Sheriff Quinta, if you hadn't gone back through some old records kept by Sheriff Eldridge . . ."

"Yup, that report sent over from Utah inquiring about some missing miners chanced to tie in with what Kemmerer's foreman told me—his finding those graves out there. What Kemmerer did was to kill these miners and then steal their gold."

"The gold mine Zalba stumbled upon was worked by those men—which was what Kemmerer had wanted all along." Lankford scratched at his beard. "It sure didn't bother him any—killing, I mean."

The screen door was flung open by Angelita, who came up to them adorned in a shimmering white wedding dress, but she'd taken off her lacy bonnet, and with her eyes directed at plainsman Lankford, she said, "Zach, I've come to claim that dance you promised me. You others—come . . . come, join us."

With a sigh Moses heaved to his feet as did the others, and they moved from the patio to the boardwalk running along it to stand with the others. The crowd parted a little, and then Moses had to shake his head through a smile at the sight of John Kornkven dancing with his girlfriend of the moment. Kornkven and the petite girl wore matching purple shirts and bandannas, and Moses called out, "Hey, John, what happened to what's-her-name . . . ?

"Oh," Moses went on. "She broke away to hook up with another cowpoke? Well, I'll tell you, son, this one's got a ring through your nose, too."

"Moses," said Celia Quinta, as she tugged at her husband's arm. "I want to dance."

"Well, yeah." He handed his glass to Josh Medran and moved out into the street to take Celia in his arms and fell into the rhythm of dancing.

Without preamble Celia informed her husband, "Beth wants to order a new lead-glass window from Denver."

"What'd'ya mean from Denver? I just got the other one paid for."

"Well, Moses, she doesn't like it. And after all . . ."

"After all, woman, I might have to stay on as sheriff asides being a rancher . . . and maybe get a part-time job as county clerk—*from Denver?*"

"Look, Zalba's claimed his bride. Isn't it wonderful that he'll regain the use of his left eye? And all of this is over."

"I expect my daughter-in-law wants me to go to Denver to pick it up, too—"

THE SURVIVALIST SERIES
by Jerry Ahern